MY HEART'S BETRAYAL

Patrece L. Tolbert

ISBN:1481894374
ISBN-13:978-1481894371

DEDICATION

This book is dedicated to my loving, encouraging and supportive grandparents and uncle: Elder William & Nealie Mae Bobo, Deaconess Illa Mae Tolbert, and James E. Bobo, Sr. who are now seated around the throne of God. Thank you for teaching me to love God more than anything and for being examples of good and faithful servants.

To all my family who listened to my crazy stories and pushed me to move forward. Thank you for your continued support, prayers, and patience. A special note of gratitude goes to my son and my mother who have always been my greatest fan club. I love you both and I pray God's continued abundant blessings over your life.

ACKNOWLEDGMENTS

I am extremely thankful to God for the gifts that He has placed inside this earthen vessel to give Him glory. I have truly learned that with God all things are possible. To my awesome son, Quincy, I am proud of the man you have become. Remember to keep God first and let Him direct your paths. To my beautiful mother, Mary, you are a great example of a true woman of God and I thank you for your unconditional love, patience, and support. To my dad, Kenneth, thanks for your support and love and always letting me know that I can do anything.

To my church family, Upper Room Tabernacle, I thank the Lord for placing me in a congregation of true believers in Jesus Christ. Thank you for your love, support, and prayers. Stay with God and never give up.

To my beautiful sisters, Penny and Kisha, thank you for all of your help, love, support. I love the both of you more than you know. To my lovely Aunt Carolyn and Aunt Neta, thanks for walking with me through the valleys and the high places and pushing me forward when I wanted to quit. I love you much.

Thank you to Thomas Boyd (CSU for life), Valerie Turner, Elder Vanessa Thornton, Linda Marie Ransey and Pandra Barnett for being my extra eyes and giving me unbiased critiques. You're the greatest! To my Central State University sister-girlfriends: Carmella Cohen, Dr. Constance Phipps, and Felicia Woods-Wallace, thank you for all you have done but most of all for always being real with me even when I didn't want to hear it. I love all of you very much. For God, For Central, For State!

To all my Toledo support, I love you guys and thank each of you for what you have taught me and poured into my life. I cherish all of you dearly. To the Beta Gamma Chapter Sorors of the National Sorority of Phi Delta Kappa, Inc., especially Exquisite 6, thank you so much for your unconditional love and support and for teaching me that true sisterhood still exists.

I thank God for matriculation through Jesup W. Scott High School and the phenomenal teachers that taught me that hard work and dedication are crucial to success. Once a bulldog, always a bulldog!

To my sister-cousin, Nikki Gray, you are such an inspiration of strength, love, and loyalty. God has great things in store for you so just continue to hold to HIS unchanging hand. To all of my family, the Bobos and the Tolberts, I love each of you and pray God's blessings over you.

To Al J. Godbott, thank you for your unconditional love and support throughout this process and all my other adventures. You are truly an awesome man of God. There are not enough words in the world to truly express the song my heart sings for you.

Special thanks to my Pastor and First Lady for your love and encouragement for me to be all that God has called me to be. I love you both very much.

Prologue

*Seasons changing are constant, the sun rising in the day
and the moon in the night are a certainty. So is the timeless
true love of best friends. Theirs is a mighty river that
rushes toward the edge of life and willingly, without
hesitation leaps over the edge to a body of calm. There, it
can just exist in truth refreshing those who are thirsty,
cooling those who are on fire, and satisfying the restless
soul. However, the heart can create illusions of love that
are really meant to disturb the calm waters of true love.
Becca will have to fight her way back from her own heart's
betrayal by turning back to her faith in God.*

Chapter 1

R-R-Ring, R-R-Ring!

"Good morning and thank you for calling First Ohio National Bank, this is Mark Simmons speaking. How may I assist you today?"

"Well Mr. Simmons, you certainly have a sexy voice and I'm sure I could think of one hundred and one ways you could assist me and none of them have anything to do with taking out a loan. "Becca fought hard to keep from bursting out in laughter.

"Ma'am please refrain from the sexual innuendos or I'll have to bring you up on sexual harassment charges." Mark was playing along.

"I thought you could only do that if you worked in the same office? We don't even live in the same city! Good luck makin' that charge stick! Becca laughed and leaned back in her black leather cushioned, swivel office chair.

"Oh, I'll make 'em stick. Don't you worry about that! I know people." Mark laughed with Becca and then regained his composure. "How are you Becca?"

"Great, Mark. How's everything goin' in C-Town?" When Becca and Mark were at Central State University, an Historically Black University, in Wilberforce, Ohio, *C-town* was the nick name for Cleveland. They often enjoyed reminiscing about their college days together.

"Alright. Busy but alright. So what do I owe the pleasure of hearing from the gracious Becca Thomas? It's been about four or five days since we've talked." Mark was really glad to hear from her. They usually spoke every other day but things had been very busy.

"Well, you know I try not to stalk you on a regular basis." She giggled.

"Whatever, Becca. Now tell me what's on your mind." Mark pressured.

Becca proceeded carefully. She didn't want to sound over anxious. "Mark, what are you doing for Valentine's Weekend?"

Mark spoke thoughtfully. "That's a three day weekend. I was thinkin' about goin' to Chicago. Why? What's up?"

Becca's heart sank a little. She wanted them to spend that weekend together—Mark, Camille, Bryan and herself. "Well, I was thinking about all four of us goin' to Hueston Woods Resort and staying in my time share cabin. But you've already made plans so never mind." There was a hint of disappointment in Becca's voice.

"Hold on, Becca! I haven't made any definite plans. Going up to the cabin sounds nice. Just you, me, and the kids? That sounds great! Mark loved spending time with all of them together. It felt like they were a real family.

Becca spoke trying to hold back her excitement. "Are you sure Mark? I don't want to pressure you into going?" Becca was smiling from ear to ear.

"Oh, like you're worried about pressurin' me to do somethin'. Please Becca remember who you're talkin' to." Mark spoke in a playful, sarcastic tone. "Besides, when have you ever been worried about pressurin' someone to do something you wanted to do? I'll answer that one myself—NEVER! He laughed out loud.

"You're just the comedian, hunh? I do care. I want you to go because you want to not because I pressured you." Becca's tone was sincere.

"Girl please! Don't try to give me that sad tone. Now what time did you want to meet there?" Mark changed the subject to keep Becca lighthearted.

"Oh, I don't know maybe Bry and I will just drive to Cleveland. That way we can all ride together to the cabin. How does that sound?" Becca was so filled with joy that she wished they were going this weekend.

Mark paused before he answered, looking at his day planner to make sure nothing would interfere with their family getaway. "That sounds great, Becca. I'll just let my boss know I'll be taking Thursday and Friday off. Tell Bryan it's on at the cabin! I owe him a rematch in arm wrestling."

"Don't worry, I'll tell him. You, just make sure you don't plan anything else for that weekend." Becca's voice changed to a stern tone.

"Alright, Becca, I hear you. I already wrote it in my planner. I just love it when you get forceful!" Mark chuckled. Just then Mark's cell phone vibrated. He looked at the screen and sighed heavily before he spoke in a serious tone. "Becca, I gotta take this call."

9

Becca could hear concern in Mark's voice. "What is it Mark?"

"It's Camille's school. I hope it's not one of her teachers again with a bad report." Mark was no longer playing. "I'll talk to you later, ok?"

"Ok. Call me if you need me and try to have a good day." Becca hung up the phone and stared at the photo of the four of them at Cedar Point last summer. She couldn't believe how good they looked together. Almost like a real family; but they were a family. Becca often had long daydreams about Mark and what it would be like to finally come clean about the way she felt for him. However, Becca was so afraid of hurting their friendship that she decided the time was just not right.

As she began to take care of some paperwork, her mind began to drift to the plans her and Mark had made for Valentine's weekend. Becca didn't hear her phone ring the first time. Her administrative assistant, Mrs. Tonya Cooper, was out to lunch. So Becca had no one to screen her calls. She answered, on the third ring in a professional tone. "Good afternoon. You have reached Solomon Christian School, Principal Becca Thomas speaking. How may I assist you?"

"Uh hello Becca is that you?" A deep familiar masculine voice questioned.

Becca's heart stopped beating for an instant and the breath left her body. She thought to herself, "It can't be! Not after six years of absolutely no contact." She decided to play it out without too much emotion. "Yes, this is Becca Thomas. Who may I ask is calling?"

The voice on the other end relaxed and chuckled, "Oh, this is Rob, the father of your only child."

She held her composure even though she was outraged that he would dare call her with a smug attitude after all this time. She decided to take the high road. "Mr. Harris, what can I do for you today?"

Rob became a little agitated that Becca was treating him so coldly. Becca why you playing'?! It's been a long time since I've talked to you and Bryan. I know that little dude is big now!" Rob smiled to himself as he spoke.

"Uh, excuse me Rob, but my son's name is Bryan William Harris, not little dude. So would you please address him as such! What do you want anyway?" Becca spoke coldly.

"You sound kinda upset, Becca. Just calm down. I know it's

been a long time since I've called; but I had to get myself together."

"Well, I'm glad you're together and thanks for calling..." Becca was about to hang up when she heard him yelling her name.

"Becca! Wait a minute. Will you just listen to me?! I'M TRYIN' TO APOLOGIZE! Girl, you can really be ridiculous!" Rob was trying to stay cool but Becca was making it very hard.

"Rob, please! You're the one that disappeared without a trace for six long years. So excuse me if I don't want to hear the lies!! I've been apologizing to Bryan on your behalf for too long! I'm through, Rob! Besides, Mark has been doing an excellent job helping me raise Bryan."

"I don't care what Mark has done! I'm still Bryan's daddy! Look, Becca, I didn't call you to argue. I just want to start doing what I should've been doing all along—being a father to my kid. So please let me see him." Rob's voice began to quiver a little.

Becca was quiet for a moment. She didn't know what to say. There were so many thoughts running through her head. "Listen, if you are really serious about seeing Bryan, then call him at home about 8 tonight. Our number is (419) 474-0000. If you don't call, I will know that you have not changed and I will not expect to hear from you again. You will not get my baby's hopes up and then send them crashing to the ground. Got it!" Becca was not playing about her son. He had been hurt too much from the man that was supposed to protect him.

"I understand Becca." Rob's heart sank because he knew that Becca was telling the truth. He also knew he was going to have to work hard at regaining Bryan's trust and her love. "But I'm gonna show you that I've changed. As a matter of fact let me give you my new number."

"Yeah, and don't forget the name of the woman you're living with now. So I'll know who she is when she answers the phone." Becca spoke sarcastically.

"See Becca, you're not hearin' me! I just said things are different. I have my own apartment and a job. I work at the University of Cincinnati in the security department and I'm takin' classes part time to finish my degree." Rob spoke in a boastful tone.

Becca was speechless. It all sounded good but she had been here before with Rob. She sure wasn't going to believe that he didn't have some other woman on the side. "Well that's great. I'm happy for you. I hope you stick with it this time. I have to go." She felt her heart melting a little and she didn't want to go easy on Rob, not yet!

"Ok, please tell Bryan I'll call at 8:00 sharp. I won't let him down." Rob's voice became low and sexy. "Will you have some time to talk to me too, Becca?

"Why? You need to just concentrate on Bryan. I don't have time for games!"

"But, Becca, there are things that I need to say to you too. You were always the one that I truly loved. Becca, I still…"

"Well, Ok, then, I will tell Bryan that you called. I'm sure he'll be anxious to talk to you. Have a good day!" Becca hung up with Rob still calling her name. She did not want to hear any more lies. Her life was complicated enough. But she couldn't help thinking what if Rob really had changed? Bry could finally have a full time dad. Becca knew that no matter how much Mark filled in, her son still missed his real dad. Then, she thought, "Why is Rob trying to mess with my head? I could never go back to him – could I?"

As Becca was sitting with her head in her hands, she didn't hear the bell ring for dismissal until Bryan came popping through her door. "Hey mom, what's up? How was your day?" Bryan was smiling as he stood beside his mother's desk.

Becca looked at her son. Then, she got up and threw her arms around him. "I love you, Bry! Don't you ever forget it!"

Bryan was stunned, "Ok ma, ok! Can I get two dollars for the vending machines?"

Becca reached into her pocket and pulled out some money. She decided to tell Bryan about his dad on their way home.

Chapter 2

"But what if I don't want to talk to him?" Bryan was confused. He didn't know what to feel after hearing that his dad had called the school today.

"Well then you don't have to talk to him. But wouldn't you like to hear what your dad has to say?" Becca touched Bryan's arm as they just sat in her gold, 2012 Dodge Durango with tan leather interior, parked in her two-car garage.

"Mom, it's been a long time since I've talked to my dad. Why is he calling now?" Bryan asked.

"I don't know Bry. I guess he needed time to get himself together. He says he wants to make things right with us." Becca opened the door and slid out of the truck and grabbed her briefcase out of the back seat. "It's ok for us to listen, Bryan. Here, do you need your book bag?"

Bryan opened the door and hopped out, "No, mom. Sis. Dunn said we didn't have homework for the weekend." Bryan walked into the house and sat down on the couch and turned on the cartoon network.

Becca followed him in after closing the car doors. Then she pushed the button to let down the garage door and locked the inside door. She walked to the kitchen, hung her keys on a hook and walked to the family room to push play on her digital answering machine. There were three messages. The first two were bill collectors, she skipped pass them and went to the third one. "Do you want a snack before dinner, Bry?"

"Yeah, I'll have a lunchable and a fruit punch Gatorade. Thanks mom." Bryan answered.

As the last message played, a big smile danced across Becca's face. The familiar voice that always made her stomach jump was speaking, "Hey beautiful! I just called to say I can't wait to see you and Bryan next month. Bryan, if you're listening get ready for a wrestling rematch! Make sure you're taking care of your momma. If you get time, call me before your she makes you go to bed. I love you guys." *Beep* and Mark's voice was gone.

"Mom, why don't you tell Mark that you like him? You guys have been playin' this game for too long."

"You're completely right, Dr. Phil! Why didn't I think of that?"

Becca replied sarcastically. "Anyway, we're best friends and that's enough for right now. Things are good just the way they are. Neither one of us needs any more stress than we already have." Becca turned and opened the fridge and pulled out a bottle of water, a turkey and cheese lunchable and a Gatorade. Every time she thought about Mark, a silly grin would creep over her face. She knew what she had just told Bryan wasn't the truth. But she wasn't sure about the way Mark felt for her and Becca didn't think she would be able to withstand that kind of rejection.

"You know Valentine's weekend would be a good time to tell Mark you want him to be your boo, mom." Bryan spoke sarcastically and made obnoxious kissing noises. He just couldn't stop laughing.

"Here boy, take your snack and go sit down before I pop you!" Becca laughed with her son and swatted him on the behind as he went back to the family room to watch his cartoons.

"Hey Mom! You're the greatest!" Bryan yelled from the couch.

"Lord, I thank you!" Becca rejoiced in her spirit because she remembered from where God had brought them. "Bryan, I ordered pizza from Gino's for dinner. So when the delivery man comes, the money is in here on the island counter. I'll be upstairs changing my clothes."

"Yes!" exclaimed Bryan. "Mom you must have read my mind 'cause that's what I've been thinking about all day. Don't worry I'll take care of it!" Bryan was very mature for an eleven year old. Becca knew she could trust him to take care of getting the pizza. Not to mention the fact that he was about as tall as some thirteen year old boys.

Becca placed $20 on the counter and started toward the stairs but then stopped and turned back to Bryan. "Oh yeah, Bryan, make sure you don't inhale the whole box before I get back down here. I would like to get at least two slices of pizza."

"Ok mom ok, you're makin' me miss Dragon Ball Z!"

Becca proceeded up the stairs to her room where she sat on her king size, cherry wood panel bed. Her heart was so full that she began to sob. "Lord, what am I going to do? I love Mark so much but I'm too scared to tell him! What if he just wants to remain friends? I just couldn't handle that humiliation. Lord, what am I suppose to do?! God please touch my mind because You know I can't trust my heart." Becca laid back on her bed and cried. Then the phone rang. She picked up her cordless and looked at the screen. It read Robert Harris and a Cincinnati phone number. Becca let the phone ring two more times before she answered it. She spoke dryly, "Hello."

"Hey Becca, it's me, Rob." He spoke with confidence and pride.

"Yes, I know. Caller ID, it's the latest thing." Becca replied sarcastically. "Hold on, I'll get Bryan."

"Wait a minute, Becca. I want to talk to you first." Rob's voice became very tender. "To be honest I'm a little nervous about talkin' to Bryan after all these years. Did you tell him that I'd be callin' tonight?" Rob thought he was in control but when he heard Becca's voice, his confidence was shaken.

"Yes, Rob I did. To be honest with you he was not all that thrilled!" Becca was a bit agitated with Rob. She really didn't want to talk to him. "You're his dad, so just open your mouth and talk. Trust me you can't do any more damage than you've already done. Anyway, I have a bit of a headache and I don't feel much like arguing with you." Becca started walking toward her door to yell down for Bryan to pick up the phone when all of a sudden Rob said something to her that stopped her dead.

"I'm in love with you, Becca Thomas and I want the three of us to be together again!" Rob breathed a sigh of relief. "Baby, I'm so sorry for hurting you but you are the only woman I've ever really loved. I think that's why I got scared and ran." Rob spoke with sincerity.

"What in the world are you talking about Rob?! How dare you! After all this time decide to tell me some crap like that! Oh and I guess I'm just supposed to melt like butter and let you back into my heart. You must be out of your mind. I don't trust anything that comes out of your mouth!" Becca was furious.

After a brief silence, Rob spoke very clearly and with boldness. "Becca, I'm gonna get you back! I know you still love me; I can hear it in your voice. Now, may I please speak with *our* son?" Rob remembered how Becca used to love for him to be forceful with her. It would always leave her speechless. Tonight was no exception.

Becca sighed with disgust and yelled to Bryan from her room. "Bryan! Pick up the phone. It's your dad!"

"I got it momma!" Bryan called back. "Hey dad, how ya' been doin'?" Bryan's voice was filled with hope and excitement.

Becca hadn't heard him sound that happy in a long time. She lay back down because her head was reeling. All she could do was pray for the Lord to help her make good decisions regarding her future and more importantly Bryan's. "NO MORE CONFUSION!" Becca shouted into the atmosphere. She fell asleep to the sound of her son's laughter while talking to his long lost father.

It was about 9:30 at night and all Mark could think about was why Becca and Bryan had not called him back. Usually, when he left a message for them they would call back immediately. It was now about five hours later.

"Uncle Mark, what are you doin'? Are you ok?" Camille noticed that her uncle had been a little preoccupied this evening.

"Oh nothing, Camille, I was just thinking about some stuff at work." Mark shook himself and gave her his attention. "Are you ready for bed?"

"Not yet. You didn't read my bedtime story! Has Auntie Becca called yet?" Camille inquired as she crawled into her full sized princess canopy bed with purple Cinderella comforter that Becca bought for her two years ago. "I sure hope she calls before I fall asleep. Don't you?"

Mark answered under his breath, "More than you know."

"What did you say Uncle Mark?"

"I said yes, I hope she does too. But if she doesn't we'll call her first thing in the morning. Now, get under the covers and we'll read Snow White." Mark and Camille sat on the bed and laughed about the seven dwarfs. Camille began to fall asleep under the sound of Mark's voice. He closed the book, whispered a prayer over her, and turned off the ballerina lamp on her nightstand.

Mark walked down the hall to his room and sat at the foot of his bed on the oatmeal colored Berber carpeted floor. He allowed his mind to wander back to the death of his brother, Ryan. Ryan was older by three years. They were very close. Sometimes, Mark felt like the oldest. Ryan always told Mark that if anything ever happened to him, his daughter was to live with Mark. Her mother had left Ryan three months after Camille was born and never tried to contact them again. Ryan made sure that all the legal paperwork was in order before his unit was called to go overseas. Mark agreed, thinking that Ryan was just being overly cautious and expecting his big brother to return unharmed. So when news arrived a year ago last month that Ryan had been killed during a training exercise in South East Asia, the whole family was devastated. Especially Camille, her dad was her world. Ever since that day, Mark has been taking care of Camille like she was his own biological daughter.

This is one of the reasons Mark's and Becca's bond had grown so strong. They both fulfilled a void in each other's lives. Mark is the missing father in Bryan's life and Becca is that missing mother figure in Camille's. Mark, Becca, Bryan, and Camille have all experienced loss in some form or another. There is nothing that Mark wanted more than to give Camille and Bry a stable family. But he knew that Becca had been through a lot with men and he just didn't know if she was ready to put her heart on the line one more time, even if it meant obtaining real love.

Ring, Ring, Ring.

Mark jumped. The phone startled him a little. He leaned over toward the night stand and grabbed it. He hoped it was Becca. He cleared his throat, looked at the caller ID then the clock, which read 10:30 and pressed the talk button. He spoke dryly, "Hey Lena, what's goin' on?" Mark's disappointment could not be hidden from his baby sister.

"Well you don't have to sound so happy to hear my voice." Lena was concerned after hearing her brother's tone. "Why do you sound so depressed?"

"Do I?" Mark cleared his throat again and stood up. He walked to the right side of his bed that faced his bay window that looked out over a small pond. "I was just thinking about Ryan. But I'm ok. You know the older Camille gets the more she looks like him." Mark's voice quivered slightly.

"Do you want me to come over? I'm not doin' anything tonight." Lena was trying to be helpful but she knew nothing would help her brother when he got into these kinds of moods. They had to just run their course. But Lena wanted Mark to know she was there for him if he needed her because she missed Ryan too.

"Lena, thanks for offering but I'm alright. Besides, yo' man should be callin' pretty soon to check up on you, right? I know how much you love talkin' to him." Mark chuckled half–heartedly to let Lena know that he was feeling a little better.

"Yeah, whatever, Mark! I know you better than you think. But if you need me, please call. I'll be there in a flash! I don't want you to be depressed." Lena spoke tenderly.

"Seriously sis, just hearing your voice has made me feel a lot better. Thanks. I'll give you a call tomorrow." Mark made himself sound normal so Lena wouldn't be alarmed.

"Alright, tough guy, have a good night." Lena hung up the phone and made up in her mind that tomorrow she would definitely stop by to see her brother. There was more going on with him than he wanted to share.

Mark sat on his bed staring at a picture of Becca and Bryan. He spoke in a whisper as his heart grew heavy with a long kept secret, "I love you, Becca Thomas. But how do I tell you?" Mark leaned back on his pillow and fell asleep to dreams of a new life and a new family—maybe.

Chapter 3

"Mom, mom! Are you going to make breakfast? I'm starving!" Bryan called to his mother.

Becca struggled for clarity. Her dream of Mark proposing to her and whisking her off to some romantic island was still fighting for her attention. Becca could hear Bryan's voice but she also wanted to feel Mark's soft full lips kissing her neck and his strong masculine hands gently caressing her shoulders. When all of a sudden, Becca felt the whole room shake. Bryan had done one of his famous dive bombs into her bed. "Boy! Why are you so silly? You could have really knocked the wind outta me!" She yelled at him. However, when her precious son looked at her and gave her that goofy one sided smile she couldn't help but laugh with him.

"Mom, I love you! Now, what are you cooking this morning? I hope it's your yummy pancakes and eggs with bacon and cheese."

"Well keep hope alive, son! Oh and I'd suggest you be more concerned with cleaning that room than feeding your face this morning."

"But mom, what about cartoons? Today is Saturday! You know my routine: first, I wake you up to cook; second, I go downstairs to watch cartoons on the big screen; and third, I take a shower and clean my room. You can't mess with tradition, Mom!" Bryan looked so sincere and handsome pleading with his mother.

"Tradition, huh? Well, if my memory serves me right, tradition says you never make it to the step where your room actually gets cleaned. So, what I'd like to do is start a new tradition. First, clean your room; second, take a shower; and third, eat your breakfast. I'll even throw in a perk. You can watch TV in your room while you're working." Becca was adamant. She knew that if she didn't put her foot down with him, his room would not get cleaned again. So, it didn't matter what kind of puppy face he tried to give his mother she was not going to back down.

"But mom the new Power Ranger episode is coming on today and Teenage Mutant Ninja Turtles! Please, just let me watch those two and I promise I'll clean up. Mom, come on now, please for your favorite son." Bryan was practically begging.

Becca turned from making her bed and looked at her son

standing in the middle of the room and smiled at him ever so lovingly, then replied in a stern, diplomatic tone. "Bryan William Harris, I will make this final offer to you. This is non-negotiable. If you don't do exactly as I have instructed you, then you won't only miss cartoons this morning, but for the entire month. Your phone privileges will be cut off and no game systems. Oh yes, and that skating party that your little friend, Erica, invited you to, forget it! Now, do you have anything else you would like to say?" Becca did not crack a smile.

Bryan just dropped his head and said, "No Ma'am." Then he walked off to clean his room.

Becca hated to have to crack the whip on Bryan but she had to let him know that she was serious.

Becca slipped on her burgundy satin robe and matching slippers, went into her bathroom, brushed her teeth and washed her face. She pulled her braids back into a ponytail and headed downstairs.

As Becca walked into the kitchen, the phone seemed to beckon for her to call Mark. However, the thought of Rob and the things he said to her last night would not go away. Becca thought to herself, "How can Rob really think that I could ever go back to him. I spent all those nights worrying about him, not knowing if he were dead or alive. Um—I'm just not the same person!" She spoke the words out loud as if trying to convince herself.

Ring, Ring, Ring!

The sound of the phone caused Becca to jump back into consciousness. She remembered instantly that she was supposed to call Mark last night. But, after talking to Rob, she was confused, angry, and just mentally worn out.

Ring, Ring, Ring!

Becca pulled herself together and picked up the phone. "Hello." She spoke the greeting trying to make her voice light. There still seemed to be heaviness in it.

When Mark heard Becca's voice he knew something was not quite right. He also knew that just asking her outright what was wrong would not be a good approach. So, he decided to just play it cool and let her tell him in her own time. "Well hello to you. How's everyone this morning?" Mark wanted the conversation to be easy so he didn't mention about her forgetting to call last night.

"Hey, honey, everyone is fine. Except for Bry who is about to get the punishment of his life if that room is not cleaned properly!"

"Really? What did he say this time? Bryan's mouth always gets him in trouble." Mark chuckled. "I guess he's just like his mom."

Becca gave a sarcastic laugh. "You're just so smart! Anyway, I told him to clean that room this morning and he wanted to negotiate with me about why he should do it later. But we came to an understanding that either the room gets cleaned now or he would have to sacrifice a month of no extra activities. Needless to say, he is upstairs getting it together." Becca put on some hot water for a cup of herbal tea and began pulling out her electric skillet and mixing bowls to start the pancakes.

"Do you need me to speak to Bry about taking care of his chores? He never pulls that when he stays with me." Mark was serious. He did not play when it came to children being respectful. Mark also tried to be there for Becca when it came to disciplining Bryan. He knew that it could get rough raising a young man.

"No, well, yes, maybe when we go to the cabin next month we can find some time for you two to be alone. I hope you can get him to listen and take heed." Becca answered Mark with concern.

"Oh, he'll listen. We will have ourselves a nice little man to man conversation. Bryan has a lot of changes going on inside of him that he does not understand or know how to deal with. Mark paused for a moment and then said, "Becca, I'll tell you what, I can take a personal day on Tuesday and come to the school. I'll pick up Bry at lunch time and spend the whole afternoon with him. I'll even have Lena take care of Camille for me that day. That way I can stay for awhile without having to rush back. If that's ok with you?"

Becca began to feel the butterflies in her stomach go into hyper drive. She knew if Mark said it, it was definitely going to happen. Mark was such a good man. She often wondered why they never dated in college. But everything has its own season and there were lessons they both had to learn before they could become the people they both were today. "OK? Of course it's OK. I'm not even going to tell Bryan that you're coming to visit. He is going to be too surprised when he sees you walk in that classroom." Becca was so excited she didn't know how she was going to keep this secret from Bryan for the next three days.

Mark was so glad that he could be there for Becca and Bryan. He knew they needed someone in their corner and he desired to be that person. "I'll leave as soon as I take Camille to school. So I should get to Toledo about 10 or 10:30."

"That sounds great!" Becca had to calm herself as not to seem to anxious. "I-I mean we can't wait to see you. Should I plan on you staying for dinner?" Becca was trying to downplay her enthusiasm.

"I don't think that'll be a problem. I might even stay the night." Mark replied hopefully.

"Oh we might not be able to take all this love!" Becca laughed sarcastically.

Mark never missed a beat when talking to Becca. "Oh, well you betta' get ready because I've got a lot more to give!"

Becca was stunned. They both laughed and began to talk about stuff related to work and both their families.

Two hours later Mark told Becca he'd call back later that evening to talk to Bryan.

She hated saying goodbye to Mark. She also remembered that she had not apologized for failing to call him and Camille last night. "Mark, I'm so sorry for not calling you guys back last night. I had a surprise phone call from Rob that developed into a severe headache after talking to him. So I went straight to sleep. Please forgive me."

Mark was caught off guard. They had not heard from Rob in years. He knew that every time Rob started coming around it meant trouble for Becca and disappointment for Bryan. "Are you serious? What made him call after all these years? Was he suddenly feeling fatherly?! I don't even believe this! That dude is a trip!" Mark was getting more upset with every thought of the broken dreams and spoiled hopes Rob had left Bryan and Becca with the last time he just appeared out of nowhere. However, Mark realized that he had to be calm for Becca's sake. She said she was over Rob – but he is the father of her only child. How do you ever really get over that?

There was a moment of silence before Becca spoke. "Mark, I was saying the same thing after I talked to him at work..."

"What do you mean at work? Are you saying that Rob called you twice in one day? Oh, he really is trying to get back in good with you! I hope you're not falling for his lies." Mark was getting agitated. He had made up in his mind years ago that Rob would never hurt two of the most important people in his life again.

"Mark, I've said the same thing to myself. Now do you understand why I didn't call last night? I couldn't do anything but go to sleep." Becca knew how Mark felt about Rob. She also knew that he would not be pleased to find out that Rob wanted to try and make things work between him and her. Becca decided that it would be best not to even mention all of that to Mark right now. It would cause too much drama and she just didn't want to deal with all of that at this moment. "Mark, please don't let Rob's little phone call throw you off. We'll just deal with the situation as it comes. Anyway, we have a great Valentine's weekend trip coming up so let's just concentrate on that, ok? Is Camille excited?"

Mark realized that Becca was adamant about changing the subject—a little too adamant. But he didn't want to cause her anymore stress. Mark went along with her. "Yeah, she's very excited. I think I should've waited 'til the week of the trip to tell her because she's gonna be buggin' me all month! What about Bryan? How does he feel about it?" Mark asked.

"Oh, he is looking forward to the vacation also!" Becca was trying not to let Mark hear the weight in her voice. I just hope he and Camille don't fuss with each other the whole weekend." Becca and Mark had to laugh at that statement because the probability of those two clashing was very high.

"Mom, mom!" Bryan called out to Becca as if the house was on fire.

"What is it Bryan? And stop callin' me like it's an emergency!"

Mark was on the other end laughing at Becca.

Bryan stepped into the kitchen where his mom was on the phone and mixing pancake batter at the island counter.

"Mom, I'm sorry. I just wanted you to know that I finished cleaning my room! Aren't you proud of me?" Bryan was so pleased with himself.

"Do you see what I'm dealing with, Mark? Now this boy wants praise for somethin' he should have done last weekend! I just don't get it!"

Bryan rose up at the sound of Mark's name. "Mama, mama can I speak to my Godfather? Please!!"

Becca handed Bryan the phone and told him to settle down. "Hey Mark! How ya doin'? Did mom tell you that my Dad called last night? I still can't believe it! Don't you think that's great?" Bryan was excited he was talking a mile a minute. He wouldn't even wait for Mark to respond before he asked another question. Mark had to just jump in the conversation wherever he could.

"So, is your dad going to come see you, Bry?" Mark tried not to sound upset. He knew how happy his God-son was and he didn't want anything to ruin Byan's moment.

"Yeah, I think so? I hope my dad comes to see me." Bryan whispered the latter phrase prayerfully as if saying it too loud would keep it from coming true.

It pained Mark to hear the desperation in Bryan's voice. No child should ever have to anxiously seek out the attention of their own father. "Well I'm sure he'll be by to see you soon. I love you little buddy. Remember, I'm always here for you." Mark was holding back his emotion over the situation.

"Ok Mark, I'll remember." Bryan repeated obediently sensing a funny tone in his voice. "Are you ok?"

Becca turned quickly to look at her son when she heard these words. "Bry, let me speak to Mark." By the time she got the words out of her mouth, Bryan placed the receiver back in its cradle.

"Mom, Mark said he had to go but he would call you later. Can I watch the rest of my cartoons now?" Bryan ran to his mother and hugged her really tight.

"Sure, Bry, I'll call you when breakfast is done. I love you, Mook." Becca kissed Bryan on his forehead as he released her and ran up the stairs.

Becca stood by the sink and dropped her head as a river of emotions began to flow through her. She never wanted to hurt Mark but she knew that is exactly what had happened. Becca prayed in a soft whisper, "God, please show me how to handle this situation. Don't let Rob hurt my baby boy again." There were quiet sobs in between her words. "And God please help me to now if Mark loves me as much as I love him." Becca reached for a paper towel to the left of the sink on the marble counter top, wiped her face, and finished cooking while humming *Order My Steps.*

Rob sat in his large one bedroom apartment staring at a picture of Becca, Bryan, and himself about six years ago. Rob had truly regretted not being a father to Bryan and leaving Becca for another woman. Becca scared Rob. Her dreams and goals were always larger than life. Rob was used to the street life and Becca would have nothing to do with it. She wanted so much more for Rob; but, he wasn't sure if he could live up to her expectations. So he chose the familiarity of the streets and all that came with it.

Becca was devastated when Rob told her that he was living with another woman and that it was over with them. She never saw it coming. He had given her no clues or at least none she wanted to acknowledge.

Rob clutched a picture of Becca and Bryan to his chest and spoke out loud. "Your feelings for me haven't changed Becca Thomas and I will get you back. I ain't gonna lose my baby's mama to no Mark Simmons!" Rob was determined to finally be the man Becca needed him to be—husband and father. But would the streets release their hold on him and would the cost of his freedom be too high a price for Rob to pay?

Chapter 4

Mark was up at 5:00 Tuesday morning. He wanted to make sure he made it to Bryan's school by 10:30. Mark put on a pair of dark blue denim jeans, a cream colored turtle neck sweater, which accentuated the firmness of his upper body. He put on his tan Timberland boots and brown ¾ length leather jacket. He looked in the mirror one last time before leaving the house. Mark's beard was tightly trimmed and he had just gotten a fresh haircut the evening before. He put on his favorite cologne, Kenneth Cole, grabbed his keys, briefcase, and garment bag. Mark had decided to stay the night that way he could spend more time with Bryan and Becca.

He had a two hour ride ahead of him. It was now about 7:00. He told Camille to put her cereal bowl in the dishwasher and grab her coat and book bag so they could leave. Mark figured by the time he dropped her off at school and filled up his gas tank, it would be close to 8:00. This would put Mark in Toledo by 10. Just like he had planned.

Camille was disappointed because she could not go with her uncle. She even started crying in the car and giving him her sad face. He almost cracked, but Camille needed to be in school every day. She was still a little behind in her reading.

"But why can't I go with you, Uncle Mark? We always go to Toledo together. And I wanna see Auntie Becca too!"

"Camille you can' t this time. You have to go to school. Besides, you're going to see them next month."

"And so are you! So why do you have to go today?" She folded her arms in protest.

"Camille, baby, remember when Auntie Becca came and spent the day with you at your school? Well I'm doin' the same thing with Bryan. Can't you understand that?"

"I guess so. I just miss you when you go away. Can you and I do something together when you come back?" Camille softened her tone and placed her hand on Mark's.

"We'll see. But you better do well in school and with your Auntie Lena! Ok?" Mark's tone was stern.

Ok Uncle Mark. I'm gonna do real good in school and with Auntie Lena! You're gonna be so proud of me!" Camille replied with new found enthusiasm.

They pulled up in front of Camille's school and Mrs. Snelling, Camille's reading tutor was going in the door. She stopped and waved to the both of them. Mark rolled his niece's window down and spoke pleasantly, "Good morning, Mrs. Snelling."

"Good morning, Mr. Simmons. I can walk Camille to the cafeteria for you."

"Thank you, I'm on my way out of town. Oh, by the way, my sister will be picking up Camille from school today." Then he turned his attention back to Camille. "You have a good day." Mark gave Camille a kiss and a big hug. "I'll see you tomorrow evening. "Remember, you better be good. I love you, babe."

"I love you too, Uncle Mark! Have a safe trip and give Auntie Becca a kiss for me. Bye!" Camille jumped out of the car and threw her pink Bratz backpack over one shoulder. She ran up to Mrs. Snelling who was holding the door for her.

Mark was definitely gonna try to give Becca, Camille's message. While driving down the turnpike, Mark couldn't help think about Rob tryin' to ease back into their lives again. He couldn't believe that man had the guts to even try this again. Mark remembered how Rob had left Becca and Bryan in a mess the last time. Then, Rob did what he does best—disappeared. Bryan was hurt and Becca felt so stupid for letting him get close to them.

Bryan told Mark one night, when he had went to stay in Cleveland for a week. "I wish you were my dad." Then, Bryan asked with overflowing feelings of abandonment, "Mark, why doesn't my daddy love me? I've tried to be a good boy, but maybe I did something to send him away again?" Bryan just broke down and fell into his Godfather's arms.

Mark was angry and choked up. How could this precious child that he watched grow up into a great young man think that he could do something so bad it would drive his own father away. "Bry, you could never do anything bad enough to push your mom and me away. Your father has personal issues that he needs to deal with. It has nothing to do with you. Don't you ever think badly of yourself like that again. God is raising you up to be a strong witness for Him! Sometimes we have to go through the valley in order to appreciate the mountain top. I'm so thankful that God allowed me to be a part of you and your mother's life. No matter what, little buddy, your Godfather has got yo' back!"

"I love you Mark!" Bryan sobbed.

"I love you, too, son." Mark hugged him tighter and then pushed him off the couch. "Now it's time for Wrestle Mania!"

Bryan laughed and dove on Mark's back, sending him crashing to the floor. They laughed and played until they were both extremely tired. A bond was strengthened between them that night that couldn't have been stronger if they shared the same DNA.

Mark wiped his eyes as he drove toward Toledo. He was more determined now than ever to protect Bry and Becca from Rob!

Becca was sitting at her kitchen table filling out some teacher evaluation forms from her observations last week. She had made sure that Bryan wore his best uniform and shined his school shoes. He couldn't understand why his mom was makin' all that fuss over a school uniform. "There's only so much you can do with navy and white, momma. Are we goin' somewhere special today?" Bryan could not take it anymore.

"No I just want you to start taking pride in the way you look when you go to school! Do you have a problem with that?" Becca was so nervous and she did not understand why. "Mark comes to visit all the time! It's not like we just met. Pull yourself together, Becca!" She was thinking so hard she didn't feel Bryan tugging on her arm.

"Momma, momma – Ms. Thomas! We're gonna be late for school if we don't leave right now!" Bryan was almost yelling before she snapped back to reality.

"Well it's a good thing you know the principal then? Now get in the truck and let's go, boy." Becca laughed with her son as they drove to school.

"Becca, Becca are you ok?" Tonya Cooper was Becca's administrative assistant and prayer partner. Tonya kept the office in meticulous order at all times. She was Becca's right hand and sister in the Lord. Tonya was about 45 years old, married to a successful lawyer, and they had one child, Marion, who was a successful surgeon at one of the local hospitals. Marion had two beautiful children. Her husband had died 2 years ago in a terrible car accident. But thank God she had her parents. Tonya came to work at Solomon Christian School because the Lord had led her there. She was always praying – for the school, teachers, students, parents and especially for Becca. When you walked in the office you could smell the coffee brewing and feel the Spirit of God moving.

"Becca did you hear me? I said your 10:00 appointment is here." Mrs. Cooper touched Becca's arm. Becca was startled. She smiled and said, "Alright, but give me a few minutes to collect my thoughts."

"Becca are you sure you're alright? I mean you seem a little out of it." Tonya looked at Becca with concern.

"Thanks for your concern, Tonya, but I'm fine. There's just a lot of stuff in my head that I need to sort through." Becca let out an exhausted sigh.

"Well, you remember to pray and trust God. Keep yo' mind stayed on him and let Jesus keep you in perfect peace, Becca. Things and situations are gonna get bad but we have to grab hold of our faith in Christ and believe that HE is in control of everything." Tonya walked over to Becca and gave her a big hug.

Becca was in awe of this woman whose faith seemed to never waver. Tonya had a relationship with God that Becca wanted so badly. Becca knew that she was someone very special. "Tonya, thanks, I needed a little extra encouragement this morning. I know God will work it all out in His time. It's just the waiting period that messes me up!" Becca gave a little chuckle and dabbed the tears from her eyes.

"Well, Becca it's through the waiting period that our faith is made perfect. Now, get yourself together and I'll send in your appointment in about ten minutes. Don't you worry honey, everything will work out." Tonya exited Becca's office and closed the door quietly behind her.

Becca walked over to her full length mirror, fixed her cream colored, single-breasted, cashmere blazer. Under which she wore a scarlet red silk, with lace trim, camisole. She smoothed her matching cream colored cashmere, tea- length skirt with a sleek split that rose graciously just above the right knee. Her hosiery was ultra sheer coffee that made her legs look bare. On her feet she wore scarlet red, two-inch leather heels. Becca's left wrist was dressed in a gold and platinum Rolex watch with diamonds surrounding the face. Her right wrist wore a one carat diamond tennis bracelet. Becca's mom always taught her that a woman should never have to wait on a man to buy her anything. So, if there was something, especially jewelry, that she wanted, Becca felt she owed it to herself to get it.

Becca tightened the hair pins in her French roll. With her braids pulled back, her diamond studded earrings sparkled beautifully against her warm walnut brown skin. Becca turned once more in the mirror. It had taken her a few years to realize how beautiful she was. Once that revelation came, she was able to stick to a diet and change her way of life. It had taken a year to lose 100 lbs. Now, she just wanted to lose 50 more to reach her goal weight. Then she would be completely off of her medicines. But she loved how good she was looking in her clothes. Mark had been so supportive through her weight loss. He made sure to fix meals that she could eat and if they had dessert, Mark prepared some type of low carb, sugar-free dessert just for her. He always encouraged her and told her how pretty she was.

Becca walked over to her desk and pressed the button to page Tonya. "Mrs. Cooper, please send in my next appointment. Thank you." Becca then took a seat behind her mahogany desk and reached for a new enrollment folder.

Mrs. Cooper opened her office door and said, "Ms. Thomas this is Mr. Harris, your 10:00 appointment. As Mrs. Cooper entered the office and stepped near the desk, Becca rose from her chair, her mouth dropped open and her knees buckled. Mrs. Cooper looked concerned and reached to steady Becca. "Are you alright?"

Becca was shocked and angry. She was staring at a 6'5, 300 lb, brown-skinned man. He was dressed in a navy blue cotton, long sleeve camp shirt with khaki colored Dockers and some beige Karl Kani boots. The man was clean cut and shaved. He would look like a prime catch for someone who didn't know him.

"Hello, Becca. How are you?" asked Rob in a deep, sexy voice never taking his eyes off of her.

Mrs. Cooper looked at him with confusion in her eyes. "Do you know our principal, sir?"

Before he could answer, Becca found her breath and her strength to stand up straight again. "Yes, he knows me. This is Robert Harris, Bryan's dad." There was an awkward silence.

"Oh, oh I see. Well I didn't know Becca or I would've informed you earlier. And Mr. Harris, you should've been a little more forthcoming with your identity. Well, I'll leave the two of you alone." Mrs. Cooper started for the door but Becca stopped her.

"Tonya, please do not let my son know that Mr. Harris is here. Thank you." Becca whispered to Mrs. Cooper as she touched her shoulder.

Mrs. Cooper nodded and shut the door quietly.

"Well, well don't you look good! How's about a hug for yo' baby's daddy." Rob stood in the middle of the office with his arms open and a big smile on his face.

Becca could not believe this man. He had just called Friday and now he was standing in her office on Tuesday. She was speechless.

Rob put his arms down after Becca brushed passed him and grabbed a bottled water out of her little dorm-sized fridge in the opposite corner of her office. Becca needed something to calm her nerves. But what she did not know was that Rob was watching every move she made. He could not believe how gorgeous Becca looked. Rob had always thought Becca was beautiful but today she was radiant. Rob wanted so much to take her in his arms and hold her and kiss all the pain away. But he decided to be cool and take things slow. Besides, he didn't see a ring on her finger so she must not be married. However, he was disturbed by all the pictures with Mark and some little girl in them. They really looked like they were more than just friends. Rob decided to ignore the pictures, except the one of her and Bryan at Disney World last summer.

"Wow! Bryan is so big now! He looks just like us." Rob emphasized the word *us* as he sat in the burgundy leather winged back chair in front of Becca's desk.

"Well kids usually don't stay babies forever. That's why it's so important for parents to be an active part of their lives while their young because they grow up so quickly!" Becca spoke each word as if she were spewing out venom. Now she was walking back to her desk about 10 feet away.

"Ok Becca, I deserve that and a whole lot more, but I really need you to give me a break. I miss you guys and I want to be back in your lives." Rob was pleading with her it seemed.

Becca looked at him and couldn't help but melt a little on the inside. After all, this was the father of her son and she did love Rob at one time. But there was also a lot of pain and brokenness in her heart that he had caused. She couldn't afford to be stupid again. "Rob, look, I'm not the same person I used to be. I don't want you to think that there can ever be anything romantic between us again! You hurt me and I won't allow you to do it anymore." Becca looked at Rob with fury in her eyes. "If you want to build a relationship with your son and try to be a father to him, please be consistent. Bryan has been through enough! You got that Rob! No MORE!!"

Becca was furious and practically leaning over her desk, pointing at him. "You are to blame – no one else but you!"

Rob was impressed and a little stunned by Becca's strength and no nonsense attitude. He knew it would not be easy to win her back but he was determined to try. Rob spoke carefully and gently. "Becca, I'm sorry from the bottom of my heart. I was afraid of all of yo' dreams and goals. In my mind, I just couldn't keep up with your expectations. You wanted so much from life and I couldn't give it to you. So I just left. It wasn't right, but I had to go!" He rubbed his hand over his face and let out a heavy sigh.

Becca slowly sat down and leaned back in her chair. She could not believe the softness – the vulnerability that had washed over Rob's face. She was not use to seeing him like this. "Rob, what do you mean you *had* to go? The thing for you to have done was to stay and communicate, not run! I loved you and everything I wanted was so our lives would be better – yours, mine, and Bryan's. We could've worked through your fears together, as a family."

"Can't we still try, baby." Rob stood up and walked around the desk to Becca and knelt down beside her chair. "I still love you, woman! You have always been in my heart." Rob took Becca's hand in his and kissed it.
BEEP!

The intercom startled Becca and she slipped her hand out of Rob's gentle grasp and back to reality. "Yes, Mrs. Cooper."

"Becca, Mark is out here. He is signing Bryan out for the rest of the day. He would like to see you before Bryan comes down from class." Mrs. Cooper's voice was a little concerned.

"Tonya, please tell Mark I'll be right out." Becca was confused and rattled. She hadn't realized how quickly the time had gone by. What would Mark say when he saw Rob coming out of her office? Well, it was about to be revealed to her in living color. Becca jumped up almost knocking Rob out of the way. "Rob, I can't talk about this right now. Give me your number and I'll make sure Bryan calls you tomorrow."

"Tomorrow? What about today?" Rob stood up agitated. "And why is Mark taking my son out of school, but you won't let him know that I'm in the building! It was you and me that conceived that boy, not you and Mark! Sometimes I think you forget who Bryan's father really is, Becca!" Rob was getting angry. He could not believe he had just shared a piece of his heart with this woman and she was dismissing him for another man. Rob had always resented Mark because he was there for Becca and Bryan the way Rob knew he should've been. He always figured that Mark's feelings were deeper than just friend and Godfather and he didn't like it.

"Rob, I think you're the one that has forgotten who Bryan's father is." Becca smoothed her jacket and checked her face in the mirror by the door. "Please remember you walked out on us, not the other way around. So don't question me about who I let spend time with Bryan! You don't have that right anymore." Becca's tone was even and harsh as she turned and glared at Rob. She wanted him to know that she was in control. She opened the door to her office and spoke directly to Rob as if he were a stranger. "Thank you for coming by Mr. Harris. I'll be sure to have Bryan call you tomorrow. Have a good day."

Rob was so angry he could barely say a word. He grabbed his jacket and stormed out of Becca's office.

When Mark looked up he was shocked to see Rob standing there staring at him. The words were stuck in his throat. Finally, he pushed out a dry greeting. "Hello, Rob."

Rob continued to glare at Mark. He was trying to intimidate him. But Mark would not be broken. And to further intensify the sting of Becca's rejection, Mark side stepped Rob, kissed Becca on the cheek, and spoke flirtatiously, "Hey Becca, you sure know how to light up a room." Then Mark slipped his arm around her waist.

Words finally flew out of Rob's mouth like daggers. "Watch yo'self, dog! Becca, we'll finish our conversation later." He exited the main office and then the building. When he was back in his truck, Rob hit the steering wheel with his fists and spoke into the air. "Mark, I'm not gon' let you take what belongs to me! I have Becca Thomas!" Then, Rob started his black F-350 Truck and peeled down the street.

Mark looked into Becca's eyes and knew not to ask any questions. He just wrapped his strong, muscular arms around her and held her close to him. "It's ok Becca. I'm here now, just let it out." Mark gently rubbed her back as Becca laid her head on his shoulder and let the tears fall. Mrs. Cooper gave Becca some tissue and closed the door to her office.

Becca found refuge in Mark's strength and ability to know exactly what she needed. She wanted so much to tell him how she really felt about him but Becca was afraid. Afraid that their friendship would never be the same again if he didn't feel the same way. And what about those precious children, Bryan and Camille, that had come to depend on both Mark and Becca. No, there was just too much at stake. Instead, she would just rest in the riverbed of his warm embrace.

Bryan was so glad to see Mark. He was really surprised when his mom told him to go get his coat and book bag because he would be leaving school for the rest of the day.

The two of them went to Ruby Tuesdays for lunch. They had cheese and bacon fries for an appetizer. Bryan ordered the Cheddar burger platter with onion rings and a Sprite. Mark ordered the Bourbon Street Chicken with steamed vegetables and a Raspberry Iced Tea.

"Mark, I can't believe you came all the way here to spend the afternoon with me! This is the best!" Bryan was very enthused.

"Bry, I told you I was gonna be here for you. Besides, it's good to take a little break from everything and just relax. Don't cha' think?" Mark winked at his God-son and gave him a big smile.

"Yeah, it sure is!" Bryan shouted. How long are you staying?"

"How long do you want me to stay?"

"I wish you could at least spend the night. But, I know you probably have to get back to take care of Camille. Where's she at, anyway?"

"She's in school right now, but Lena's gonna pick her up afterschool and let her spend the night. So, I guess you get your wish, buddy, because I can stay all night!"

Bryan gave his Godfather a high-five across the table and they continued talking about everything from school to sports to girls. Bryan was having the best afternoon ever.

Becca made it home about six o'clock. When she pulled up to her house, she saw Mark's light gold Cadillac Seville parked in the drive. Her heart began to race. When she walked in the door, no one was downstairs. She placed the two bags of groceries on the kitchen countertop and walked into the family room. She could hear Bryan's T.V. turned up very loud. Becca knew they were playing some X-Box 360 game. "Hello, I'm home!" She called toward the steps but no one answered. She could hear them laughing and talking loudly. Becca set her briefcase down next to the loveseat. She pushed the blinking red button on the answering machine that sat on the end table in her family room and sank down into the bronze colored Italian Leather loveseat cushions. She took off her shoes and unbuttoned her jacket as she listened to a voice that would not leave her alone.

"Becca, please call me tonight. We really need to finish what we started in the office. I love you and tell Bryan I love him too. See ya later."

Becca pushed the erase button and breathed heavily. "I'm so tired of these games! Why won't he just leave us alone?" She laid her head back.

"What games?" Mark had come downstairs while Becca was venting and heard Becca's statement.

"Becca didn't notice Mark leaning against the wall in one of his black A-shirts that he always wore under his sweaters. He looked so good standing there. Becca had to turn away to keep from staring like a school girl. "Oh, just a wrong number. Somebody's always playin' on the phone." She laughed nervously. She did not know how much longer she was going to be able to withstand Mark's penetrating stare. Every time she turned to glance at him it was as if he were looking right through her. Becca wanted so much to tell him the truth but that would mean hours and hours of talking about Rob. Besides, Mark was only spending one night and she didn't want to spend the brevity of their time together talking about Bryan's dad. So, she changed the subject. "I was just about to put the groceries away and change my clothes so I can cook dinner. Would you like to help me?" Becca asked him as she brushed pass him to get to the kitchen. Their hands touched briefly and the smell of his cologne filled the atmosphere.

Mark watched every move Becca made. She had taken off her jacket and shoes. She slipped on some beige fluffy slippers that she kept in the family room. He was in awe of the beauty that illuminated her countenance. Mark knew how pretty she was even before she realized it. But today, when he looked at her, putting things away in the kitchen, he was struck by her inner radiance. In spite of the situation with Rob, the demands from her job, and raising a pre-teen boy, she still glowed at the end of the day and smelled of sweet honeysuckle. "Amazing." He hadn't known that he had spoken out loud.

"What's amazing?" She asked as she shut the refrigerator door.

"That the most beautiful woman in the world just tried to hit on me!" Mark smiled. "If I weren't a God-fearing man I might have taken you up on that invitation."

Becca was caught off guard and she almost dropped a jar of whole sweet pickles. "What invitation might that be, sir?" Becca was really confused.

"To help you change your clothes, of course! Don't act like you didn't say it, Becca." He started smiling.

"You are crazy, Mark Simmons! I wanted your help putting the groceries away and then I was going upstairs, alone, to change. What are you thinking about, Man of God? I oughtta call yo' pastor right now!"

Becca and Mark laughed so hard and loud that Bryan came down to see what was goin' on. "Hey, what's so funny? Hi mom. Are you cryin'?"

Becca wiped the tears from her eyes. "Tears of laughter, baby, tears of sheer laughter!" Becca hugged her son and gave him a swat on the butt.

"Watch it mom, I'm a young man now!" Bryan tried to give his mother a serious look.

"Ok, Ok! Well since I have all of this manpower in one room, why don't you guys finish putting the food away while I go change into my play clothes?" Becca did not wait for an answer. She just grabbed a bottle of water out of the fridge and headed up the stairs. "Oh yeah Bry, don't forget to take out the trash! Thanks guys!" She laughed the rest of the way upstairs.

Mark yelled after her, "Yes masta'! We won't forget the trash!" He and Bryan continued to laugh. Bryan, however didn't think it was as funny as Mark did. But that was alright because he was just glad to have Mark there with them.

Becca was standing in front of her antique full length mirror. She had taken off her skirt, stockings, and camisole. She stood there in just her black bra and panties. "I can't believe it!" She thought to herself. "I think Mark was flirting with me. Naw, maybe not. He's always acting silly. Or was he? Becca, just calm down. Don't get yourself all excited over nothing. Remember you don't want to end up having sex with Mark – you want him to marry you! So, remain a virtuous woman!" Becca often had to talk to herself that way in order to fight that fornicating spirit that at one time held her captive.

Becca slipped on some navy sweatpants. She pulled on a long

sleeved, v-neck orange t-shirt and placed her bare, manicured feet back into her slippers. She also took off her watch and pulled her hair back in a ponytail. Then, she went into her bathroom and washed her face with some Noxzema and brushed her teeth. Becca hung her clothes up and went back downstairs to start dinner.

After dinner, Mark and Bryan did the dishes and put the food away. Becca was at the dining room table finishing some paper work. It was almost 9:30. Mark told Bryan to take his shower and get ready for bed.

"But Mark, I should get to stay up later because you're here." Bryan gave Mark a hug.

"Don't even try it! If you were at my house you'd been in bed by 9:00, so the way I see it you already got to stay up later. It's all in how you look at it. Now go kiss your mother and get upstairs." Mark was firm with his voice.

"Yes, sir. Thanks for a great day. I love you." Bryan hugged his Godfather again and went to go kiss Becca goodnight. "Love you, mom. I've got to go to bed, now."

"Alright, now you give your teeth a good brushing and I'll be up to check on you later. I love you too, son. Sweet Dreams." Becca kissed him on the forehead and whispered a prayer over him before she sent him on his way.

Mark sat in the chair next to Becca. So he could see what she was working on. "How many more evaluations do you have to finish?" Mark asked.

"Last one. Why, did you wanna go for a midnight walk or something?" She smiled at him very coyly. Becca was always coming up with some fantastic escapade for Mark to embark upon. He hated telling her no but sometimes her bright ideas were a little much.

"No, I just want to talk to you before we have to go to bed." Mark smiled back at Becca and then stood and walked into the family room.

Becca looked up from her paperwork and watched Mark walk into the next room and sit down on the couch. She didn't know how but it seemed as if her love for Mark had grown even stronger during this visit. She wanted so badly to run into his arms. The feeling was so intense she thought she would just burst! But Becca refused to take a chance on declaring her feelings for Mark. He meant so much to her and Bryan and it was just too high a risk to take. So she closed her binder, placed her reading glasses on the table, and went into the kitchen. Becca pulled out two crystal flute glasses and a bottle of sparkling white grape juice she had chilling in the freezer. As she poured it into the glasses she could tell it was perfectly chilled because it was slushy. She knew Mark would like that. Then she placed the two glasses on a tray with the half full bottle of sparkling white grape juice and proceeded to the family room.

When Mark saw her enter the room with the tray, he immediately jumped up and helped her with it. He motioned for her to sit down on the sofa next to him and handed her a glass. Mark spoke gently and with great concern, "Becca, how are you, really?"

"I'm fine, great in fact, especially now that my best friend is here!" She spoke quickly and with too much excitement as she took a long sip of her drink. "How's everything going with you? Is Camille doing alright? I sure miss her."

"Listen Becca, I have known you for too long. Don't try and change the subject! I'm fine and so is Camille. She misses you too. But I know you are not ok. I saw how flushed you got when Rob was in your office this morning. How long has he been back?" Mark was very intense. He wanted so much to protect Becca and Bryan from Rob's hurricane of lies and empty promises.

Becca looked up from her empty glass and spoke carefully, trying not to let her true feelings betray her. "Mark, I was just shocked, I mean he'd just called the day before and then to have him show up at my office a few days later. It was weird! All those feelings I thought I had dealt with – the anger, confusion, and disappointment – it just all came flooding back like a gigantic eighty foot, angry ocean wave. I was completely caught off guard." Becca dropped her head and allowed defenses to drop.

Mark slid closer to Becca, took her empty glass and set it on the table, then wrapped his loving arms around her. He just rocked her gently as she laid her head on his chest and cried. Mark and Becca had a language all their own that surpassed words or feelings – it was almost mystical the way they understood what each other needed. They sat that way for almost an hour before Mark broke the communing of their silent thoughts. "Becca, please don't let him back in your life. You guys have been through enough. I can't stand to watch him hurt you again. Please Becca. Whatever you need I'll give it to you. No matter what it is I'll be here for the both of you. Don't ever feel like you can't talk to me – from your heart." Mark gently brushed the right side of her cheek with his hand.

Becca didn't want to look at him because she was afraid that her eyes would betray her and show Mark the deep feelings she had hidden from him all of these years. So she just slid her arms around his waist and rested her head on his shoulder. She softly whispered, "Mark, sing to me."

"What? Becca, why are you trying to avoid talking to me? You can't hold all that stuff inside of you forever." Mark was really concerned about her.

"Mark, please. I don't want to spend the only night you're staying here talking about Rob. Just sing something sweet – something that will encourage my soul. For me, Mark. Do it for me." Becca pressed her body against him and closed her eyes tightly.

Mark rarely said no to Becca and this time was no exception. He didn't want to push her. He knew she would open up when she was ready. He just leaned back and began to sing *His Eye is on the Sparrow*. Becca loved to hear Mark sing. It always made her smile and ministered to her soul. He sang softly until Becca fell asleep wrapped in his embrace. He brushed her hair back behind her ear and kissed her forehead. Then Mark carefully pulled the burgundy, Chenille throw blanket from the back of the sofa and spread it across the both of them. He whispered a prayer over Becca. Closed his eyes and fell asleep holding the woman with whom he had secretly fallen in love.

Chapter 5

It was a chilly Wednesday afternoon. Mark sat at his desk looking out the window watching the light snow flurries fall from the heavens. He thought about how nice it would be to have a snowball fight with the kids and Becca. He couldn't wait for their Valentine's vacation. Especially after the wonderful night he had just spent in Toledo. He could still feel Becca in his arms and he enjoyed having her there. Mark knew that the situation with Rob was still wearing on Becca and he was bound and determined to do whatever it took to keep his family safe and intact. Rob was not going to mess up their lives again.

He was so engrossed in his daydream about Becca that he did not see Shawna standing in his office doorway watching him. Shawna Lewis was one of Mark's co-workers at the bank. She was also a friend. They had known each other for about six years. Shawna was a beautiful woman – tall, slender build, light caramel skin, and long black hair. She always wore designer clothes and shoes. She was divorced with no children. Mark had been a good friend to Shawna through her divorce. Her marriage had been one filled with abuse and turmoil. So, it was understandable that she would develop feelings for the one man in her life that was kind, gentle, and loving – Mark Simmons.

Shawna cleared her throat loudly. "U-Um, Mr. Simmons. Earth to Mr. Simmons. Are you responding?"

Mark was startled. He hadn't realized that someone was in the room. He tried to wipe the silly grin off his face that he could feel forming but it kept getting bigger. "Oh, oh come on in Shawna. I didn't see you standing there. I was just thinking about some of my new accounts. What do you need?" He nervously reorganized a stack of file folders on his desk.

Shawna smirked sarcastically at him as she strutted into his office. "Come on Mark. You have to do better than that. The look on your face already told on you. So, how was your Toledo visit? I'd venture a guess that all is well in T-town!" Shawna knew how much Mark valued his friendship with Becca and his role as Godfather to Bryan. She also knew what Mark and Becca seemed to clumsily try to hide from everyone else – that they were in love with each other but both of them were too afraid to take a risk.

Mark was blushing a bit. "Yes, Shawna everyone is fine. We had a really nice time. As a matter of fact, we're all goin' to Hueston Woods Resort in a couple of weeks." Mark was trying not to sound too excited. But his face kept betraying his heart.

"Oooh, Valentine's Weekend! How romantic! Are the kids going too or just you and Becca?" Shawna was taunting him but she was also trying to get information.

"Don't start Shawna! How many times do I have to tell you that Becca and I are just friends!! And to answer your question, of course the kids are going." Mark was trying not to get agitated.

"Look Mark, it's none of my business anyway. I just came in here to drop off these reports that need to be signed off on by Friday. I'll leave you to your daydreams about those new accounts. Are we still on for dinner tonight?" Shawna was walking back toward the door hoping he hadn't forgotten.

Mark rubbed his forehead and repeated the words, "Dinner? Tonight? Oh, oh yeah at that new Chinese restaurant on the West Side. Yes, of course. We're goin' right after work, right?" Mark had forgotten all about it until she had said something. He was actually tired but he was a man of his word. She had been planning this for the last week.

"Do you wanna take my car or yours? Shawna turned around at the door.

"Yours will be fine. I'm still a little tired from the drive this morning. I'll meet you in the lobby at 5:15." Mark smiled at her.

He picked up one of the folders she had just put on his desk and began to go over the reports. Shawna watched him then stepped outside his office and closed the door. Mark was so handsome and such a gentleman. Even though she could tell he was tired from his trip, he still wanted to keep his promise to her. This was the kind of thing that made her want him all the more. It didn't matter that he and Becca had known each other for sixteen years and that they had all of this history. She was the one in Cleveland with him every day and Shawna was going to use it to her advantage. If Becca was too scared or confused to take a chance on Mark, too bad for her! Shawna was not and she had nothing to lose.

Bryan was standing in the door, watching for his dad, when Rob pulled up. Bryan had mixed emotions about seeing his dad after all these years but that was still his dad. Rob hopped out the car and walked up the side walk to the door. All at once Bryan swung open the door and gave his dad a big hug.

Rob was speechless. "Hi, dad, I'm glad you're here. Come on in." Rob followed his son into the house. Becca was in the family room sitting in her burgundy recliner reading a book by T.D. Jakes. She looked up and spoke softly, "Hello, Rob. How are you?"

Rob wanted so much to just grab her, pull her close to him, and kiss her gently. He remembered how soft and warm her lips were. He desired to feel her love again but he knew it was too soon. So he just touched her shoulder as he spoke. "Hey, Becca. I'm great now that I'm finally getting' to spend some time with my boy. Thanks for lettin' me come over." Rob walked over to the sofa and sat down next to Bryan.

Bryan was so excited about having his dad there he was talking a mile a minute. He told Rob about his school camping trip he had just gone on back in the fall. Then he told him about the summer before last when he played soccer for a community league. Bryan also started whispering to his dad about the girls he liked in school. That's when Becca took it upon herself to leave the room so they could have some privacy. "Bryan, I'm goin' upstairs to my room and finish my book. If you need me just holler." Becca turned her attention toward Bryan's dad. "Rob, I'm glad you kept your promise. I really hope you continue to build your relationship with our son. He is quite a young man – just extraordinary."

Rob looked up at Becca standing by the recliner in a pale blue silk blouse and a straight black jean skirt with a split on the side. Her braids were pulled back in a pony tail with three braid ringlets lightly cascading the side of her face. Becca didn't have on any makeup except for the dark berry lip liner and clear gloss which when mixed together gave a soft wine color to her full lips. He couldn't believe how beautiful she looked standing there. Rob was almost intimidated by Becca's strength. It was like she had found a place in herself where she was really happy and that joy radiated from every part of her. "Becca, I'm here if he needs anything. You just go relax. I'll let you know when I get ready to leave."

She smiled politely and walked toward the stairs. When she got half way up the stairs, Becca looked back to catch another look at her son enjoying his father. But, to her surprise, Rob was watching her. Their eyes met and he winked at her and mouthed the words, I love you. Then, he turned his attention back toward Bryan and the pictures he was showing him from their trip to Florida. Becca continued up the steps, clutching her chest and praying. "Lord if you don't keep me I won't be kept!"

When it got to be about 10:00, Becca didn't hear any noise from downstairs. She got concerned and walked out of her room to the top of the stairs. But as she was getting ready to take a step down, she noticed the light on in Bryan's room and voices talking low. She stepped back and walked down the hall to Bryan's room where the door was cracked open. Her heart became full as she watched her son laying in his father's arms watching a video on T.V. Becca could see that Bryan was sleep and Rob looked like he was almost out for the count himself. She didn't say a word. She just turned around and went back to her room. It wasn't about her or Rob it was about Bryan. And she wasn't about to interrupt their long overdue father and son time. Becca closed the door to her room and went into her bathroom to take a shower and get ready for bed. She thought about how a part of her still loved Rob and wanted him to be a permanent part of their lives. But she also couldn't get pass the fact that Rob had lied to them so much over the years and the wounds were still tender.

Rob laid Bryan back in his bed and covered him with the football comforter. He clicked off the T.V. and kissed his son on the forehead. "Things are gonna be different this time Bryan. Daddy promises." Rob turned the light off and walked out of his son's room closing the door behind him. He was headed toward Becca's room to tell her he was leaving when he heard the shower running and Becca singing. Rob decided to sit in the oversized recliner that was situated across from her bed by a window. He didn't want to disturb her; but then again it would be nice to hold her wet, uncovered body in his arms and make love to her all night long. Becca and Rob never had a problem satisfying each other in the bedroom. It was when their feet hit the ground that things got crazy.

Becca turned the shower off, reached for her oversized paisley green bath towel that hung on the wall next to the shower door. She dried herself off and then wrapped the towel around her body. She walked over to the mirrored medicine cabinet and pulled out a small bottle of body spray. Becca sprayed it all over herself. The smell of sweet honeysuckle filled the room. After she finished, Becca walked into her bedroom and plopped down on her bed. She grabbed some lotion that was sitting on the night stand and began applying it to her legs and feet. Then her arms and when she was just about to unwrap her towel she heard a voice from across the room that scared her to death.

"Do you need some help wit' dat, baby?" Rob leaned forward into the light so Becca could see him. He decided to test the waters to see if they were still inviting.

Becca let out a hushed cry, "Whew, Jesus! Are you crazy?! She tightened the towel back around her and sat up straight on her bed. "Rob Harris, why are you in my room. You need to excuse yourself so I can put on some clothes." Rob watched Becca for a moment. He knew that she was feeling something because even though she protested she still hadn't moved off the bed. So, Rob got up and went over to her side of the bed and sat down. He didn't say a word. He just stared at her seductively as if he could see right through her thick bath towel.

"Rob, Rob, what is wrong with you? I asked you to please leave my room. Why are you looking at me like that?" Becca knew she needed to get up from the bed but it was like a magnet had drawn her down and she could not escape.

Rob touched her hand gently and then slowly caressed her arm working his way up to her shoulders. Becca felt herself softening and her deep rivers begin to flow. Rob knew that there was still a part of her that loved him and he was determined to resurrect it. "I'm sorry Becca. I love you more than you know." Rob leaned in close to Becca. So close that he could feel the change in her breathing. He lightly touched her lips with his and felt her push back. He slid his arm around her waist and pulled her into him. They kissed passionately until something struck Becca deep down in her soul. She pulled away abruptly and jumped off the bed.

"Rob you've got to go! I'm not the same woman and I won't be taken for granted. Please let yourself out the front door. Becca went back into the bathroom and locked the door. She refused to exit no matter how hard Rob tried to coax her out. When Becca heard his truck start up, she exhaled and slid to the floor. "Please Lord not again! I don't want to make the same mistakes! Help me Jesus!" Becca began to sob profusely. She was confused and it seemed the storm in the pit of her stomach had started to rage. That only meant one thing – a path of devastation and destruction. She had to find a way to stop the familiar betrayal of her heart before it snatched her freedom.

As Mark and Shawna were driving back to the office to pick up his car from the parking garage, they laughed and talked about how good the food was that night, some of their co-workers, and Camille's progress in school. But Shawna really wanted to talk about Mark's visit with Becca. She needed to know how much alone time they had spent together and if they had somehow crossed the friendship line. So she decided to very carefully start walking through that mine field. "So, Mark, how is Becca doing these days? It's been awhile since she's been up here. Is everything alright?"

"Yeah, she's fine. Just continue to pray for her and Bryan. Their goin' through a delicate situation right now. But thanks for askin' 'bout them. I'll be sure to tell them that you were concerned." Mark didn't always understand the tension he felt when the three of them were sometimes together. Occasionally, he would catch himself explaining to Becca why he and Shawna had done something together or gone somewhere together and he didn't know why. It also seemed like Shawna's attitude would change a bit when he talked about Becca. But Mark just dismissed the feelings as paranoia and moved on.

Well what did you guys do while you were there? Shawna was trying not to be transparent but it was hard because Mark would only give her so much information. "I mean if I'm not getting' too personal."

Mark looked at her with that silly grin he always got when talking about Becca. "Shawna, what do you mean too personal? We're just talkin' about Becca. Bryan and I hung out during the afternoon and then Becca cooked a big dinner for us that evening. I helped Bry with his homework, Becca had some evaluations to finish, and then Bryan went to bed. Becca and I did our normal up most of the night talking routine until we fell asleep. I got up this morning. Becca cooked breakfast for us. We got dressed and we all left the house together." Mark laid his head back on the leather head rest of Shawna's 2013 black Acura Legend. He could feel the exhaustion starting to overtake him.

"You and Becca always stay up late talking when you guys get together. Why is that Mark?" Shawna asked curiously.

"I don't know I guess it's because we don't get to see each other on a regular basis. So we just try to spend as much time with each other as possible. Why do you ask?" Mark's eyes were starting to close.

Shawna had to try and cover her curiosity by acting like it was no big deal. "Oh, no reason. It's just peculiar that a man and a woman who are not romantically involved can find so much to talk about all the time." Then she decided to change the subject. "Hey Mark, since you're so tired why don't you just leave your car at the garage and let me take you home. I can pick you up for work in the morning too. I'd hate for you to be driving home and get into an accident because you fell asleep behind the wheel. Ok?"

"Well, ok only because I'm extremely exhausted. I couldn't move another step if I tried." Mark let the sleep fall down around him as the steady movement of the car rocked him.

Shawna was amazed at how handsome Mark looked even asleep. She was positive that this was the man for her. Whatever she had to do to get closer to Mark Simmons, she was going to do it.

Back at the motel, Robert was laying in his bed thinking about the kiss he shared with Becca that night. He knew that his efforts were not in vain. He also thought about how mature his son was getting to be. He was angry with himself for missing so much of Bryan's life. But now that he was back he would do whatever it took to become a permanent part of Bryan and Becca's life again. Rob knew it wasn't going to be easy but he was willing to buckle down and get to work. The first thing he needed to do was to try and get Becca to trust him again and that would definitely take some time. But at least he now knew that she did still have feelings for him – especially after that kiss. Once Rob regained her trust it would be easy to win her heart. He knew deep down that a piece of it still belonged to him. But there was a factor he hadn't banked on and that was Mark Simmons. He knew they were good friends but it seemed like they had become more since Rob had been gone. Even Bryan seemed to think of this Mark character as a father. All of that was going to cease. Rob knew he had to get Mark out of the picture and that was going to take some careful planning. Rob would be damned if he'd let this dude sneak in the back door and steal his family away – not when he was finally ready to settle down and commit. Rob rolled over on his side and as he closed his eyes, his mind became fixed on what he must do. First thing tomorrow morning he would start looking for a job in Toledo and then find himself an apartment. Rob would not be separated from Becca and Bryan any longer. He dreamed of the time when he would hold her dripping wet body again and be bathed in her warm, soft kisses.

Chapter 6

It was Sunday morning and Becca was hurrying Bryan around the house so they wouldn't be late for Sunday School.

"Why do I have to go, mom? My class is boring! Those kids are bad and Sis. Watkins has to yell at them most of the time. It's crazy! Why don't we just go out for breakfast then be on time for morning service?"

Becca looked at her son with amazement. He was growing up so fast and learning to articulate himself so well. But she didn't have time for his mess this morning. "Bryan Robert Harris, I don't have the time or the patience to fool with you this morning! Get yo' rusty behind in that shower, put on yo' clothes, and let's go! If you don't I will beat yo' behind until it hurts for you to sit down-- you got that!!"

"O.K. mom, O.K. you don't have to bring violence into the conversation. I was just making a suggestion. I'm getting in the shower right now. I'll be ready in twenty minutes." Bryan ran off to his bathroom in the hallway and left Becca sitting at her vanity. She was putting on her makeup when the phone rang.

"Praise the Lord and good morning!" Becca answered the phone cheerfully.

"Hallelujah and good morning to you, sunshine! How are you feeling today?" The familiar voice sang to her.

"Hey Mark. I'm blessed and highly favored of the Lord. How about you?" Becca smiled so hard she just knew Mark could see her. She loved when he called her on Sunday mornings.

"Likewise, likewise. Are you guys getting' ready for church?" Mark questioned.

"Tryin'," breathing a sigh of exhaustion." That boy of yours knows he can work a nerve early in the morning!" Becca chuckled. "How about little Ms. Camille, I know she is doin' exactly what she's suppose to right?"

Mark grunted, "Becca you must be smoking' this morning. Make sure you go straight to the altar when you get to church!" He started laughing. You know those kids are so much alike it's scary! As a matter of fact she just got in the shower." Since Mark knew Rob visited with Becca and Bryan last night, he was curious about what happened. "So, Becca, how was your visit with Rob? Is Bryan O.K.? And what type of false hope did he give Bry this time?"

Becca was a little shocked by all the questions Mark started throwing at her. She had to be careful not to say too much. Mark always had an uncanny way of pulling more information out of Becca than she was ready to give. "Well, why don't you try not to be so subtle," she laughed. "Just say what's on your mind!"

Mark answered in a sarcastic tone, "Well you don't have to tell me anything if you don't want to."

"Stop playing Mark, you know I was going to tell you the juicy details. But, nothing fantastic really happened. Rob and Bryan sat in the family room talking about any and everything. It was as if they had not lost any years. It was quite unbelievable." Becca paused unconsciously not realizing she was smiling at the thought of her son with his father. She inadvertently became silent until she heard Mark calling her name.

"Becca, Becca, BECCA!" Mark found himself shouting through the phone. "Are you still there?"

"Y-Yeah, man, and you don't have to yell." Becca spoke with agitation. "That's all that really happened. Rob stayed until Bryan fell asleep while they were watchin' a movie in his room."

Mark trying to hold back his concern, "So, Rob saw Bryan's room?

"Yeah?"Becca responded cautiously.

"And what else did Mr. Harris see? Did you show him the phone bill? What about your utility bills? Oh and maybe the house note? Was he interested in seeing any of that?" Mark made sure Becca could hear his distaste about the whole situation. "I mean it's your business how you deal with him but I sure hope he left an envelope on the table with some monetary show of affection."

Becca was upset that Mark would think she was that easy. She had to take a deep breath before she said something that both of them would regret. "Look here Mr. Simmons, I'm a grown woman and I am well aware of my son's father's obligations, even better than you." The tone in her voice was unmistakable. "Oh by the way, how was dinner with Shawna last night?" Becca asked in a retaliatory tone.

Mark felt the mood in their conversation change drastically. He knew instantly that something happened between Rob and Becca, whether it was physical or emotional. He decided to back off and give Becca some room to breathe. "Dinner was fine. I was tired so she drove me home. Becca, I wasn't trying to make you mad. I just don't want Rob to hurt you guys again. But I know you are able to handle the situation. Listen, I have to finish getting dressed for church. I'll call you later."

Becca breathed heavily, "I'm sorry Mark. I just have a lot going on right now. I thank the Lord for you and please don't stop looking out for me, OK?"

Mark was silent for a brief moment then cautiously responded. "Have a good time at church and tell Bryan I called. Good-bye Becca." Mark hung up the phone and sat down on the edge of his bed staring at the wall. He didn't know if he should be angry or worried. But he did know that sometimes you have to let some things go in order to hold onto them. Maybe it was time to step back from Becca and let her find her own way.

Mark was so deep in thought he didn't hear Camille come into his room. She was standing beside him in her purple robe and matching slippers that her Auntie Becca had bought for her birthday. Camille spoke softly, "Uncle Mark, are you OK? I thought I heard you yelling." She put an arm around him and kissed his cheek.

"Everything is fine baby girl. I love you. Now, go put on your lotion and stockings and I'll bring your dress to you when I'm done ironing it." Mark did everything he could to try to hide his disappointment and irritation with Becca and the whole situation.

Camille hugged her uncle, turned and skipped out of the room. She instinctively knew this was no time to cause problems.

As Becca and Bryan pulled up at House of Judah Worship Center, she felt a peace rest on her. She was very tired and confused. What did Mark want from her? What does Rob want? And more importantly what does Bryan need? These were the questions that flooded her mind all the way to church. As they rounded the corner, walking from the parking lot to the front of the church, Becca stopped dead in her tracks as Bryan took off running towards a familiar figure standing by the church door. All Becca could say was, "You've gotta be kidding me." She was so stunned at what she saw that she didn't have the time to grab Bryan before he took off running down the sidewalk and landed in his father's arms. She began walking toward them cautiously all the while praying in her spirit.

"Dad, Dad! Bryan was so excited to see his father. "I didn't know you were coming to church this morning." Bryan hugged his dad tightly.

"Yeah, well I thought I'd surprise you." As Rob held his son he looked at Becca, now standing a few feet away. "I told you that things were going to be different this time." Rob smiled, "Good morning, Becca, and how are you?"

Becca was stunned but she quickly regained her composure. "Good morning, sir. I am fine. What do we owe this pleasure?" Becca pulled her three quarter length black fur coat together.

"I told you I wanted us to be a family and that means in every area. So I thought I'd come out to see where my family goes to worship." Rob was smiling at her as if he could see straight through to her heart.

Becca responded coarsely, "First of all we are not a family. You made sure of that when you walked out on us six years ago. We share a wonderful son but that is all. So, if you want to see where he worships that is fine just don't try to make it something that it will never be. Second of all, you could have at least warned me that you were coming today. You think I like all these little surprises you keep throwing at us?"

Rob, knowing that Becca doesn't like to make scenes in public, stepped closer to her and reached out and pulled her into his arms and embraced her as two of the church sisters walked up behind them. He whispered softly in her ear, "I still love you." Then he released her and took Bryan by the hand and walked in the church.

Becca was so shocked that she did not notice Sister Lynette and Sister Marie standing behind her.

"Well Praise the Lord, Sis. Becca. Who was that going in the church with Bryan? I've never seen him before." They looked at Becca in a peculiar manner waiting anxiously for her response.

Becca responded very cautiously and without emotion, "He is Robert Harris, Bryan's Dad. "Becca immediately walked into the church. She did not feel like giving anymore answers to fuel the speed of the church. Service had already started when she walked into the sanctuary. Becca had to prepare herself for the curious stares that would be shot her way all through the service. This particular morning Becca was wearing a navy blue suit with a silk lime green shell underneath. Her braids were pinned up with a few of them hanging around her face. Her navy pumps had rhinestones that accented the heel of the shoe. Becca looked very professional; which was one of the things that always attracted Rob to her. She was so different from the other women he would mess around with-- Becca was a lady.

Bryan was so happy to have his dad in church with him. Becca slowly walked up the far aisle to the seventh pew from the front and sat beside Bryan. Rob sat on the other side of Bryan. Becca made sure not to make eye contact with Rob throughout the whole service. Afterwards, people came up and spoke to Becca that had never spoke to her before. She was so ready to get out of there. But she was trying not to be rude. Not to mention the fact that every time they got close to the door to leave someone else was calling her name. Then, it didn't help any that Rob would take that opportunity to drape his arm around her waist as if they were a happy couple. Becca was getting nauseated.

"Praise the Lord, Sis. Becca! How are you?"

"Oh Pastor Samson, Praise the Lord, I'm fine. I enjoyed the sermon today because I've been praying for wisdom." Becca put on a smile to hide the confusion in her heart.

Pastor Samson noticed that Becca was somewhat uncomfortable so he introduced himself to the gentleman with her. "Good to have you visiting with us today. I'm Pastor David Samson and what is your name?" Pastor held out his hand.

Before Rob could speak, Bryan yelled out, "This is my dad, Pastor!"

Rob smiled and shook Pastor Samson's hand. "My name is Robert Harris and I'm glad to be here today."

"Oh yes, Mr. Harris, I've heard about you. You live in, uh, Cincinnati, right? How long will you be in town?"

"Yes sir that's correct. But I may be relocating to be closer to my family. You know I've made some mistakes but I'm ready to do things the right way. Who knows you may be officiating a wedding soon." Rob smiled confidently and pulled Becca closer to him.

"Ok Rob I think it's time to go. Pastor, I'll see you at Bible Study. Tell First Lady Melinda I missed her today. God bless." Becca took Bryan's hand and walked quickly out of the front door to her vehicle. She was hoping that Rob would just disappear.

"Wait, wait mom, dad's coming. We have to invite him over for Sunday dinner. Momma, you're walking too fast!" Bryan kept trying to wiggle loose from her grasp.

Becca did not stop until she got to her car. She could not believe Rob's behavior. Enough was enough.

"Hey little man why don't you and I give mommy some time alone and go to Golden Corral and then maybe to a movie. We'll catch up with her back at the house." Rob was standing close to Bryan smiling at Becca.

"Please momma, please can I go with my dad. I'll be good. That way you can relax. We'll be home later." Bryan was excited.

Becca hated Rob for putting her in this situation. "OK baby boy. You just be careful and if you need me call. Do you have your cell phone?"

"Yes mom. Come on dad, let's go." Bryan grabbed Rob's keys out of his pocket, ran to his dad's truck and hopped in the passenger side front seat.

Rob walked up close to Becca and hugged her gently. "We'll be home about six or seven, baby. We can sit down and have a serious conversation then, OK?" Rob kissed her on the cheek and walked confidently to his truck. He jumped in on the driver's side and pulled off laughing and talking with his son..

Shawna's number appeared on Mark's phone as a missed call at 1:00 P.M. It was about 2:00 when Mark got out of church. He hit the speed dial button as he pulled out of the parking lot with Camille riding shotgun. "Well hello pretty lady how are you this afternoon?"

"Hey Mark, I'm fine. How are you doing?" Shawna tried not to sound over excited.

"Oh, I'm doing, just trying to make it. How was church today? I know the choir brought the house down." Mark tried to hide his sadness.

"It was good. We had a guest speaker today. I think that's why we got out earlier. Sis. Teresa sang pastor's favorite song, *"I Won't Complain"*, and she tore it up. The church went up in high praise. You should've been there Mark." Shawna spoke with such excitement.

Mark was uplifted just hearing Shawna's enthusiasm about the service. He always thought Shawna was beautiful and that she had a great personality. Shawna had gone through a terrible divorce that left her heart broken. When she met Mark, he was able to help her heal. Now, they were good friends but she still could not touch his soul the way Becca did. "Yeah maybe I'll visit soon. Well, Shawna

I'm getting ready to go in the house to warm up dinner. How about I call you a call later?"

Shawna tried to hide her disappointment in the conclusion of their conversation. "Ok Mark, but first tell me what you cooked today. I know it's something really good."

"Oh, nothing special, just some roast w/potatoes and carrots, green beans, fried corn, and some hot water corn bread. For dessert, I just whipped up a pound cake. If you haven't already eaten you are more than welcome to come over. The food should be ready in about thirty minutes."

"Well, since you invited me I'll be over in twenty. Do you want me to bring anything?"

"No Shawna, we're good. I'll see you in a few." Mark hung up the phone and began pulling food out of the refrigerator. Camille ran upstairs to change her clothes and finish up some homework. Mark was trying desperately not to think about his dispute with Becca that morning. He wanted to call her but thought it would be better to just give her some space. He decided that if Becca wanted to talk to him she would have to call.

As Shawna pulled up in the circular driveway of Mark's home and parked, she pulled down her visor and checked herself in the mirror. Her makeup was flawless. As she stepped out of her black Acura Legend she wore a pale blue pant suit that was tailored to her tall thin fashion model sized body with silver mule heels. Her black trench leather coat trimmed in fur swayed as she glided up the sidewalk to the front door. Shawna was confident that she would make Mark forget about Becca today.

Mark heard the doorbell ring and walked to the door to answer it. When he opened it, his breath was taken away by her beauty. He caught himself and immediately reached out to take her hand to guide her into the foyer. Once there, Mark took her coat and hung it in the closet. He greeted her with a warm smile and big hug. He complimented her on how lovely she looked.

"Well thank you sir. You don't look so bad yourself. And it sure smells wonderful in here. Where is Camille?" Shawna walked into the kitchen to find Mark's sister, Lena sitting there. "Hey Lena, what's going on? I haven't seen you in awhile." Shawna was a little disappointed because she thought that she would be able to spend time with Mark and Camille alone.

"Hey Shawna, I'm doing well. How have things been goin' with you?" Lena stood up and hugged Shawna.

"You know the same old stuff. Working hard and trying to take care of my business. We ought to go out to lunch sometimes, Lena." Shawna sat in the chair across the table from her and crossed her legs.

"Do you want something to drink Shawna?" Mark asked as he walked toward the fridge.

Shawna looked at Mark seductively and spoke steadily, "Oh something cold and wet would be great." She winked at him and smiled coyly.

"Ok then, well all I have to offer you is soda or fruit juice or maybe some bottled water." Mark was smiling back at Shawna.

"Bottled water is fine. And we'll discuss what you have to offer later." Shawna took the bottled water from Mark and turned her attention back toward Lena.

Mark couldn't believe the vibe that Shawna was giving him. He had no idea she was feelin' him like that. He excused himself from the kitchen to go get Camille for dinner. When he walked into her room, she looked up from her desk and smiled at him like her father used to do. He wanted to break down and cry at the thought of his older brother and the joy Ryan brought to his life when he was alive. "Hey babe, come on it's time to eat. Are you hungry?"

"You know I am Uncle Mark!" Camille jumped into his arms and gave him a big hug and kiss. "Did Auntie Shawna come over yet?" Camille could barely hold her excitement.

"Yes, she's downstairs."

"Come on, Come on Uncle Mark let's go downstairs and see her." Camille pulled her uncle towards the steps. But Mark stopped short.

"Camille, go downstairs and tell your Auntie Lena to start fixing the plates for everyone. I have something I need to do before I come back down."

"Got it Uncle Mark, see you downstairs. You betta' hurry or I won't save you any food." Camille took off down the steps and greeted Shawna with a big hug and gave Lena the message.

Mark stood at the top of the steps listening to everyone downstairs laughing and talking--enjoying themselves. He kept trying to figure out why he could not stop thinking about Becca and Bryan. He started walking toward his bedroom and sat on his bed. Mark pulled out his cell phone and stared at it. Just as he was about to dial Becca's number, it appeared on his phone screen. He didn't know whether to answer it or not. Finally, he felt himself calm as he listened to the familiar voice.

"Mark, are you there?" Becca spoke carefully and softly.

Mark found his voice and answered, "Good afternoon, Becca. I'm surprised to hear from you." His voice remained steady and calm.

"Yeah, well I wanted to apologize for earlier this morning. I don't like it when you're disappointed in me. I just want to make the right decision for everyone involved."

"Becca, I'm not disappointed, I'm concerned. I don't want that man to hurt you and Bryan again with his empty promises. You guys mean so much to me. Don't you know that by now?" Mark's voice became tender.

"Oh Mark what am I supposed to do about this situation. Bryan is so happy to have his dad back in his life. I mean you should've seen him at church today when Rob showed up. Bryan was practically beaming with joy."

"Rob showed up at your church today? He really is pulling out all the stops. I guess you all sat together like one big happy family. I'm sure that rumor mill is working overtime tonight." Mark was getting agitated again. But he was trying to be understanding.

"Yeah, I'm sure it is. But that's Ok I know how to ignore foolishness. How was your service today?" Becca did not want to make Mark upset so she decided to steer the conversation in a different direction.

"Oh it was good. The Lord blessed and we praised HIM awhile." Mark paused a moment. There was an awkwardness between them that neither one could seem to break through. Mark could not take it anymore. "Well Becca I have guests for dinner so I better get back downstairs. Tell Bryan to call me later if he still has time for his Godfather. Have a good evening." He pushed the end call button and sat on his bed for a moment in a daze. He did not hear his sister come up the stairs and enter his room.

"Mark, Mark what are you doing? We're trying to wait on you so we can all eat together and you're up here staring off into space. What's goin' on?" Lena was concerned about her big brother.

"Oh I'm good. I was just talking to an old friend. You guys didn't have to wait on me. Just eat. I'll be down in a minute." Mark crossed to the other side of his bedroom to his master bathroom and closed the door behind him. He stood on the gold marble floor in silence until he heard Lena's footsteps walking down the stairs. He could hear Camille downstairs laughing with Shawna. Mark knew that this charade he had been playing with Becca would have to come to an end soon. His heart could not take much more and he refused to lose her to Rob. Mark leaned against his porcelain sink, looking in the mirror, "Lord, what is going on? YOU know I love Becca, why can't she see this man means her no good. Help me Lord! Please show me what to do." Mark splashed cold water on his face and took a white washcloth and dried it. He left the bathroom and returned downstairs to his guests.

Becca could not believe the tension that had taken root between her and Mark. She began to talk to herself. "This is crazy! Why is he acting like this? He knows I'm just trying to do what's best for my son. Rob does not have a place in my heart anymore." Becca was just plain old tired of the drama that Rob had brought with him. She realized at that moment that she could not play with this situation but she had to deal with it quickly if she did not want to jeopardize her close friendship with Mark. As she sat on her bed contemplating everything and praying for guidance, Becca heard footsteps on the stairs. Her heart began to speed up. She put a sky blue sweater over her black tank top and pulled up her black cotton pants, and slid her bare feet into her black footies. She took a warm towel and dabbed her face where she had been crying. Then she put a small portion of lotion in her hands, rubbed them together, and smoothed it over her face. Becca gave herself one last look in the mirror and as she walked out the door she whispered, "Jesus, please help me and kill my flesh."

Rob told Bryan, as they made it to the top of the steps, "Bryan, go change your clothes and make sure you get that homework out and do it. I need to talk to your mom for a minute. I'll check in on you before I leave." As Rob turned to the left to walk towards Becca's room, he saw her standing in her doorway. "Hey babe, I was just coming to talk to you. How are you feeling? You look like you could use a back rub." He started toward her and stood as close to her as he could, trying to read her body language.

Becca was silent but her spirit was in a heated battle with her flesh. "I am fine, Rob, and I'm glad you want to talk because some things need to be clarified. As a matter of fact, why don't you just go downstairs and have a seat in the family room and I'll be down as soon as I check on Bryan. OK?" She eased pass him and headed toward Bryan's room; but Rob reached out and gently grabbed her arm.

"Wait a minute Becca. We can just talk in your room since we're already up here. I think that would be more comfortable. I'll even sit in the chair across the room." You don't have to be afraid of me." He was very confident and staring at her intensely.

Becca knew this was a setup. Her spirit was yelling at her, "RUN GIRL RUN!" She was bound and determined not to get caught up in Rob's nonsense again. So she stood with boldness and all asurety pulled her arm from his grasp and said, "Rob I will see you downstairs in few minutes. There are some cool beverages in the fridge and some fruit on the table. Please help yourself." Becca did not wait for his response. She turned and proceeded to her son's room.

Rob stood there in awe of Becca's new found will power. He realized at that moment that winning her back was not going to be easy. He walked down the steps to the kitchen, grabbed a bottle of fruit juice and continued into the family room. He sat down on the love seat, picked up the remote control, and started scanning though the cable channels. As he stared at the T.V., he thought of ways to get Becca to let down her guard. But what would he have to do differently. Rob began devising a plan in his mind about how to get the one great love of his life to want him again.

When Becca came down the stairs she grabbed a bottle of water out of the freezer. It was just the way she liked partially frozen. She unscrewed the cap and took a drink from it, let out a sigh of satisfaction, then walked into the family room. Seeing Rob sitting on the loveseat, flicking through the channels relaxed and comfortable made her think back to the time when they were a couple and she would take care of all his needs. All she ever wanted was for them to be a real family. Not playing house but being together as husband and wife. But he wasn't ready then. Now, just out of the blue, this man who has made a multitude of empty promises and frivolous excuses wanted to just pick up where they had left off. She could not believe it. "So Rob let's talk. We need to get a clear understanding of what's going on between us because I will not allow my son or myself to experience the type of pain you caused us to feel before. It wasn't right then and it sure isn't right now!" Becca continued to stand in the doorway, leaning against the wall and taking a sip from her water.

"Becca, please come sit down next to me and let's talk." He scooted over so Becca could slide in next to him. He watched her continue to stand there struggling over whether or not to sit down next to him. Rob never took his eyes off of her.

Becca cautiously walked over to where he was sitting and sat down. She knew this was a big mistake. Her mind became clouded with all kinds of past images of the two of them together which flooded her heart with emotions that she had not had in a very long time. All she kept thinking was does he love me for real or is it my heart's betrayal creating another illusion of love. Becca felt Rob slip his arm around the back of the loveseat and drape her shoulder. She shuddered a little. He smelled so good and it was exhilarating to be pursued. "Rob, why are you here?" She looked straight ahead she didn't want to get caught up in yesterday's memories. "I really need you to be totally honest with me."

Becca took another sip from her bottle of water. As she did a couple drops of water trickled down the side of her mouth. Rob immediately wiped the wetness away from her face. He turned her head toward him and just looked into her eyes. "I already told you that I want my family back. I know I messed up before but you have to give me another chance to make it right, baby. You and Bryan mean the world to me and I need you. Trust me, if you allow me back in your heart this time, I will do things the right way. I never stopped loving you, Becca and I want us to spend forever together." Rob leaned in close to her face and touched her lips lightly with his. He wanted to see if she would reciprocate the kiss.

Becca's insides were melting and she could feel a fire burning wildly deep within her. She could not believe that she actually wanted to allow this man to penetrate her heart and her body with all of his love. Becca knew this was wrong but it felt so very right. "Rob, I can't. As much as I may want to be with you, I know that I'm worth more. You have not communicated with us for six years and now after a few days in town I'm suppose to lie down and allow you to disgrace my temple. I don't know who you've been with, where you've been, or what you've been doing for the last 72 months. I will not allow this type of behavior in my life anymore." Becca calmly stood up by the loveseat. "If you would like to see Bryan tomorrow that will be fine. He has a basketball game at 5:00

P.M. at the school. You and I really need to keep our conversations about Bryan and things will work out a lot better. It's late and I think you should go. I'll tell Bryan you said good-night." Becca started walking towards the front door.

Rob was shocked. He just knew he would be waking up next to Becca in the morning. Instead, he found himself headed for the door to another lonely night. "Becca, you need to get yourself together and stop playing with me. I told you I love you and I wanna be with you. How much more do you want? I have two more days left to be here and then I have to go back to Cincinnati. Don't make me wait too long. I'll call Bryan tomorrow." Rob slipped on his jacket and headed to his truck in agitation.

Becca closed the door behind him and began to thank the Lord for the courage to stand in the midst of temptation. She ran up the steps and went into her son's room. Bryan had fallen asleep at his desk. She woke him enough to get him to bed. "I love you big boy."

"I love you too momma." He turned over and went back to sleep.

Becca felt a peace come over her. She was learning to be content with Jesus and how to read the writing on the wall.

Chapter 7

Mrs. Cooper was not going to allow Becca to stay in this depressed state. Becca had not been herself for the past couple of days. "Becca, remember that the joy of the Lord is your strength. Whatever you're going through it will pass. If there's something that you want to talk to me about, I'm here for you." She set a cup of coffee in front of Becca and eased down into the chair across from Becca's desk.

"I'm fine Tonya and I appreciate your words of encouragement. It's just that with Rob's surprise appearance after all these years and Bryan's excitement over having his dad back, things have been a bit overwhelming to say the least. I am so tired of everyone wanting more from me than I can give! Peace, that's all I want." Becca rested her head in her hands as a waterfall of pinned up emotions saturated her face.

Mrs. Cooper walked around Becca's desk to where she sat and knelt down beside her. She laid her hand on Becca's shoulder and held the other one toward heaven and began to pray fervently for Becca's peace of mind. Mrs. Cooper's prayer was so powerful that the anointing of the Holy Spirit filled the office. Their praises could be heard through the office door.

"It's gonna be alright, Becca. As long as our GOD is still on the throne, we don't have to worry. Hallelujah!" Mrs. Cooper started toward the door then stopped and turned back toward Becca. "Remember daughter, God knows the thoughts that He has toward you, thoughts of good and not evil to bring you to an expected end."

"Thanks sis for all your encouragement and prayers. You are truly a God send. I'm gonna pull myself together and take you to lunch. Get Ms. Perkins to cover for you this afternoon and we'll leave about one o'clock." Becca walked over to her file cabinet, unlocked it, and pulled out her make-up bag and looked at herself in the mirror that hangs just inside the right side door.

"Ok Becca, sounds good." Mrs. Cooper opened the door and stepped into the outer office. "Should I close your door?"

"No, just leave it cracked." Becca stared at herself in the mirror and smiled slightly as she touched up her makeup from the tracks of tears that stained her face. She knew she had to make some tough decisions but with God everything would work out for her good.

Mark and Shawna were sitting at a table in a small little café drinking cappuccinos, mocha for her and caramel macchiato for him. They had gone there for lunch.

"What's going on with you Mark? You seem distracted." Shawna sipped her coffee.

"Oh I'm alright Shawna, I just have a lot on my mind." Mark took a bite of his honey roasted turkey and swiss cheese on wheat bread sandwich.

"Well, I want you to know that I had a great time last Sunday. Camille is getting so big. I've been missing your cooking, Mark. I'm glad to know that you haven't lost your touch." Shawna looked at Mark staring off into space as if the weight of the world was on his shoulders. He was like a robot in his response. "Is it Becca?" She spoke slow and soft.

"WH-What are you talking about, Shawna? Is what Becca?" Mark seemed agitated. He took a couple of sips from his cappuccino. Mark was thinking that he really didn't need someone trying to pick apart his emotions right now.

"Hey don't get upset. I'm your friend remember. I just want to help." Lena told me that you and Becca have been having problems. I know how close the two of you are and how much you care about her." Shawna leaned in close to Mark and placed her hand gently on his. "I'm here for you."

Mark sighed heavily. "Yeah, I know Shawna and I'm sorry. I just don't know what to say to Becca anymore. Everything I say to her makes her angry. It just doesn't make sense."

"It's not your fault, Mark. Maybe she's going through something in her personal life. I know you guys share a lot but maybe she can't share this. But you can't beat yourself up over it. You have been a really good friend to Becca. As a matter of fact, to the outside world you guys act as if you're a couple." Shawna chuckled a little. She was fishing for a response from Mark about his true feelings for Becca.

Mark sat up straight and pulled his hand back from hers. "I know it's not my fault. But I don't want to see my God-son get hurt again. I know he loves his dad. But his dad keeps making promises he just can't keep. Becca chose me to be his Godfather for a reason and I'm just trying to live up to my responsibilities. That is all! Anything else is a mute point." Mark pulled out his wallet to pay for their lunch.

"Ok, ok Mark I hear you loud and clear." Shawna grabbed his arm as he was about to stand and walk away. She knew she had pushed too hard. "Mark, I'm sorry. Please sit down and talk to me. I just don't like to see you upset and distracted like this." Shawna leaned in closer to him so that the positioning of her upper torso highlighted her modest bust line. Her smooth light caramel skin seemed to glisten as the afternoon sun seemed to slightly expose her hidden secrets.

Mark sat back down and couldn't believe that Shawna was trying to make a pass at him. He was always so caught up in Becca's drama that he never paid much attention to Shawna's advances. But this one he was reading loud and clear. Mark had always thought that Shawna was beautiful and often wondered why she was still single. "Shawna, there is no need for you to apologize I've just got a lot of stuff going' on. Trust me I see what you're trying to do and I appreciate your concern." As Mark laid his hand on top of hers, he gently touched the side of her face with the back of his other hand. "Maybe we can go to that new restaurant downtown by the river tonight and I'll buy you a late dinner?"

Shawna perked up quickly. Her stomach was doing back flips at the thought of spending an evening alone with Mark. Her plan was working to get Mark's mind off of Becca Thomas. "That sounds just great Mark. I'll meet you at your house about 8:00." She smiled at him seductively and winked her eye.

"No, Shawna, I'll pick you up at your place. Like a real date. I think I need to clear my head for one night." Mark stood up next to Shawna, reached out his hand for her to take it and stand. Mark wrapped his arms around her waist and pulled her close to him as he whispered in her ear, "Thank you for being my friend and putting up with my mess. Come on now, we better get back to the office." He stepped to the side and let her lead him out of the café.

Shawna led them smiling all the way.

Bryan could hardly concentrate in class. His hopes were soaring through the sky. He had never spent so much consistent time with his dad. Things had been going great. Not only that, but it seemed as if his mom and dad would get back together too and they would all be one big happy family. Except for the fact that his mom seemed a little agitated with his dad and he didn't know what for. But that really didn't matter as long as his dad continued to show his mom that he had changed for the better. Bryan was going to hold onto the dream of having his family together again.

his thoughts now were how to get his mother to visit his dad in Cincinnati. He would have to think of something very clever as not to arouse her suspicions.

On their way home, Becca and Bryan stopped at the Market to pick up some fresh fruit and vegetables. Becca was going to make homemade Beef Stew tonight. Bryan decided to use this time to advocate for his dad.

"Hey mom you know that dad really thinks you're pretty. What do you think about my dad?" Bryan was curious. He had to know if there was anything of substance left between them.

"Does he now? I think your dad really loves you and he'll say anything to make you happy." Becca chuckled trying to hide her curiosity about what Rob had said about her.

"Ma, why do you have to act like you don't think about my dad? It's ok if you still like him. He has really changed and he wants us to make things right!" Bryan was getting excited. "Come on mom tell me what you think about dad."

"I don't know what you want me to say, Bryan. I used to love your dad very much but sometimes feelings change. My only concern now is that your dad spends time with you and develops a relationship with you. I love you Bryan and you're my only concern." Becca smiled at her son briefly and turned her attention back to the road.

Bryan watched his mom as she pulled their truck into the driveway. He could tell that she was not telling him the complete truth and that something else was on her mind. He would have to work a lot harder to get her to open up.

As they entered the house they were laughing about some of Bryan's fantastic stories. Becca was laughing so hard that all she could do was fall onto the loveseat crying and begging for Bryan to stop. Bryan fell down next to his mom and just hugged her. He loved to hear her laugh. He wanted so much for his mom to be filled not just with happiness but with joy that would last through the good times as well as the bad.

"Mom, do you have joy?" Bryan lay next to his mom with his head on her shoulder.

Becca sat up a little and looked at her son. He was growing up so fast and becoming a little man. "I think so. I know that I'm happy."

"Naah mom, I asked if you had joy. Happiness is something that can change depending on your mood or what's going on around you. Joy is solid. It doesn't change. Just like the big Willow tree in our backyard. No matter how the wind blows, it never uproots the tree. The leaves may blow away, the branches may even break but the tree is not uprooted."

"Wow!" was all Becca could say. She was amazed at her son's intelligence. He seemed to be getting smarter and smarter. She always knew God had His hand on Bryan's life but she never saw it more clearly than now. "Son, you are so special and you are completely right. How did you know the difference?"

"I listen in Bible Study class. I know you think I don't pay attention but I do. I even heard Pastor tell about the difference on Sunday morning." Bryan had a satisfied look on his face. He liked catching his mother off guard. "Mom, you still have not answered my question."

Becca paused, stood up and looked down at her son. She knew at that moment that whatever decision she made had to be what was best for Bryan's interest not her own selfish desires. "I love you son and I know that the joy of the Lord is my strength and as long as I keep my relationship with HIM in order I can face any situation with joy." She rubbed the top of his head and went into the kitchen to start dinner.

Bryan sat up and realized that his mother was a lot stronger than he thought. He knew that she would make the right decisions.

Just as he pulled out his homework, the phone rang. Something in the pit of Becca's stomach dropped. She knew before Bryan answered the phone that it was Rob. All she could hear in the spirit were these words, "Don't lose your joy! Protect it at all costs!!" Becca began to rejoice as she pulled out chicken to fry and spaghetti to warm up.

"Hey dad, how are you doing?" Bryan was so happy to be talking to his dad once again.

"I'm doin' fine son. Was school good for you today?" Rob was glad to hear that Bryan was glad to hear from him. He was really trying to be a good dad this time.

"Yeah dad, I had a fantastic day! How was yours? Are you

coming over this evening? I had so much fun with you yesterday." Bryan was so overjoyed. All he wanted to do was spend as much time with his father as possible.

Becca listened to her son talk to his dad with so much excitement. She hoped with all that was in her that Rob would not disappoint her baby again. Becca knew the importance of a male child having his father in his life. She did not want him growing up wondering if his father loved him.

"Mom, mom can I spend the night with my dad tonight at the hotel? He said that there is an indoor pool and we can go swimming. Please momma please! Bryan was pulling her arm and holding the phone to his chest with the other.

"Let me talk to your dad, Bryan. You go on and finish your homework." Becca remained calm. Bryan handed her the phone and walked away pouting. "Hello, Rob."

"Hey baby. How are you doin'? I sure missed you last night. Did you dream about me?" Rob dropped his voice to a seductive tone.

Becca sighed heavily but kept her composure and focused on the issue at hand, allowing Bryan to stay overnight with his dad. "Why would you ask Bryan to stay with you and we have not discussed it? What exactly were you thinking? Were you trying to make me look like the bad one in this situation? Becca could no longer hide her agitation.

Rob responded nonchalantly, "How are you going to look like the bad one if you say yes? I mean it's not like you're going to say no. I'm the boy's father or don't you remember the hot passionate love we made the weekend Bryan was conceived? Now, I was thinking that I'd pick him up about 6 p.m. and he'll be absent from school tomorrow." Rob smiled to himself confidently. He just knew that she would never deny him time with their son.

Becca paused briefly to collect her thoughts before she responded. She could not believe that he had the audacity to think that she would just trust him to take their son for an overnight visit and they hadn't been in touch with him in 6 years. "You must be crazy, Rob! Or either you still think I'm that same gullible idiot that you left. Whichever it is, let me set you straight! There will be no overnight visits until I'm sure you are reliable and consistent. It's going to take some time for you to build trust again. Until then you're more than welcome to come visit him and take him out during the day. Now if you can't handle that, just go on back to Cincinnati and leave us alone. Got it!" Becca was proud of herself.

"OK Becca well then I'm coming over right now so that I can spend as much time as I can with my boy and will discuss the rest later. Bye." Rob hung up the phone knowing he had caught Becca off guard. She was expecting him to go off; but not this time. He had a surprise for Becca tonight. He knew her better than she knew herself and he was going to give her something that she had been missing for a long time. He grabbed his keys and headed toward the door.

"That joker really has a lot of nerve! I don't believe him!" Becca rubbed her hand across her forehead. "I just don't understand that man! He must be crazy!!"

Bryan ran into the kitchen unsure of his mom's response but with high expectations. "Mom, mom what did dad say? Can I go with him? Did you tell him yes?" Bryan could hardly breathe waiting for his mother to answer him.

Becca was so upset; but, when she looked at her son her anger seemed to subside. She sat down in one of the white metal, floral cushioned kitchen chairs and pulled him close to her. "Baby you know that I just want what's best for you. I want you to understand that sometimes mom has to make hard decisions that you may not get but just know that I'm thinking of your best interests. OK?"

"Ok mom. But what did you tell dad?" Bryan was squeezing her hand.

"Well I'm not letting you go spend the night by yourself but your father is going to come over and spend the rest of the evening with you here. I will go to my room so you guys can have some bonding time. I hope you understand boo." Becca tried to rub his face.

Bryan pulled away from his mom with an attitude. "Why don't you trust my dad? He wouldn't do anything to hurt me. Don't you know that?" Bryan jerked away from his mother and leaned against the refrigerator.

"Bryan, you better watch your tone. Now, I don't have to explain anything to you so I suggest that you deal with it and go upstairs and wash up, change your clothes, and put your books away. I'll let you know when your father gets here." Becca started going through the mail that was on the table. She did not see the tears that began to flood Bryan's face as he turned and stormed upstairs without a word.

As Rob drove out Secor to Sylvania, his mind was on Becca and Bryan. He knew that tonight was his last night to try and change her mind about him because tomorrow he had to go back to Cincinnati. If he could he would love to get Becca to let him move in with her so they could all be together. He could no longer bear the thought of another man touching her. But he had to get rid of Mark's meddling self! He was tired of trying to compete with that imposter. Bryan was his son and Mark needed to have his own kid. "I'm sick of that GQ wanna be Father of the Year! I think I may need to give that sucka' a call." Rob was thinking out loud. In the midst of his thoughts he heard his cell phone ring. He answered without looking at the caller id. "Yo, what's up?"

"What's up with you Rob? Where you at? I know you not still sniffing around that sedity hoe!" The voice was slightly rough with a street flair.

Rob almost wrecked his truck when he heard the voice. He could not believe it was her. "What do you want Toya? Why are you callin' me?" Rob spoke harshly as he pulled over to the side of the road. This was the last thing that he needed right now.

"I wanna know when you're comin' home to yo' woman! Or are you gettin' what you need in T-Town. I hope you told her that you're getting married! Don't play me Rob. I'm not on yo' bull boy!" Toya was very angry with Rob because he had lied to her yet again. When Rob left Cincinnati five days ago, he said he was going to find his son and tell him that he was going to have a stepmother and wanted him to be at the wedding. But when he got to Toledo, Rob stopped returning Toya's phone calls.

"Toya, I'm busy! I'll just call you later. Now stop sweatin' me girl!!" Rob was disgusted with her nonsense. He thought he had that situation under control. He didn't want anything to get in the way of having Becca back in his life.

"Oh, I'm sweatin' you? Well why don't I make a call to yo' little baby mama and let her know everythang! Then, maybe you'll start callin' me, Sweetie." She responded in a sarcastic tone. " Yeah, I'll wait for you to call but I betta' not have to wait too long!" Toya hung up the phone with force. She sat back on her sofa and screamed with anguish. Sometimes she hated that man and sometimes she loved him with everything in her.

It was ridiculous the type of relationship they shared. All she could think was that she was going to kill him or he was going to be the death of her; especially now that she was six months pregnant. He was driving her insane. Rob told Toya that he was going to clear up some stuff in Toledo so he could see his son on a regular basis. Toya had gone through this nonsense with her first child, Casey, and her father, Tony. When he left her for a girl from his past, she swore that she would never put herself in a relationship like that again. So, when she met Rob it seemed as if things were going to be different. Especially when he suggested they get married a couple of months after she told him she was pregnant. The pieces of her life that had been torn apart seemed to be mending themselves back together. So if Robert Harris thought he was going to walk out of her life for some old fling that didn't even understand him, he'd better think again. Because it will be a cold day in Hell before she let him go. Toya lay back on her sofa and began to talk to her baby girl. "Don't worry baby girl, momma's not gonna let daddy leave us. We're gonna be one big happy family- you, Casey, me and daddy. Watch and see." Toya began to hum a lullaby as she fell back into an abyss of sleep with thoughts of Rob searing her mind.

Chapter 8

Rob made a right turn onto Doty Street off of Sylvania, traveled down two blocks and pulled into the third paved driveway from the corner and turned off his truck. He sat there for a few minutes trying to get his focus back. He realized that he could have a much better life with Becca than Toya. "Toya" He whispered her name through an agitated sigh. All he could think was that he wanted to go off on her so bad for pressin' him about callin' her. He was trying to spend time with his son. Rob knew he would have to deal with her some kind of way. But tonight nothing was going to interfere with him spending the night and makin' love to Becca.

Before he left his apartment, he had taken a shower and put on some Usher Cologne. He noticed that Becca really seemed to like it the last time he visited. Rob pressed and put on his Roca Wear black Jeans, Roca Wear black cotton button down, and a lime green t-shirt, with his Roca Wear black boots. He shaved his head and oiled it then trimmed his mustache and beard. He put his diamond stud earring in his left ear. Rob knew he was looking good and there was no way Becca would be able to resist. He had even stopped by the florist on his way over and bought Becca half dozen red roses with baby breath. He was going to do all the right things tonight. He jumped out of his truck, grabbed the roses but decided to leave his overnight bag in the car. He didn't want to seem over confident. Rob walked to the front door and rang the bell. He could see Becca's silhouette walking toward the door. When she opened the door, he smiled seductively, handed her the flowers and stepped inside. He could tell by the look on her face that she was pleasantly shocked. "Good evening, Becca. How are you?" Rob leaned down, kissed her on the cheek then whispered in her ear. "You look very nice tonight, baby." As he stepped back away from her, Bryan ran into the foyer and jumped into his dad's arms. Rob's attention turned completely to his son.

"Thank you" was all she could whisper back. Becca was becoming intoxicated by the smell of Rob's cologne. It wasn't real heavy but just enough to lightly dance around the room as he walked pass her. Becca had to quickly shake herself because she was not expecting Rob to come over dressed well and smelling that good. Oh and don't forget about the roses. Becca was outdone. Once she pulled herself together she walked into the kitchen through the dining room as not to disturb Bryan and his dad in the family room. "Lord what is goin' on here?" She whispered to herself. "I don't think Rob has ever bought me flowers. This is craziness!" Becca was really confused. All she knew was that the father of her only child was here in her home, playing with their son as if no time had ever passed, and Bryan was so excited. She was in the kitchen preparing a snack for them so they could watch "Roscoe Jenkins", a movie she had picked up from the video store. Becca could hear a still small voice speaking to her, "Don't get caught up in the hype!" Becca knew this was a set up but then again maybe things were happening the way they were supposed to. She decided not to give it to much thought but to just enjoy her family. She paused right before she stepped into the family room and whispered to herself, "My family—that sure sounds good."

Rob jumped up and grabbed the tray with pink lemonade slushies, popcorn, and fruit snacks on it from Becca. "Here, let me help you with that honey. You go on over there and sit on the sofa next to Bryan. The movie is just about to start." Rob winked at her as his hand gently touched hers when he took the tray. He could tell she was melting and it wouldn't take long to sop her up.

Bryan patted his little hand on the cushion next to him for his mom to sit down. It was the middle seat. Rob sat down on the other side of her and handed her and Bryan their drinks. Bryan grabbed the hot buttered popcorn. Rob put his arm around the back of the couch. Becca could smell his cologne mixed with his manly deodorant even the more. Her insides seem to be on fire. "Is this ok Becca? I don't want to make you uncomfortable or cross the lines."

Becca looked at him and almost got lost in his beautiful brown eyes. "Uh, Please don't flatter yourself, Rob. I'm cool." Becca was lying through her teeth and she hoped to God that he couldn't see right through her. She turned her attention to Bryan. "Are you comfortable baby? Do you need anything else?" She rubbed his leg.

"No mom. Shh! The movie is on." Bryan sat as close as he could to his mom which pushed her closer to Rob. Bryan felt good being with his mom and dad. He hoped the movie would never end.

"Mark, did you hear what I just said? Earth to Mark

Simmons!" Lena was beginning to get a little upset. This was the second time in their conversation that her brother had drifted off in thought with a far away look. Mark laid back on his brown chaise lounge with one leg stretched out on the lounger and the other hanging off the side. Lena sat across from him on the matching sofa sipping her mango flavored water. She was trying to tell Mark about the latest drama with her boyfriend. But Mark just was not listening.

"I hear you, Lena. I've just got a lot on my mind right now. I even have a date tonight that I should be getting ready for. So please excuse me if I don't have time to get caught up in yo' self made relationship drama, sis." Mark was a little upset with his baby sister because it was like she could not see what these no good men were doing to her. Mark was tired of her getting hooked up with these married men that just used her. "Lena when you get tired of his nonsense then you will shut him down and stop playing second fiddle. You're worth so much more than that, my dear sister." Mark rubbed his forehead.

"Forget you, Mark. You don't know what I deal with everyday. I just thought I could talk to my big brother but apparently that's not the case!" Lena stood up and grabbed her purse and walked to the steps. Camille, Camille come on let's go. Your uncle has a hot date." Lena glared at Mark. "You can pick up Camille tomorrow afternoon." She turned to Camille and told her to grab her backpack and walked out the door.

"Love you Uncle Mark. Have a good time tonight and try not to be so serious." She kissed him on the cheek, gave him a big hug and ran out the door to catch up with her Auntie Lena.

Mark got up walked to the door and closed it. He was tired of Lena getting an attitude every time he tried to be honest with her. It was just juvenile the way she would respond. He shook his head and walked up the stairs to get ready for his date with Shawna. "Lord, I just don't know what's going on. Maybe I should try to call Becca one more time before I leave. Mark strolled into his room and sat on the end of his King sized Oak Panel bed and pulled out his cell phone to call Becca. However, just as his call was getting ready to go through, a familiar number popped up. "Hey lady, how are you doing'?"

Shawna sounded happy and satisfied. "I'm doing fine. I'll be even better when you pull up in front of my apartment. So about how much longer will you be?" She laughed coyly.

"I should be there in about thirty minutes. I hope you're ready to get down tonight because I've caught my second wind." Mark laughed. It felt good to think about something else for a change, to not worry about anything.

"Well, Mr. Simmons, you are the one that better get ready because I'm gonna take you on a ride tonight that will make your head spin. I'll be anxiously awaiting your arrival. See you in a few." Shawna hung up the phone and went into her bathroom and sat down at the vanity. She began to apply her makeup and put the finishing touches on her hair. Shawna was excited because her and Mark were finally going on a real date. She could not wait to be alone with him. "Mark Simmons, you will be mine tonight. You won't be thinking about Becca this time. I promise you that." Shawna began humming an old Boyz II Men song, *I'll Make Love to You,* as she finished getting dressed.

As the movie ended, Becca looked down at Bryan asleep lying on her lap. She whispered to him, "Bry, Bry it's time to go to bed. Get up hon, get up."

Bryan was so delirious he could barely stand up straight. "Can you and dad tuck me in tonight, mom? Please?"

Rob looked at his son and winked. He did not give Becca a chance to answer. "Sure we can. Listen Bryan, your mom and I can put aside our differences to make sure your needs are met. Isn't that right, Becca?" Rob knew that Becca would not disappoint their son no matter how much she didn't like him-- or did she?

Becca graciously conceded and guided Bryan upstairs with Rob following close behind. "Come on big boy let's get you to bed." Becca told Bryan to go to the bathroom and brush his teeth before he went to bed. Then she looked at Rob. "Can you go in there and make sure he washes his face and brushes his teeth the right way. I'm going to turn down his bed." Becca walked into Bryan's room with Rob's eyes on her the whole time. She felt so uncomfortable and desired all at the same time. Becca knew she had to stay focused or she would drown in her own carnal desires.

Rob couldn't help but keep his attention on Becca as she moved around their son's bedroom making sure everything was ready for him to get a good night's rest. Rob knew this was his chance to penetrate her will and inject himself back into her life. Rob turned his attention back to Bryan as he was wiping his mouth with a towel.

"Dad, are you gonna spend da' night with us?" Bryan barely was able to form the words to ask the question he was so sleepy. "I don't think mom will mind?" Bryan yawned and stretched his arms. "Anyway, I know that mom misses you being around. Please stay, Dad." Bryan slowly walked out of his bathroom holding his Dad's hand.

Rob could not believe that after all this time his son still wanted them to be a family—and maybe Becca too? "We'll see son, we'll see." Rob helped Bryan climb into bed and tucked in one side of the bed. "Are you cool, Lil' Dude?"

Bryan smiled with his eyes barely open. "Luv ya mom. See ya in the morning." Bryan closed his eyes and fell asleep immediately. Becca picked up his clothes off the floor and placed them in Bryan's dirty close hamper. Rob kissed his son on the forehead and stepped outside in the hallway and leaned against Becca's sage colored wall. Becca stepped out of Bryan's room and pulled the door shut gently behind her as not to wake him. Becca turned to walk down the hall, thinking Rob had gone downstairs.

"Whew!! Shh!" Becca dropped her voice to a whisper, "What are you doing out here lurking in the hallway?" She started to step around him but he grabbed her arm as she walked pass him and he turned her around to face him.

"Baby, don't you know how much I miss you and want to be there for you in every way. I love you Becca girl and I need you TO-NIGHT!" Rob's whisper became more intense as he pulled her close to him and draped his arms around her waist.

The more Becca tried to pull away from Rob the more he tightened his grip and the more she could feel a volcanic heat rising up within her; one that she had been trying to keep suppressed. "Stop it, Rob! This just cannot happen. You're no good for me and I'm sick of bein' hurt. So, why don't you just go on downstairs and sleep on the couch and that way you can see Bry in the morning before you leave to go back home." Becca managed to pry herself free and walk away from Rob toward her bedroom. But what she didn't understand was that Rob was not taking no for an answer. He was a man on a mission.

Rob followed close behind Becca. He was tired of talking. So he snatched her passionately, pulled her to him, and kissed her soft lips as if she were a cool drink of water in a desert of severe heat and drought. Rob kissed her until she kissed him back. His tongue found its rest on top of hers. Becca felt sensations all through her body that she had not felt in a very, very long time. It seemed as if she would give in to Rob's temptation.

It was as if Becca had become a deaf mute to the Spirit of God. Inside of her a tumultuous struggle was taking place. "Lord, I need your help, Please right now!" At that very moment Becca became nauseated and had to run into her master bathroom to vomit. She just didn't understand it—at first.

Rob tried to go after her but when she got in the bathroom she locked the door behind her. Rob could hear her gagging. "Are you ok, Becca? Is it something that I did?" Rob was confused at what just happened.

Becca spoke in a stuttered tone, "J-just g-go on downstairs and I-I'll b-be ok? Rob went downstairs and decided to wait for Becca to get herself together so that he could really share his manhood with her. However that never happened. When Rob went back upstairs to check on her after about 30 minutes, Becca was in the bed sleep with the door to her room locked. Rob realized that this new Becca was a lot stronger than the Becca he used to know. But that was ok because Rob was up for the challenge. Too much was at stake for him to be defeated. Rob went back to the sofa in the family room and pulled a blanket and pillow out of the back hallway closet. Then he stretched out and figured he needed to try to break Becca down another way.

Becca heard Rob when he knocked on her door but she did not move. As a matter of fact, she breathed harder and sat up in her bed. She had decided to let her spirit man take over and act like the queen God intended for her to be. Becca began to pray hard, "Lord please help me to stand! Please don't let me yield to temptation again. I need you JESUS, right now." Becca decided not to say another word to Rob because she didn't trust her judgment at that moment.

The live music was loud in a sophisticated jazz club nested next to the river with the reflection of the city skyline lights dancing across the water. It was hot in that swank little club as Mark and Shawna slow danced to sultry notes. Shawna made sure her body was pressed against Mark. The whole atmosphere was intoxicating. Mark knew he would forget himself if he became anymore inebriated. "Hey Shawna why don't we walk out on the back deck and get some air?" He stopped his rhythmic swaying and reached for

Shawna's hand to lead her through the crowd of people.

"Ok Mark, that sounds good. It's all about you baby. I'll follow you anywhere." Shawna followed Mark out of the club. She stood next to him, leaned up against the rope that was separating them from the undeniable enticing of the night's air. Mark looked at Shawna and smiled coyly. He leaned into her and kissed her gently on the cheek.

"What was that for? Don't get me wrong I'm not complaining just want to know where we're going with all of this?" Shawna felt very warm inside and wanted to get an idea of what Mark was thinking.

"Let's not go into anything deep. Just enjoy tonight and our good time. I'm sick of always worrying about the future and trying to second guess somebody. Look, aren't you having a great time?" Mark turned out toward the water and took a deep breath. His profile against the moonlight was vulnerable and burdened. He didn't want to let Shawna see that side of him that he had only shared with Becca. "Come on are you ready to go? I think it's going on 2 a.m. I want to make sure I treat you like a lady and I behave like a gentleman."

Shawna stared at him as her heart began to melt. She knew that she had to spend at least one night knowing what it felt like to have this man inside of her. She didn't care how wrong it was or what would happen to their friendship afterwards. She stroked his arm gently as she moved in closer to him and rested her petite hand on his chest. Shawna looked up at Mark to see if his body language was objecting to her advances. He was not. So she slipped her arm around his waist and laid her head on his chest and began to speak softly and seductively. "Mark, please don't worry about who needs you or what's going to happen tomorrow." Shawna could feel his body relaxing and his breathing steady. As she looked up toward Mark, she did not know that she would be meeting his gaze at her. Their eyes locked on each other and Shawna seized her opportunity and was not disappointed.

Somewhere in the back of Mark's head he could hear a distant voice saying, "No, don't do it. This will not satisfy you. Make a choice this day." Mark pulled back from Shawna abruptly. He shook his head in confusion and immediately became sick to his stomach. He leaned over the rope and emptied out what seemed to be all the contents of his stomach into the water. He was baffled and weak.

Mark barely was able to speak. "I'm sorry, Shawna, I don't know what happened. Maybe I drank to many Tequila Shots. Everything was going so well. Shoot! I don't believe this crap! Becca can spend time with her deadbeat ex and play house with no issues but I try to spend one night with a beautiful, vivacious woman and start puking like a teenager. Somebody's playin' a sick joke on me." Just then he began to throw up again.

"Oh don't you worry about all of that Suga' Daddy, I'm still gon take care of you. Now where are your keys so I can drive us home." Shawna was determined that tonight would not go down as a total waste. And she was going to do whatever it took to get his mind off of Becca Thomas. "I got you Mark as she allowed him to shift some of his weight on her as they walked back through the club to the exit. This was definitely going to be a night to remember.

Shawna pulled up at her apartment about 30 minutes later. Mark was passed out in the passenger seat, snoring. She watched him sleeping and then decided to move forward with her plan. She turned off the car and walked around to the other side and opened Mark's door. The cool air rushing in on him all at once startled him awake. He was barely lucid. Shawna instructed him on what to do next all the way to her house. "Mark I need you to swing your legs out of the car and stand up so I can help you walk to my door. Can you do that for me?"

"Yeah baby, I can do whatever you want me to do." Mark was trying to sound sexy but his words were slurred and his breath smelled like rotten onions. He really didn't know what he was saying either. All he knew was that this woman was familiar to him. As they crossed the threshold to her apartment the sweet smell of potpourri made Mark want to throw-up again but he was strong and pushed it back down. Shawna helped Mark over to her suede like micro fiber sofa. Before he sat down, she started unbuttoning his shirt and pants. "Wait a minute, Shawna, HOLD UP, HOLD UP! You can't just strip a man down to his underwear and have your way with him." Mark was starting to get his wits about himself and realizing what was going on.

Shawna started laughing so hard she almost fell backwards. "Mark Simmons, you are in no condition for me to take advantage of you. I just want to throw your shirt and pants in the washer because they stink from you getting sick. Besides you are in no condition to drive yourself home. So you can sleep on my couch tonight and I'll fix you breakfast in the morning. If you want to take a shower tonight, which I would appreciate, the guest bathroom is right on the other side of the dining room. There are towels and I think there is a brand new toothbrush on the sink. I will get you some sheets and a pillow. Now, do you think you can make it in there on your own or do you need me to help you get out of your underwear and t-shirt as well?" Shawna winked at him and smiled.

"NO, no I think I got it. The alcohol is starting to wear off." Mark started to walk towards the bathroom but stopped and turned back to Shawna. "Thanks Shawna, I really needed this tonight. I'm just sorry that I had to get sick. You're really a good friend." Mark continued to the bathroom, turned the light on and shut the door. A few minutes later the shower started running.

Shawna thought to herself, "Oh Mark, don't thank me yet because the night is not over. I still have some surprises for you." Shawna walked to her bedroom, pulled out a turquoise satin and sheer night shirt with matching panties. She went into her bathroom and ran a hot shower. When she finished showering she stepped out and let her body air dry as she brushed her teeth, fixed her hair and sprayed a light, fresh body spray scent all over her body. She walked back into her bedroom humming *I'll Make Love to You*. Shawna slipped on her night shirt and pulled up her satin panties. She rubbed lotion on her arms, hands, legs, feet, and inner thighs. She turned on her CD player low and sat down on the edge of her bed and waited. Ten minutes later she heard a knock at her door. She smiled and responded, Yes Mark, Come on in."

When Mark opened the door, Shawna was sitting on her bed looking good enough to eat. He could feel his manhood rising. He was afraid to move because he knew his next step would change their relationship forever. The battle going on inside of him became even more intense when Shawna stood up and her night shirt opened enough to reveal her caramel breasts peaking through, calling to Mark just for one touch.

"Come here, Mark. I need to talk to you." Shawna's voice was soft and filled the room until it seemed as though there was barely enough room for the two of them. She leaned against one of the poles on her queen sized Elizabethan Canopy bed running her tongue over her full lips.

Mark was so confused from the lingering effects of the alcohol, the chaotic situation with Becca, and these strong feelings for

Shawna that had never surfaced before. Inside Mark was trying to hold a conference between his head and his heart. Things were not going well. He took a step towards her as he spoke slowly, "Shawna, you are gorgeous and-and I so want to do things to yo' body that I know are a sin!" Mark paused breathing irregularly. He decided to close his eyes and finish the rest of his sentence. He figured it would be easier than looking at this highly erotic nymph. But what he didn't factor in was Shawna's boldness. When Mark opened his eyes, he could feel her warm breath on his lips. "Wh-What are y-you doin', Shawna? This isn't gonna work. We're friends." Mark was finding it harder to fight and breathe at the same time.

"Baby just relax. Don't analyze this tonight. Just let it be what it is. I'm not gonna hurt you I just wanna help you release some of that locked up energy. Come on baby-- I'm here, she isn't." Shawna kissed Mark lightly on his lips, cheeks, and then more passionately on his neck. She could feel him responding to her. "It's on now." She thought to herself.

Mark got lost in the warmth of Shawna's touch and the feel of her soft skin so much and so that he didn't even remember walking over to the bed and how Shawna ended up on top of him slowly kissing his bare chest. "Shawna, we need to stop. Ok, ok that's enough." All of a sudden Mark's mind played a flashback of a vacation that he and Becca took with the kids a year and a half ago. He could see Becca's face as if she were right in front of him. He knew this one impulsive act would change everything. "Shawna get off me right now! This is not gonna happen tonight or any other night. I'm sorry." Mark grabbed her arms and pushed her away from him onto the bed. He jumped up and grabbed his t-shirt and started toward the door. Mark could hear Shawna yelling at him but he knew he could not stop or he would be drawn back into her jungle of temptation.

"Where are you goin'? I don't believe you! She's not even worth your time. Shoot! Both of ya'll are screwed up!! Shawna was like a spewing volcano. Her words burning everything in its path. She buttoned up her night shirt and grabbed her satin robe and tied it following Mark into the living room.

Mark picked his pants up off the floor pulled them on and grabbed his shirt and jacket. He sat down in the chair and put on his shoes and grabbed his keys off the table. He stood up and turned toward Shawna standing by the sofa. Mark spoke calmly, "I'm not gonna take any of this to heart Shawna because I know you're just talkin' from the embarrassment and the alcohol. Look I already called my cousin, Bruce, to come get me and his wife is gonna drive my car home. I'm really sorry about the misunderstanding. I'll just wait out on the porch for my ride." Mark walked to the door and felt a sharp pain in his back.

"YOU'RE A JERK, MARK SIMMONS!!" Shawna was breathing hard because she had just thrown a shoe at him. "She's just gonna suck you into her destructive world and drain the life out of you." Shawna ran toward her front door and slammed it in Mark's face. Then she slid to the floor crying in anger and embarrassment. Swearing the whole while and vowing to get even.

Mark sat outside on the steps to Shawna's front porch waiting on his cousin. He held his head in his hands whispering to himself. "Thank you Jesus for keeping me from myself. Please forgive me for getting myself into this situation and thank you Lord for getting me out! YOU are awesome. Now help me Lord stay focused and not get swallowed up in self pity anymore. I trust YOU because you promised to keep me in perfect peace if I keep my mind situated on you. Help me Lord, help me." Tears began to roll down Mark's face as he felt the presence of GOD surround him and he knew he would never be the same.

Chapter 9

Becca knelt at the sanctuary altar praying to the Lord for guidance. It had been about a month since she almost slipped up and slept with Rob. She was so conflicted in her heart. Did she just desire Rob because it was the familiar or was there something still unresolved between them? What about their son? It was obvious that Bryan needed his dad. How was she going to handle all of this? Then, there was Mark and the secret love that she felt for him. But the unsurety of mixing romance with almost two decades of unconditional friendship was too overwhelming. "Lord, please teach me how to live holy amongst all this temptation to settle for a less than abundant life." Becca was so tormented that she just screamed out loud in the presence of God. "AHHHH!! I NEED YOU, JESUS!" Becca sobbed at the foot of Jesus and it was almost as if she could feel His arms around her. This particular morning all Becca did was lay in the abundance of the Lord's comfort. She felt so much peace that she didn't even realize three hours had passed by. When she stood up she felt a little woozy. Becca picked up a tissue from the front bench and wiped the tears from her face. She was so engrossed in thanking the Lord that she did not see one of her church sisters walking up the aisle until she spoke to her.

"Hey sis, how are you? Is everything ok?" She hugged Becca and they sat down on the bench together.

"Well praise the Lord, Sis. Misty. I'm blessed. I'm just seeking God for some direction in my life. You know, sometimes I feel like whichever road I take it's the wrong choice so I become stuck and stagnated." Becca was trying to get answers that deep down inside she already knew. But Misty was one of her spiritual friends and prayer partners so she felt like she could trust her.

"Becca, sometimes the Lord wants us to just stand still and rest in HIM. There is something He may need to purge out of you before you can move forward and bring HIM glory. You know it's all about allowing ourselves to be used for HIS purpose. Maybe you need to change your requests and ask God for purging not just direction." Misty placed her hand over Becca's to comfort her. "Why don't you let me pray with you sis? Then, let's go to lunch and just spend some time together. I have a feeling you don't need to be alone right now. OK?" Misty gave Becca a warm, encouraging smile and began to pray.

Becca could feel the Spirit of God even stronger now that Misty was there too. It's was always amazing to Becca how the Lord God Almighty would come and commune with His people in their strongest hour of need. She really did love God and pleasing Him was more important than anything in her life. She was so grateful for the Lord sending Misty in the church that morning. Her friendship and unbiased encouragement was much needed. By the end of the prayer, Becca felt rejuvenated and strengthened. It was clearer to her what she had to do. But she decided to enjoy the rest of the afternoon with her sister in the Lord. They left the church on their way to the Olive Garden for lunch and somehow ended up at Wal-Mart's before they departed company to go to their respective homes. Becca thanked the Lord all the way to her mom's house to pick up Bryan and go home.

"How's everybody doin'? Becca's mom was standing at the sink washing Collard Greens for Sunday's dinner. Her granddad was in the basement tinkering with some of his old tools and sharing old stories with Bryan. When Becca walked in the house she could smell Sweet Potato Pies cooking in the oven and roast in the crock pot, "UM, UM, UM mom, you sure have the house smelling good! You know we'll be over for dinner after church tomorrow, right?"

Fran Donaldson was a beautiful and strong-willed woman of God. She loved her only daughter and grandson very much. She felt so blessed to see her daughter doing well for herself and taking good care of her son. "Well of course I know ya'll are coming over. Mr. Bryan Harris has already made that clear. He even said he would be here with or without you." Fran laughed while drying her hands so she could hug her daughter. "Don't look so serious, Becca, you know that boy is not going anywhere without his mother. How was prayer?" She went back to the sink and resumed her duties.

"Ah, mom, I'm not thinking about that spoiled little boy. Prayer was real good. Where is my wonderful child at anyway?" Becca sat down at the kitchen table, picked up the glass that was sitting there on the open paper bag and began crushing graham crackers.

"Oh he's in the basement with your grandfather doin' the man thing. Whatever that is?" Fran laughed as she started tearing the greens and placing them in a big pot on the stove that was already simmering with smoked turkey parts. She glanced at her daughter sitting at the table crushing graham crackers like she used to do when she was a child. Fran would have to keep an eye on her because she would eat the crushed buttery graham crackers. "So, did you get some answers from the Lord about Robert?"

Becca couldn't believe her mother. It never failed that her mom always seemed to know what was bothering her or causing her stress. "How do you know there is an issue with Rob? Everything is not always about a man when it comes to me." Becca put the glass down and stared at her mother. How was she supposed to tell her mother that she had almost given into Rob's temptation? She decided it would be better to just hold onto that piece of information. "Just know that I'm gonna trust GOD completely on this one, mom. Becca went to the top of the basement steps and called to Bryan to get his shoes and coat on and get ready to go.

"Becca, you know that I love you and I just want what's best for you. I pray for you and my grandson all the time. As long as you seek after the Lord, I know you guys will be ok." Fran walked over to her daughter and took her hand gently and smiled at her. "You are such a beautiful girl. I hope that one day you'll see how much God has blessed you. You don't have to settle for anything or anyone." She kissed her on the forehead and went back to cooking dinner. "So, when do you guys go on your vacation with Mark and Camille? Bryan is so excited."

"Oh, we're leaving early Thursday morning and we'll be back on Saturday evening. It should be a really nice time for the kids." Becca sighed and sat back down waiting on Bryan to put his shoes on. "Shoot, I'm not even sure if Mark wants me to even go."

"What happened? You and Mark always have a good time together. Why would he not want you to go? Nothing can be big enough to cause a permanent riff between you guys. I'm sure things will mend themselves."

Becca looked at her mother and just smiled. She knew how much her mom loved and respected Mark. He had really become a son to her over the years. She decided not to go into their argument they had the other night. "Your right, mom, we'll be fine. I'll talk to you tomorrow and Bryan will probably call you tonight. Love you." Becca stood up and walked out the door said good-bye to her granddad and told Bryan to get into the truck.

"You ok mom. You seem a little sad." Bryan put his hand on his mom's arm as they rode down the street towards home.

"Yeah, babe, I'm fine. I just got a lot on my mind." Becca tried to straighten her face so as not to worry her son. She knew she had to talk to Mark tonight before the trip so that they could get passed the big wedge that was starting to form. She didn't like it and they had to talk.

It was about 10 p.m. and Mark was sitting on his bed going over some contracts from work when his phone rang. He looked at the caller ID and saw that it was Becca. He took a deep breath and pushed the talk button. "Hello, Becca. How are you tonight?" Mark spoke in a slow, steady tone. He was trying not to be emotional.

"Hey handsome. We haven't talked for about a two or three weeks. I sure have missed you. Whatcha' been up to? And how's Camille?" Becca tried to keep her voice light and normal.

"WOW, Becca, you sure have a lot of questions. I'm surprised you even had time to think about me and Camille. I mean, you've been so busy trying to make Rob feel at home. I'm just impressed that you have the energy to even call." Mark couldn't hold back any longer. It was getting harder and harder to temper his comments with tenderness.

Becca was shocked by the sharp sarcasm that Mark was shooting at her. It was out of character for him. "Well, Mr. Simmons, since you think you know everything that's going on-- I'm surprised that you're even speaking to me. But there are things that I have to deal with in my own way! And know that I'm not planning on making the same mistakes I have in the past. I'm just tryin' to do what's best for my son."

Mark could never stay upset with Becca for long. "Becca are you crazy?! I'm only trying to protect you and Bryan. Remember, I was there six years ago when he left you in a terrible state. So don't try to get funky with me. I'm the one that loves the both of you. But that's neither here nor there. So, have you decided to move to Cincinnati with Rob?" Mark sighed heavily.

Becca couldn't believe that Mark was acting like this and saying all of these silly things. She wanted so much to tell him how much she loved him but Mark was so angry. "You just have all the answers don't you? She was agitated. There was an awkward pause. Becca decided to change the subject. "Are we still going on vacation next week?"

Mark decided that it was best to just let it go. "Of course. Everything has been paid for. What time will you and Bryan get to Cleveland?" Mark tried his best to be unconcerned.

"We should be there about 8a.m. Thursday morning. Is Camille excited?" Becca had so many emotions flowing through her that she didn't know what to say. "Please tell her I can't wait to see her and that I love her very much." Becca thought it best to go ahead and end this gruesome conversation.

"She is excited and she really misses you Becca. I'll have her call you tomorrow. Tell Bryan I'll hit him up later. You have a good night." Mark was getting ready to hang up the phone when he heard the softness in Becca's voice.

"Mark, don't be upset with me. I'm sorry for not sharing things about Rob with you. I know you were the one that helped me put the pieces back together. I just wanted to make sure that those feelings were dead. Do you understand?" Becca spoke carefully trying to mend their friendship.

"I'll talk to you later and I do understand-- more than you know." Mark hung up the phone with a sense of heaviness. He didn't know what to make of the conversation he just had with his best friend. He loved her so much that he could not bear the thought of Rob's chaos engulfing their lives again. Maybe they would be able to work things out at the resort.

The hot pink satin and lace peek-a-boo thigh high night shirt with fur around the hem fell beautifully against Toya's dark brown sugar skin. Her make-up was flawless with soft berry lip gloss. Her hair was pulled up in a pony tail with crimps gently brushing her shoulders. White candles were lit all around her bedroom. She sat in the chair in the corner with one leg draped over the right arm. She smelled of citrus and white gardenias. Even though her six month baby bump was visible, she still looked radiant. Toya was determined to show Rob how much she loved him and that Becca was not woman enough to handle him. She thought to herself, "Rob Harris, I'm gonna give you the ride of your life tonight."

As Rob entered the house, all he could think about was the good time he had share with Becca and Bryan a month ago. He just wished he could have made love to Becca at least one of the nights he was there. But he knew he had touched her emotionally. All he had to do was just continue to stay in contact with her. He would have to plan his next move carefully. "Um, what's that smell?" Rob spoke out loud as he closed the front door behind him and dropped his work bag by the door. He was hoping that Toya would be sleep. He didn't want to deal with her nonsense tonight. He walked to the back of the apartment and opened the bedroom door. Rob was in shock. "What is goin' on in here?" Rob was loud until he turned to the left and saw Toya in the chair. She was glowing he thought to himself. "Hey babe. You sho' look good." Rob was grinning from ear to ear.

Toya licked her lips seductively and parted her legs so that Rob could see her hidden secrets. "Hey, you big sexy bear, did you miss me? I sure have missed you." She rose from the chair and met Rob in the middle of the room. Toya was so close to him she could feel his heart beating. "So what's up?"

Rob could feel his manhood coming to attention. She looked good enough to eat. It was not his intention to have sex with her because he didn't know how much longer he was going to be with Toya. But the way she looked tonight, with his baby inside of her, he had to taste her just one more time.

After Toya and Rob laid together about an hour, both of them were exhausted; but there still seemed to be some tension in the air. Rob just wanted to enjoy his woman and feel his baby moving inside of her. He didn't want to deal with her insecurities about Becca. "Toya, you sho' did work me tonight! Rob kissed her on her neck and shoulder. "I didn't expect all of that when I came home. Shoot, I had no idea you could still move like that!" He chuckled and slapped her playfully on the butt. Then, he got up and strutted to the bathroom.

Toya was smiling in the dark. She spoke with confidence. "See, baby, I know Becca ain't never gave it to you like that! You betta recognize! I'm all the woman you need." Toya sat up in bed and smoothed her hair back in place. "TOYA! Ooh baby, you don't have to worry 'bout nobody!" Rob helped her stand and watched her walk to the bathroom. He knew Toya was a freak; but he would never make her his wife. Even though the sex was fantastic, Rob could not stop thinking about Becca and what she was doing at that very moment. When he heard the shower come on and the bathroom door close, Rob grabbed his phone and dialed his heart.

"Hello." The voice was groggy but familiar.

"Hey lady, what's up?" Rob was trying not to talk too loud. "Were you sleep?" He walked over to the lounge chair by the far window and rubbed his forehead. He also grabbed the flat sheet off the bed and wrapped it around his lower body before he sat down.

"Of course I was sleep, Robert. Why are you up so late?" Becca pulled herself to an upright position, leaning against her headboard. With her free hand she wiped her eyes so that she could focus on the digital clock across the room. Becca was trying to figure out why Rob was playing games at 3:00 in the morning.

Robert loved to hear Becca say his name. He began to see flashbacks in his mind of them together, before they had their son. "Baby you know I just can't get enough of you. Besides, I wanted to check on you and Bryan to make sure everything was ok. How's my big boy doin'?" Rob looked back at the bathroom door to make sure Toya was still showering. And she was.

"Sleep!" Becca blurted out in a louder more agitated tone. "Which is something you should be doing. Goodnight Robert." Becca was about to hang up the phone when she heard two words glide out of his mouth like butter sliding across a hot skillet.

"Marry me!" Rob couldn't believe that these words were coming out of his mouth. But he could not take them back-- and he wasn't sure that he wanted too.

"Wh-What did you say?" Becca knew that she must be delirious with sleep because she just could not have heard what she thought she had.

"You heard me. I wanna be yo' man for life and I don't want nobody else to have you. I love you, Becca! So stop playin'." Rob was serious and he needed to get away from Toya. He could see that she was becoming too possessive and controlling. He needed more than a chicken head. Rob had experienced a little piece of Becca and Bryan's life and he wanted to be a part of it. He saw how happy they were without him and he didn't like it. Besides, Rob was not gonna give Mark Simmons a chance to take his family away from him. Rob also knew the kind of woman Becca was-- kind, classy, and strong. He knew she would take care of his new child like it was her own.

Becca was in shock. All she could say was, "I have to go Rob, Bryan is calling for me. I'll talk to you later." She gently hung up the phone and curled up into a fetal position and began to pray. "Dear God what do I do now? That man has got to be crazy! I can't go through this nonsense again. I don't know if he's lyin' or what! Lord, You have got to regulate my mind and order my steps on this one." Becca paused and squeezed her pillow tighter. "Maybe he has changed. I mean there was something different about him when he was here and Bryan really enjoyed being with his dad. Oh I just don't know!!" Becca buried her face in her pillow and screamed. She was tired and decided not to think about any of this nonsense for the rest of the night. Besides, she was still trippin' from her earlier conversation with Mark. Becca looked at her clock again it was almost 4:00. She closed her eyes and went to sleep trying to rest in her faith.

Chapter 10

Becca and Bryan made it to Cleveland with no problems. They even arrived a half an hour earlier than what they were supposed to. They were now riding in the rental van that Mark had secured for their trip so that everyone would be comfortable. It was a chocolate brown 2010 Chrysler Town and Country with beige interior and leather seats, all power with a DVD player in the back for the kids to watch movies on the way to the resort. After sixty minutes of singing silly songs, telling corny jokes, and idle conversation, Bryan and Camille were sound asleep. Now it was just Mark and Becca left alone to fill the empty silence that saturated the van's atmosphere. Becca decided she would break the silence first.

"Mark, do you need something to drink or for me to drive the rest of the way? I am rested and I can take over now." Becca was really trying to make this trip a success but it was becoming a little difficult.

"No Becca, I am fine. Just relax and enjoy the drive. We should be there in about another hour and a half." Mark tried to make his voice not sound like he was carrying the weight of the world on his shoulders. "Did you bring a book to read or paper work?"

"Yes. I brought both but I thought you and I would be able to talk about this tension we have between us. I know you can't still be upset over this Rob situation. I mean it's not like I slept with him and came back to tell you that we're getting married and Rob is moving us to Cincinnati. I mean give me some credit!" Becca shifted in her seat at the sound of the word marriage coming out of her mouth. It had only been three days since Rob proposed to her. She still had not spoken to him. Every time he would call she would make sure Bryan answered the phone and she would disappear into another part of the house to avoid speaking with him.

"Look Becca, this whole situation with Rob is ridiculous. If you want to be with the father of your child, who am I to stop you. So let's talk about something else." Mark just wanted to have peace this weekend and not lose his cool. But the more Becca brought up Rob's name, the more it irritated him. All Mark could think about was the hurt and pain he watched become Becca's permanent mask for about six months after Rob's last disappearing act. Nothing he could say or do seemed to snap her out of the lethargic state she had fallen into only time and a lot of prayer brought her back to normal.

Becca turned and looked at Mark. His face was serious. She could not believe that he was disconnecting himself from her. Becca decided that it would be best to leave that subject alone and try to just enjoy the weekend. She turned her attention back to the road and let herself get lost in the ministering sounds of the music that was encompassing their vehicle.

Becca was awakened by Camille's shout, "Is this the place, Auntie Becca?" She was so excited that she started shaking Bryan. "Wake up, Bry, Wake up!"

"Yes sweetie, we're here. Isn't it beautiful?" There was a sound of renewed hope in Becca's voice as she spoke to Camille. She glanced over at Mark and caught a glimpse of his profile that had a slight glimmer of a smile. She knew that things would work themselves out. "Look at that pool you guys and they have a horse stable. Are you up for a ride, Mark?" She looked at him and winked her eye.

"Wouldn't you like to know?" Mark smiled back at Becca. He just couldn't help himself when she looked at him like that. Maybe they would be able to get through this nonsense again? He was willing to try. "Ok guys let's grab our luggage and get to our cabin." Mark unlocked the back of the van so that everyone could get their bags. "Hey Brian, you help me with the big stuff and let your mom and Camille go and check us in at the front desk."

Becca grabbed her black Coach Saddle Bag purse and slipped into her black fur lined leather, three-quarter length jacket. She also picked up her red overnight bag. "Camille, let's get inside and let the guys handle the heavy lifting because we are delicate flowers." Becca laughed and winked at Camille.

"Auntie Becca, you're silly!" Camille laughed and took Becca's hand and walked up the path into the front doors with Mark smiling at the sight of his two favorite ladies together.

Bryan was glad to have some alone time with his Godfather. "Mark, are you gonna be upset with my mom for the rest of the trip?" Bryan was following behind Mark through the vast automatic glass sliding doors. As they entered the lobby area, Bryan's mouth fell open at the high cathedral ceilings. "WOW, Mark! This place is 'da bomb."

"You right, boy. Your mom sure did well with this vacation." Mark place his hands on Bryan's shoulder in a fatherly way and spoke gently. "Bryan, I'm not upset with your mom. I just want the best for you guys and sometimes we just don't agree about what the best is. But I still love you and your mom. Mark walked over to Becca and Camille with Bryan in tow. "Did you get the keys to the cabin?"

"Yes I did. We can catch the shuttle in the rear of the building that will take us to our cabin. Let's go." Becca was trying not to grin so hard. She felt so complete with her family. No matter how tense things may have become between Becca and Mark when they were away from each other, everything would just fall into place when they were in the same space. It was just unbelievable.

"Mom, can Camille and I go to the game room before dinner? PLEASE!" Bryan was just itching to get a look at the place and play some arcade games.

"I don't know Bryan. We're almost ready why don't we all go down together?" Becca didn't know the resort that well and she was very protective of the children.

"Wait a minute Becca. I'm sure that Bry will be responsible and look out for Camille. They will both behave themselves well. And besides, I still need to iron my clothes. No sense in having them cooped up in this room. How about it Becca? Can they please go?" Mark walked over to where she was standing and draped his bare arm around her shoulder and squeezed her gently. "The next shuttle will be here in five minutes and I'll go out and talk to the staff chaperone."

"Oh you guys think you're funny. Everybody wants to gang up on me hunh? Well how am I supposed to say no to all of you?" Becca looked at all three of them staring at her. Even the kids had come over to her and started hugging her waist. "Ok, Ok but Bryan you make sure you take your cell phone and call us if anything doesn't look right. Stay in the arcade at all times! Mark and I will come and pick you guys up from there. Then, we can go to the dining hall together for dinner."

Camille started jumping up and down and thanking Becca and Mark for letting them go. "Thanks a lot Auntie Becca and Uncle Mark. We'll be on our best behavior." Camille went and sat on the sofa and put on her white Nike sneakers.

Bryan rushed to put on his black Air Force One tennis shoes. "Thanks mom, you're the greatest!"

"What about me, big guy? I'd like to think I had a hand in changin' yo' mom's mind." Mark laughed and playfully punched Bryan in the arm.

"Thanks Mark you're the greatest too!" Bryan pretended to jumped at Mark as if he were going to tackle him. They laughed together until Camille became impatient.

"Come on Bryan, we're going to miss the shuttle. I hear it coming."

"Hold on a minute, Camille. I'm going to walk you guys out front." Mark grabbed his jacket and slipped his boots back on. "Are my wonderful children ready? Then let's go." Mark turned his attention back to Becca standing by the fireplace. "Becca I'll be back in a minute."

Becca stopped them just before Bryan shut the door. "Mark, here, they need money." Becca had her wallet in her hand walking towards them pulling out bills.

Mark had a confused look on his face. Now Ms. Thomas, do you really think I was going to put these beautiful children get on the shuttle with no money? Man, Becca, give me a little credit!" Mark turned and went back out the door without taking the bills she held in her hand.

"What am I thinking? Unbelievable Becca Thomas! You know Mark way better than that." She thought to herself. "Now, don't go acting crazy." Becca went back into the Master bedroom where she and Mark's luggage were. He had already laid a pair of jeans on the ironing board to press. So she went over and began ironing the blue Ecko jeans. She made sure the creases were sharp. Becca began singing an old Glen Jones song, *"All I Need To Know"*. The words sounded so good to her that she did not hear Mark come back into the cabin nor did she see him standing in the doorway.

"Sing it girl!" Mark laughed. Becca wasn't the best singer but he loved to see her in action. She had such passion that it made up for her deficiency in vocal technique. He looked at her ironing his jeans, singing, and smiling. Mark's heart began to melt. "Well, well Ms. Thomas, I guess you're the next American Idol. We better see about getting' you an audition with Simon and Randy as soon as possible!" Mark plopped down on the bed and kicked off his shoes.

"Oh stop it boy! You're always makin' fun of my singin'. I

think that you're secretly jealous. But it's ok 'cause everybody can't be blessed with this talent." Becca busted out laughing so hard that tears started rolling down her cheeks.

"Becca, I want to apologize for my harshness. I just can't stand that sorry excuse for a man, Rob. He brings out the worse in me." Mark sat back against the headboard of the king-sized bed." He sighed heavily and looked at Becca now ironing his white button down shirt. "Becca you don't have to do all of that. Just come over here and sit down. I've missed talking to you these last few weeks." He patted the other side of the bed.

Becca put the iron down and walked over to the bed and sat down in the middle facing Mark with one leg bent on the bed. "Mark, don't you think we need to hurry up so we can get the children?" She gently pulled two of her braids behind her ear.

"We have some time. I spoke with the youth chaperone on the shuttle and she said that they had activities for the kids in the auditorium for an hour and then she would accompany them to the arcade until we got there." Mark put his legs up on the bed and crossed them at the ankle. He was very relaxed. "Look Becca, I just wanna spend some time with my best friend. Is that ok?"

Becca smiled coyly and loosened up a little. Then she asked a question that seemed to make Mark somewhat uncomfortable. "So, how's Shawna? You haven't mentioned her much." She looked at him trying to read his reaction to her question.

"Oh, she's alright. I haven't seen much of her lately." Mark rubbed his forehead and leaned forward. "Why, do you miss her?" Mark was being sarcastic.

Becca made a mocking expression. "No. I'm just making conversation. Shoot, you said you wanted to talk." Becca was getting agitated with Mark's smart responses. "Besides, you're the one that told me you guys were going out to dinner about a month ago, but you never called and told me how everything went."

"Fine, Becca. Everything was fine. We ended up having a great time. There's really nothing to tell." Mark decided it would be best not to go into the catastrophic details.

"No need to get defensive. That's your business and I don't want to interfere with your secret rendezvous." Becca chuckled to herself.

"I said nothing happened so just lay off." Mark stood up and walked over to his suitcase and pulled out his underwear. "Becca, I'm tired of playing games. I'm going to take a shower and put on my clothes so we can have dinner." Mark walked into the bathroom and closed the door behind him. He could not believe that Becca was asking all these questions about Shawna, when Rob's actions were the ones that needed to be scrutinized. He shook his head and stared at himself trying to figure out how to handle Becca's curiosity.

Becca continued to sit on the bed stunned at Mark's reaction. She did not mean to cause more tension. A tear started to fall down her right cheek. She loved him so much and the last thing on her mind was to make him upset. "What is really going on? Have I just stepped into the Twilight Zone or what?" Becca stood up and walked over to the dresser and stared at her reflection in the mirror. "Lord, I need a little help. Please salvage this weekend and bless us to mend our friendship."

The shuttle ride to the main lodge was more quiet than Becca would have liked. She decided to not push Mark into a mechanical conversation. She looked out the window at nature's beauty. It was dusk and everything looked peaceful. Becca hadn't realized that they were pulling up at the front steps until she felt the warmth and protection of Mark's hand on top of hers squeezing gently.

"Becca, we're here." After the shuttle came to a complete stop, Mark stood up and stretched out his hand to help her stand and guide her into the aisle. He loved helping Becca. Even something as menial as making sure she didn't trip or holding the door for her as she walked into a building. Mark could always feel her humility; which made him want to do more for her. "Do you have everything?"

"Yes, Mark, I'm ok." Becca walked forward to the front of the shuttle and stepped down the steps. She could feel some of the other women getting off the shuttle looking at her in a curious manner. Trying to figure out why this gorgeous man would want to be with her, especially the fashion model types. But Mark never made her feel insecure. It always felt like she had his undivided attention. "Do you see the kids?" Becca inquired while walking through the main lobby holding onto Mark's arm.

"No. They're supposed to be in the arcade area. Let's walk over there. I think it's that area all the way in the back by the water fountain and restrooms." Mark and Becca walked over to the arcade laughing and talking about the different types of people that were waiting around in the main hall for the dinner bell to ring. It was almost six o'clock.

Becca saw Camille and Bryan first. They were playing air hockey. "There they are." She pointed them out to Mark. She caught Bryan's eye and waved. They moved closer to them. "So have you guys been having a good time?" Becca released Mark's arm and walked over to her son as Mark made his way over to Camille.

"Yeah, mom, we've had a blast! Look at what I made in the activities' group." Bryan was proud of his boondoggle. It was red and gold the colors of his mom's sorority. "Do you like it mom?" Bryan was so excited.

"Well of course. As a matter of fact, I love it. I wish you would have made one for me." Becca coyly smiled at her son.

"It is yours mom. You're silly. You knew it was for you. This one is mine." Bryan pulled a black and gold one out of his pocket with little animal charms hanging off of it.

"Wow, that's cool dude. You are just so talented." Becca gave her son a big hug. "Are you hungry?"

"You know it! I hope they have some fried chicken tenders and macaroni and cheese. Um, Um, Um!" Bryan rubbed his stomach and grabbed his mom's hand. "Let's go."

Becca slowed him down. "Don't you think we should wait for Camille and Mark?"

"Ok, but she's so slow. I had to keep hurrying her up the whole time. Sometimes I think something's wrong with her." Bryan had a disgusted look on his face.

"That's not nice, Bryan. Now straighten up your face. Here they come." Becca shook her head. Sometimes she just didn't know what to think about her son. She turned her attention to Camille. "Did you have fun too, Camille?"

"It was ok. Bryan kept rushing me and I didn't get a chance to finish my bracelet. So the lady gave me a plastic bag to put in my beads and yarn." Camille looked at Bryan and rolled her eyes.

Mark saw her and squeezed her hand in reprimand. "Camille that's not nice. Now let's go I think I hear the dinner bell ringing." Mark held onto her hand as they followed behind Becca and Bryan. Mark hadn't noticed earlier how cute Becca looked in her blue wide legged jeans and red cashmere v-neck sweater that he had bought her for Christmas. She had her hair pulled back in a pony tail which showed off her 1ct. diamond stud earrings and her tan colored boots. Becca was just radiant as she walked past the oversized fireplace just outside the dining hall. Mark was so caught up in her beauty that he didn't hear Becca ask him about the vacant table for four she spotted by the window with a view of the pond with pink lights reflecting off the water.

"Mark, Mark is this table ok?" Becca turned around to meet his stare and it made something jump in the pit of her stomach. She felt like a school girl on her first date. "Mark, are you feeling alright?" She touched his arm.

"Yeah, yeah, that table is fine. This whole place is nice. It doesn't matter where we sit." He smiled at her with all the warmth and love that he had in his heart.

"Ok then. You and Bryan go on over to the table and Camille and I are going to the ladies' room." Becca reached out her hand for Camille and the two of them walked off in the opposite direction. Camille talked the whole time but Becca missed most of what she said because all she could think about was the way Mark looked at her. She was trying desperately to not read more into the look than what it was but something deep in her heart knew there was a hidden secret.

"Auntie Becca, are you listening to me?" Camille had used the restroom and was now at the sink standing by Becca washing her hands.

"I'm sorry honey would you please repeat what you just said?" Becca handed her a paper towel and commenced to freshening her Very Berry lip gloss.

"Can I try some of that? My lips are dry too." Camille was only nine but she loved makeup. Her uncle would not let her wear any except a little gloss every now and then. Camille looked at Becca with her best angelic expression.

"Ok, Camille but just a little. Poke your lips out and I'll put it on." Becca always wanted a daughter and being with Camille filled that void in her life. Even though they didn't see each other every day, Becca tried to make sure that Camille knew how much she loved her as if she were her very own daughter. "Oooh wee! Look at that diva. You are just too gorgeous, girl!" Becca smiled at her and brushed her hair.

"Thank you Auntie. I know I look good just like you. We are both divas. Wait until Uncle Mark sees us!" Camille liked spending time with Becca alone. "You ready to go out Auntie?"

"Yes, sweetheart, I am. Let's go show these guys how good we look." Becca opened the door for Camille to walk through and followed her. They walked across the dining hall with their heads high and their diva attitudes on. When they made it to the table Mark and Bryan were staring at them.

"Good grief mom what took ya'll so long?" Bryan looked at Camille curled up his lips. "What is that on yo' mouth? Did you get some red punch before you came back to the table?" He turned back toward Mark. "Can I please get in the buffet line now?" Bryan looked as if he were starving.

"Hold on Bry. We need to say grace over our food. Everyone hold hands." Mark reached for Becca's and Camille's.

"I don't wanna hold his hand Uncle Mark. He's always making fun of me." Camille grabbed hold of her uncle's hand with both of her hands.

"Girl, you betta' cut it out. Now hold Bryan's hand and the two of you stop actin' up. I did wear my belt tonight so don't think I won't use it." Mark gave Camille and Bryan a look that let them know he was not playing.

"Yes, Uncle Mark." Camille reached out and loosely held Bryan's hand.

"Yes sir." Bryan held her hand and his mom's.

Becca was just amazed at how well Mark handled the kids. It was like he knew exactly what to say and how to say it. All she had to do was back him up. As they bowed their heads, Becca listened to Mark pray over their family and give thanks to God for blessing them to be in such a beautiful place. Becca loved to hear Mark pray. It felt so good to hear a strong man submit to God and give Him honor and glory. This is what she wanted in a husband. This is the part that always seemed to be missing. No matter how she tried to force it in other relationships, this was the void. That is why she had to be careful not to make the wrong moves with Mark and disturb the delicate balance of their friendship but every time they were all together like this it made it harder and harder not to scream out how much she loved this man. "Amen. Mark, why don't you take the kids up to the buffet and I'll wait till you guys get back."

"That's not necessary. We can all go together. This is a family function. Bryan get yo' momma and let's grub." Mark winked at Becca and they all went up to the buffet. Dinner was wonderful. They laughed and talked and laughed and talked some more. Mark laughed so hard he thought he would pass out from lack of oxygen to his brain. This is what family is all about he thought.

It was about ten o'clock by the time they made it back to their cabin. Camille and Bryan were so tired. But Becca made sure they both got their showers and brushed their teeth. She greased Camille's parts and put a stocking cap on her head. She watched Mark show Bryan how to brush his waves and put his wave cap on. "Ok, you guys say good night to Mark." She watched them one by one hug and kiss Mark good night and she saw Mark's pride. No one would ever be able to tell that these children were not his biological offspring. It was just inspiring to watch him with them. "Alright, that's enough let's go." Becca marched them off to their room on the other side of the cabin. There were two oak twin beds, two night stands, a closet and two chester drawers in their room. She helped both of them into bed and prayed with them. Becca gave Camille and Bryan kisses and hugs. They were sleep before she turned out the light.

When Becca walked back into the living room, Mark looked up from the fire he had just started and beckoned for her to sit next to him on the sofa. "Are you thirsty?"

"Why yes, kind sir. What do you have to quench my thirst?" Becca spoke in her professional tone.

"Hmm, let me see. How about a tall glass of chilled pink lemonade?" Mark handed the flute to Becca and picked up the other glass for himself.

"Where did this come from?" Becca had a confused look on her face.

"Oh well I have connections." Mark pulled the white fur cover over their legs. "Now, let's make a toast."

Becca couldn't believe what was going on. She pinched her leg hard under the cover to make sure she wasn't dreaming. "Are you serious, Mark?"

"Why yes fair lady I am. Now I'll go first." Mark cleared his throat and looked straight at Becca. "To my intelligent, beautiful, and gifted best friend who has never really understood what she means to me. I hope that all of your dreams and desires come true and that we will continue to grow old together. I know that I am blessed to be your friend and I never want to know what it is like to not have you in my life. Cheers." He gently touched her glass with his and they each took a sip.

Becca was speechless. This was just incredible. There were so many thoughts running through her head at one time that she had to scream inside herself for everything to just stop. "It's my turn. Mark Simmons, what can I say? You are every woman's dream. Your relationship with God, your relationship with your family, and your friendship with me it just leaves me breathless. I have never known a man on this earth with your capacity to love and care. You inspire me. I also feel blessed and privileged to count you as a friend for almost two decades. It's amazing to me that we have managed to stay friends longer than some couples have been married. And things have not always been perfect but somehow we find our way back to the friendship. Please know that I love you very much and no matter what happens in this life I will always be connected to your heart. Cheers." Becca touched Mark's glass gently and they drank from their glasses again. This night had turned out to be magical almost like a fairy tale.

Mark put his arm around Becca and pulled her close to him. They watched the fire blaze and let their hearts speak to each other in their own secret language. Mark felt Becca lay her head on his shoulder. He was so full of love for her that all he could do was sing. He began to softly sing the song he heard her singing earlier that evening.

Becca felt like she was in one of those romance movies she loved to watch. It was surreal. She pressed herself closer to him and draped her arm around his waist. As he sang she could feel the warmth of his breath on her forehead. It was intoxicating. Becca took a chance and lifted her head to say something to break the intensity of the moment but just as she did Mark looked down at her and a magnetic force pulled them together. She felt the heat of his breath and the softness of his full dark lips against hers. All Becca could do was yield to his kiss. She felt his arms wrap around her and pull her gently into him and she finally exhaled a symbolic breath that she had been holding for the last twenty years.

Mark was finally passionately embracing the woman that he had secretly loved for a very long time. When their lips parted, no words were spoken for fear that anything said would erase what just happened. Mark just held Becca tighter as she rested her head on his heart. He knew it was telling her secrets that he had hidden there a long time ago. He just continued to sing softly and rub her back. They fell asleep in each other's arms afraid to let go.

Chapter 11

Becca rose early the next morning feeling refreshed and full of hope. She took a shower, put on her black one piece bathing suit and slipped her navy jogging suit over it. She put on her socks and white tennis shoes. She walked quietly through the living room where Mark was still sleeping on the oversized sofa. He had stretched out and looked so peaceful. Becca went to the kids' room where they were already up. Bryan was playing with his PSP and Camille was playing with her Nintendo DS. Becca closed the door behind her and motioned for them to talk softly because Mark was still asleep. "Do you guys want to go swimming this morning before the pool gets crowded?"

Camille and Bryan both replied with big smiles, "Yes!"

"Ok well you need to put your suits on right away. Bryan, you go use the master bathroom and Camille you use this one. But you guys have to be quiet. I'll make up your beds for you." Becca helped them pull out there bathing suits and there sweat pants and shirts.

The sun seemed to be shining extra bright as they walked up the road to the main lodge where the indoor pool house was located. Becca told Bryan and Camille that they would eat breakfast after swimming. It was about 8:00 a.m. when Bryan jumped into the pool. Camille was right behind him. Becca took all their clothes and put them at a table in the corner of the pool house. She slipped out of her jogging suit and pulled a ponytail holder out of her red tote bag. "How's the water?" Becca asked as she walked to the end of the pool where the steps were.

"It feels good, mom! Come on in." Bryan ducked his head underwater and started swimming toward her. Bryan had always loved the water ever since he was a baby.

"Yeah Auntie Becca it feels nice." Camille was leaning against the wall of the pool enjoying the water.

Becca stepped down in the water. It felt ice cold at first. The further into the water she submerged herself, the shorter her breaths became until her body finally adjusted. Becca went over and stood by Camille. "How you doin' over here, lady?"

Camille smiled at Becca and said, "Ok. I need a little help with my swimming, Auntie." Camille wanted to get out in the water like Bryan but she was still a little scared.

"Ok, just hold onto me and I'll walk you out to the middle." Becca walked with Camille staying close to her side. "Isn't this fun?"

"Y-Yeah, Auntie, but I'm still a little scared." Camille was holding on tightly to Becca.

Becca talked Camille through holding her breath, floating on her back, and even kicking her legs in the water. Then Becca beckoned for Bryan. "Get that noodle over by the wall so Camille can use it, please."

Bryan did as his mother asked and even showed Camille how to use it. "Yeah Camille, that's it. You can do it." Bryan encouraged his God-sister with sincerity.

These two never ceased to amaze Becca. She loved it when they helped each other. "Bryan, stay with Camille while I swim a couple of laps." Becca commenced to gliding through the water. It felt good to have the water caress her body. She felt so peaceful, so sure of herself. When she lifted her head at the other end of the pool, Becca saw Bryan and Camille tossing a soft Nerf ball back and forth laughing and playing. She decided to go and stretch out on the lounge chair and read her book she had brought to read.

"Auntie Becca, where are you going?" Camille was laughing at Bryan standing on his hands underwater.

"I'll be right over here. You guys enjoy the water. We'll be leaving in another hour." Becca laid a towel on the lounge chair and sat down and leaned back toward the sun. The pool house was all glass. It was like she could feel the sun smiling at her. Becca let her mind wander back to last night. She smiled unconsciously. She didn't want to think about what came next she just wanted to enjoy the warm fuzzy feeling she had on the inside.

Mark woke up to find a note on the table next to the sofa. It was from Becca saying that she had taken the kids swimming and then they were going to breakfast. A smiled crept across his face at the two intertwined hearts she drew at the bottom of the paper. Mark stretched, stood up, fixed the sofa and folded the blanket. He could still smell Becca's perfume on it. He went to the bathroom, took a shower, and put on his silver Nike jogging suit with his black nylon body glove shirt underneath. Mark decided that he would go to the gym and workout. Then he would surprise his family at breakfast.

Mark jogged up to the Lodge and went upstairs to the gym on the second floor. It overlooked the pool house and the pond. There were only three people in the gym when he walked through the glass door. A woman on an exercise bike on the opposite side of the room facing out the window, a man on one of the weight benches, and another guy was on a machine that simulated climbing a mountain. ESPN was playing on the 48" plasma screen across the room and CNN was playing on the one facing the treadmill Mark was about to get on. He felt good this morning so he set his time for a forty minute walk at a fast pace. Mark took off his jacket and stepped on the treadmill and pressed start. It was relaxing to get his heart pumping in the middle of nature's beauty and still watch over his family in the pool house below. He let out a sigh of satisfaction.

About twenty minutes later, the woman on the exercise bike across the room had finished her session. She wore an aqua blue Reebok tank top and matching pants with white tennis shoes of the same brand. She grabbed her towel and wiped the perspiration from her face and neck. She picked up her jacket and started walking toward the door when a familiar face caught her eye. She smiled boldly and strutted over to his machine. "Hey stranger, are you following me?" She smiled innocently.

Mark almost slid off the machine when he turned to see a face standing there that he would never have expected to encounter. Mark pressed the button to slow his machine down and then stop it so he could step off. "H-Hello, Shawna, what are you doing here?" Mark felt like he was in some old episode of the *Twilight Zone*.

Shawna was trying to act like she was so surprised to see him. "I'm here for a weekend getaway with a friend of mine. How about you?" She started dabbing her chest area in order to guide Mark's attention.

"You mean to tell me that you don't remember that this is the weekend Becca and I had planned to come here? Come on now Shawna, we're too old for these types of games." Mark was agitated that she thought he was that stupid and gullible. He glanced back out the window, down at the pool area to make sure Becca and the kids were still swimming. He could see Becca reading a book on the lounge chair with Camille and Bryan playing in the pool. He breathed a nervous sigh.

"Mark there's no need for you to get upset. I've known about this place for the last couple of years. I'm sorry that you think I'm following you. As a matter of fact, I don't remember anything before that disastrous date we had a few weeks ago." Shawna looked at him coldly then broke out laughing. "You were sooo drunk. It was ridiculous!" Shawna shifted her weight and placed her hand on her hip looking at Mark like there was no tension between them. "Did you guys leave the children at home?"

"Of course not, Shawna." Mark was getting upset with her nonsense. "So who is this so-called friend you're spending the weekend with? Do I get to meet him?" Mark was ready to call Shawna's bluff until a tall Caucasian man walked through the glass door dripping of perspiration. He looked to be about 6'4, 185 pounds of extraordinary muscle tone. His skin was sun kissed and his eyes were deep blue. His hair was dark with thick locks of curl. Mark could not believe this giant of a man. "Hello, sir, how's it goin?" Mark was trying to be cordial.

"Hey man, it's good to meet you. My name is Brad. Shawna talks about you a lot." Brad extended his hand for Mark to shake. Brad was a very good looking man and he knew it. He wore a crisp white, top of the line, Michael Jordan sweat suit.

"Yeah Brad, it's good to meet you too. So, how long have you and Shawna been dating?" Mark asked Brad the question but looked directly at Shawna.

Shawna interrupted the conversation and responded proudly, "Three months and counting." She smiled at Brad and took hold of his arm. "Isn't he great?" She spoke the words while looking at Mark. She was searching for some sign of jealousy.

Mark could not believe how phony Shawna was acting when she knew that just a month ago she was trying to seduce him in her apartment. "UN-BE-LIEVE-ABLE!"

"Excuse me! What is that suppose to mean?" Shawna quickly got an attitude.

Mark hadn't realized that he had said the word out loud. He cleared his throat and tried to cover up his annoyance with the whole charade. "Oh, I just meant that you guys seem like you've been together longer than that." Mark paused a moment and smiled politely. "You really shouldn't be so quick to jump on the defensive,

Shawna, it makes you look like your hiding something."

Brad's phone rang and he touched the talk button and began to speak into his Bluetooth earpiece. Shawna glared at Mark as he kept looking back at the pool house watching his beloved Becca. She figured she had to do something fast to stop their well oiled machine of friendship. "I have an idea. Why don't we all have dinner tonight? That way we can sit down and talk with one another. Sound good, honey?" Brad was on a business call but gave her the thumbs up with both hands.

Mark looked at Shawna very curiously then replied cautiously. "I-I don't know. Becca may have planned something for this evening. I'll have to check with her first.

"I thought you guys were just friends. You're talking like she's your wife, Mark!" Shawna chuckled mockingly.

"We are just friends but that doesn't mean I can't show her some respect. Maybe you're not use to that concept. I think that's where you have a problem, Ms. Lewis, not knowing when to give respect." Mark smirked at her.

Brad ended his phone call in time to hear the last part of Mark's comment. "Well, he sure has your number sweet thang!" Brad hit Shawna on the butt seductively while turning his attention to Mark. "Look buddy, why don't you get with your friend, ask her about dinner. We'll be in the lounge at 6p.m. If you're not there by 7 we'll start ordering dinner for two instead of four. How's that sound?" Brad pulled Shawna's small frame closer to him as if he were marking his territory.

Mark couldn't figure out why these two wanted to spend any amount of time with him and Becca. Then his mind wondered to what Becca was going to say when she found out that Shawna was at the same resort, the same weekend, and that she wanted to have dinner with the two of them. He could see her disgusted expression already. That is why it shocked him to hear his voice betray his heart. "Sure, that sounds fair. I guess we'll see you about 6:30." Mark stuck out his hand for Brad to shake and then excused himself to finish his workout on the treadmill.

Brad opened the glass door for Shawna, who was still standing in the same spot staring at Mark, "Uh excuse me woman, please try to remember who your boyfriend is. Now, let's go."

Shawna turned and walked out the door with Brad following close behind her. When they stepped onto the elevator they were alone. Shawna stood in the corner with her arms behind her leaning against the back wall. Brad was directly in front of her and was becoming intoxicated by her sexy body. She, on the other hand, was so busy thinking about Mark that she didn't even notice until they reached their suite and Brad pulled her down on the queen-sized bed. "What the hell are you doing?!" Shawna was angry and struggled to loosen herself from his strong grasp.

"I'm doing what you want Mark to do to you!" Brad forced her on her back and pinned her down with his masculine body. "Quit teasing me, Shawna. If you wanna pretend that I'm Mark, it's ok. I just want to feel your sexiness all over me. Don't make me suffer like this. You owe me a taste, girl!" Brad started kissing her on her neck and squeezing her tightly.

Shawna couldn't believe it. This man was crazy but she already knew she was going to have to give up something to keep him doing what she wanted. Besides, he did give beautiful diamond gifts. So in her mind the end results justified the means. "Ok Brad, ok. Just let me up so I can breathe and get in the shower to freshen up. Then I'll give you exactly what you want." Shawna looked directly into his eyes and lifted up her head towards his kissing him ravenously. She could feel Brad's strength weakening with every stroke of her tongue against his skin. Shawna loved being in control. She flipped him on his back continuing to devour him. She stopped abruptly and told him to stay right there. They both were breathing hard and she could see his manliness saluting her through his jogging pants. As she started to walk away, she was pulled back to him.

"Where are you going? I'm not through with you yet!" Brad was possessed with raw desire as he ran his hands all over her body.

"Come on and get yo' honey." Shawna wanted Brad to hurry up and do what he needed to do so she could get ready for her dinner encounter with Mark tonight. But she knew she had to stroke Brad's ego to ensure that he would keep up his part of the bargain.

Brad seized her body like he was a starving maniac. He knew Shawna liked it when he was completely savage.

It was around four thirty in the afternoon when Becca stepped out the shower. She draped her damp body with her scarlet red satin robe. She tied the belt around her waist and walked into the bedroom. Mark had taken Camille and Bryan up to the children's movie and fun night at the main lodge. She didn't know he had made it back so quickly. He was sitting in the chair in the corner of the master bedroom watching her lotion herself. "Mark Simmons! Why are you trying to scare me? And shouldn't you be getting' ready for this wonderful engagement you set up for us to attend? I'm just so excited I can barely contain myself." The tone in Becca's voice was saturated with sarcasm.

"Look Becca, I didn't think it would be a big deal. As a matter of fact, she suggested it and her giant of a boyfriend insisted. Anyway, it's just dinner." Mark rubbed his forehead as he stood up and walked over to the edge of the bed where Becca was sitting and rubbing rose scented lotion on her arms. Mark took her hand in his and helped Becca to her feet. He led her over to the mirror and stood behind her. "Do you see that woman in the mirror? She is one of the most beautiful women I have ever seen. Why do you suppose she is insecure about herself? She is strong-willed, intelligent, and caring. Her heart's capacity to love is unbelievable."

"Mark, stop it. I'm none of those things. I try to be but I keep falling short." Becca walked away from the mirror and went over to the window to hide the tear that had begun to stream down her cheek. She looked out the window and wrapped her arms around herself. "I don't know what you want me to say. I keep trying to be this hi-fashion, beautiful woman that you deserve. But sometimes it takes so much effort to be someone I'm not."

"Why would you do that? We have seen each other through some terrible times in our lives and we have always remained best friends. I have treated Bryan like he was my own son since the day you brought him on campus. Have I ever asked you to be someone other than your extraordinary self?" Mark walked over to Becca and slid his arms around her waist. "Becca, please don't think you have to compete against Shawna for my affection because you already have it." Mark kissed her softly on the back side of her neck, released her and walked to the bathroom. He looked back at her to see that she was still at the window. "I'm going to get in the shower. I'll be out in a minute. If you still don't want to go then you don't have to." When Mark closed the door behind him he spoke in a whisper to himself. "Oh Becca, don't you know that you've had my heart since the beginning?"

As they entered the resort restaurant, Becca saw Shawna first. She was gorgeous. She wore a pale blue short dress that hugged every curve of her body. Her shoes were clear with rhinestone clusters at the top of each shoe. This goddess wore sheer natural colored pantyhose that made her legs look bare. Her long dark silky hair was pulled over to the right side and held in place at the nape of her neck with a rhinestone decorated comb shaped like a crescent moon. The bust line of her dress showcased her well endowed breasts. The solitaire diamond earrings decorated her face beautifully and her make-up was flawless. Becca wanted to turn around and go back to the cabin, pack her and Bryan's bags and catch the next thing smokin' out of Dodge. This was too much. She forgot herself and let one of her thoughts slip out as she exhaled. "Your kiddin' me. This just can't be real." Becca didn't even realize that she had stopped in the middle of the floor until Mark touched her arm.

"What is it, Becca? Do you feel ok? You look like you're about to be sick." Mark was trying to help and be attentive to her but the words weren't quite coming out right. "Do you need some water?" Mark rubbed her hand as he held it in his grasp.

Becca shook herself and straightened her face. "Wh-What? Yes, Mark, I am fine. I'm not sure what just happened. My stomach felt a little queasy but I'll be alright. Come on. It looks like Shawna and her main squeeze have already ordered drinks." Becca took Mark's arm and silently commanded her feet to move.

Mark could tell that Becca was feeling insecure. He didn't

understand why though. Mark thought Becca was looking gorgeous in her magenta wrap around dress that fell just below her knees. Her shoes were iridescent and kept changing colors as she moved through the crowd and the light danced on them. He loved it when she wore her hair up because it showed off her beautiful neck. Mark was glad to see that she had decided to where the diamond floating heart necklace he had bought her for her birthday a couple of years ago. It rested on her chest just above her cleavage and complimented the diamond tear drop earrings she wore very well. "Becca, you really look awesome tonight. I don't think I have ever seen that dress before. But you're workin' it diva." Mark spoke to her lovingly as they arrived at the table.

"Well, well, well don't you guys look good tonight?" Shawna stood up and walked up to Mark and hugged him. "Mark, I love that outfit. That jacket fits you like a glove and those pants are complimenting all of your best assets." Shawna laughed seductively and winked at him.

Brad saw her game and stood up to introduce himself to Becca. "Hello pretty lady. My name is Brad and you must be Becca Thomas. Mark spoke about you earlier. You're really an exquisite beauty." Brad took her hand and kissed it gently.

Becca smiled at him and nervously pulled her hand away. "Thank you, sir. I'll tell you a secret. I wake up in the morning looking like this. No work involved at all." Becca whispered jokingly.

Brad laughed with Becca and pulled a chair out for her to sit down next to him. "Beauty and a sense of humor you really are a rare jewel. I can't believe Mark has never tried to make you his woman." Brad looked directly at Mark with a sly smirk on his face and spoke confidently. "Man, you betta' watch out because a priceless piece of artwork should be showcased, not covered up and put in the back of the room."

Shawna shot Brad a cold stare that said a mouthful. He ignored her and took a sip of his white wine.

"So Becca how are you enjoying this wonderful place?

Don't you just want to stay here forever?" Shawna smiled at Becca politely and pretended to be interested in her answer.

Becca kept her composure and decided that she was not going to let Shawna mess with her confidence. "It is quite lovely I guess that's why I picked it. But you know I'm curious. How did you find out about this resort?" Becca took a sip of the ice water that Mark had poured in her crystal glass.

"Oh, Mark told me about your vacation plans. It sounded so great I thought it would be nice for me and my friend to come up for the weekend. So, here we are." Shawna gave Becca a fake smile and sipped her white wine. Then she turned her attention back to Mark. "Mark, would you like some wine?" She spoke to him as if every word was undressing him.

Mark looked at Becca and back at Shawna. "Water will be just fine for me." Mark reached for the pitcher of water just as Shawna's hand rested on it. For a brief moment he felt an electrical surge go through his body. "Oh, I'm sorry. Please excuse me."

Brad chuckled and through his arm around Becca's chair. "Now Mr. Simmons, I know you're not trying to flirt with my girl especially with this delicious woman sittin' next to me looking good enough to eat. Don't tempt me, man. I may have to steal her from you." Brad laughed cunningly and caressed Becca's arm smoothly.

Becca spoke up immediately, out of habit. "Brad, I think you have the wrong idea about Mark and me. We are just friends." She looked at Mark and quickly looked away. He seemed to be confused by her statement but she couldn't figure out why, especially since he didn't seem to be rejecting Shawna's blatant flirtations. Becca refused to look like a fool. Not this time.

"Oh, excuse me, Ms. Thomas I didn't mean anything by the comment. It's just that I have never seen a man and a woman that were not related have the closeness that the two of you have." Brad chuckled to himself and placed his hand on top of Shawna's which was resting on the table. "The way you two carry on people would think that you guys were married." Brad laughed harder. "It really is funny."

Mark glared at him and then looked at Becca who had lowered her head to look at her menu. But he could tell her mind was not on what to order. "So, Brad, what are your intentions for Shawna? Are you guys serious?"

Shawna decided it was time to change the direction of the conversation. "So Mark how is Camille enjoying herself? Are she and Bryan getting along?" Shawna slipped her hand out from under Brad's grasp and touched Mark's arm gently. She was not going to let anything ruin this evening.

"Camille is fine and she and Bryan are getting along well. They keep Becca busy at the pool and playin' games. Isn't that right Becca?" Mark looked at her and smiled.

"Yes, that's right but I don't mind. I love spending time with them." Becca turned her attention to the live jazz band that was playing. Anything to keep from looking at Shawna and playing mind games with her. Becca was so ready for this night to end but she had to endure just a little while longer.

Brad decided to shake things up just a little more. "Becca, would you please dance with me? That is if Mark doesn't mind." Brad smiled at her flirtatiously.

Becca answered surprisingly quickly. "You know what, Brad I think that sounds great. Now, I have to warn you that I don't dance often so if I step on your toes don't be mad." Becca smiled at him politely.

Brad stood up and helped Becca out of her chair. "Well let's go then. If you two would excuse us we're headed to cut a rug." Brad allowed Becca to lead him to the middle of the room.

Mark couldn't believe that Becca was really being taken in by this slickster. He could feel himself getting a sick feeling in the pit of his stomach watching Brad wrap his arms around Becca's waist and sway her smoothly to the beat of the music. It was almost unbearable.

Shawna broke Mark's trance by touching his leg seductively. "Mark, honey, what's on your mind? You know you can talk to me about anything."

Mark was tired of Shawna's games. "Why are you acting like everything is cool with us. The last time we were together you were cussin' me out. Now all of a sudden you on me like I'm yo' best friend." Mark took her hand off of his leg and dropped it back in her own lap. "Oh and why did you just lie to Becca about me telling you about the resort? You told me this morning at the gym that you've known about this place for a couple of years. I don't know what kind of games you're playin', Shawna, but I'm not up for any of 'em!"

"Can't we just move pass that night? I had too much to drink and was not in my right mind. I'm so sorry." She was looking directly at him trying to be sincere. "The other thing with Becca a few moments ago was a misunderstanding. I'll let her know the truth. It's really not a big deal. I'm trying to smooth things out between us Mark." Shawna tilted her head a little and slightly leaned in closer to Mark.

"You know, Shawna, I think it would be better for us to just keep our relationship work related after this weekend." Mark turned his attention back to Becca on the floor laughing at something Brad had said. He could not take it any longer. "Shawna, I'm goin' to salvage the rest of this evening and ask my best friend to dance with me. I'd suggest that you stop trying to flirt with me and show yo' man some attention because this fantasy you have about us gettin' together will never happen." Mark did not wait for her to respond. He stood up and walked over to Brad and Becca and cut in. He cautiously slipped one arm around her waist and held her other hand in his. Mark could feel her body loosen and fall into sync with his rhythm. This was where he wanted to be.

Brad sat back down next to Shawna and placed his arm around her shoulder. "Well, darling, it looks like your plan has hit a snag. I think you and I should leave these two love birds alone. We can get an expensive bottle of wine and go back to our room and soak in the Jacuzzi tub. What do you think?" Brad kissed her on the cheek.

"Will you get your head in the game? This ain't over yet!

I play to win." Shawna glared at Mark and Becca dancing in perfect timing. "I'll back off tonight but tomorrow Becca is going to get the shock of her life. Mark thinks he can just discard me and I'll go quietly into the night. Well, we'll see if he feels the same way when tomorrow comes." Shawna turned to Brad in a commanding tone. "You just do what I told you to do and stop deviating from the plan. Now, let's order so we can end this nightmare."

Brad stared at her in disbelief. "You are a real piece of work, Shawna. If you weren't so sexy and great in bed, I'd leave your crazy behind up in these mountains." They dined the rest of the evening on their best behavior.

Chapter 12

Sunrise came quickly the next morning. It seemed like they had just went to bed. Becca could hear Mark and the kids in the kitchen singing and smell breakfast cooking. Becca had a smile on her face that she just could not seem to erase. What started out as a rocky night, turned out to be an enchanted evening. After dinner, Mark and Becca walked around the Lodge and then took a stroll out by the pond under the moonlight. They talked and laughed like they had not done in a very long time. During spontaneous moments, Mark would hold her hand and they would just walk in silence. Becca thought of those moments as she got out of bed and went to the bathroom to wash up. She hated that their trip was over and it was now time to prepare for reality. But for a few more hours she would just enjoy being with her best friend and their children. "UM, it sure smells good out here. Who do I have to pay to get a plate?" Becca laughed as Camille and Bryan ran and gave her a big hug. She loved them so much.

Mark took a skillet off the fire and placed his signature French Toast on a serving plate. "How's my favorite lady this morning? I know you slept good 'cause you were snorin' pretty loud this morning." Mark chuckled and winked at Becca.

"I was not snoring! Was I? Oh well, it's nothing new." Becca laughed with him. "You've known me long enough to know that when I get really tired it's on and poppin'! But I hope I didn't keep you awake." Becca now showed concern for her friend.

"Becca, please, you know I can tune you out. I slept so peacefully I didn't want to get up. But I had two rug rats that needed to be fed so you know a man's gotta do what a man's gotta do." Mark smiled at Camille and Bryan.

"Do you need me to do anything? It looks like your help put you down and cartoons now have their attention." Becca walked over to the stove to see what smelled so good.

"Nope. You just have a seat and I'll fix you a plate." Mark

wanted to take care of his family the last morning of their vacation. "Do you want two or three pieces of French Toast, Becca?"

"Man, are you crazy?! Two will be plenty. You know I worked too hard to get my weight down for your famous French Toast to send me back up the scale!" Becca chuckled and took her plate as Mark handed it to her with two slices of French Toast, two pieces of turkey bacon, and hash browns. "Thank you, sweetie. What about the children? Are you going to fix their plates?"

Mark sat down next to Becca with his plate smiling. "Now Becca, you know those kids ate early this morning. They were acting like they were about to starve. So I fixed their breakfast first. That's why they're so content." Mark said grace over their food and they ate their breakfast talking and laughing about the fun they had had over the past few days.

There still seemed to be a question in the air that neither one of them wanted to ask but definitely wanted answered. They knew their relationship would be redefined and they weren't sure if they were ready to do that. Mark spoke carefully, "Becca, I've had a great time this weekend and there are some things that we need to discuss when we get back home. I'm exhausted from dodging mine fields and I think it's time for us to be completely honest with one another. OK?"

Becca smiled at Mark with all the love her heart had to offer but before she could respond there was a knock at the door. "Hold that thought, Mark, let me get the door and then we'll continue this conversation." Becca stood up, kissed him on the forehead and walked to the door with a ridiculous grin on her face. Things were finally falling into place until Becca opened the door. Her heart dropped to the floor when she saw Shawna standing there with a black eye and clutching her stomach. Her shirt was ripped at the shoulder and she did not have a coat just an overnight bag. "What happened?" Becca asked with concern while helping her into the cabin.

Mark jumped out of his chair and ran to meet them when he saw Shawna leaning against Becca. "Here, let me help you Shawna. Just put your weight on me."

As Shawna tried to follow Mark's instructions, she almost passed out. Mark caught her before she hit the floor and scooped her up in his arms like she was a little child. He quickly set her down on the sofa in front of the fireplace. "I'm going to call for a doctor." Mark was very attentive.

The children snapped Becca out of the trance she was in. "Mom, what happened to Shawna? Is she gonna be ok?" Bryan was clutching his mother's hand.

"Auntie Becca, what should we do? She looks like someone beat her up really bad." Camille's voice quivered a little with the last statement.

Becca was finally able to get her legs to move across the floor. She set Shawna's bags down by the table. "Look, I need both of you to do me a big favor. Go into your room, take your showers, and start packing. I don't want you guys to argue or come out of the room until I come and get you. Ok?" Becca spoke in a calm and loving voice so as not to scare them. "And don't worry about Shawna, Mark is going to take good care of her."

Camille and Bryan answered together. "Ok." They walked off to their bedroom whispering to each other and stealing glances at Shawna laid back on the sofa.

"Becca, please bring me a phone so I can call the doctor and the police." Mark was hovering over Shawna like a protective husband.

"NO, Mark! I just need some ice for my eye and some pain relievers for this headache. Please I don't want to cause Brad any trouble. It was just an accident." Shawna sat straight up and grabbed hold to Mark's hand tightly.

Becca thought it was peculiar that Shawna didn't at least want the doctor to come check her out. "Shawna, please let us call the doctor. You look banged up pretty bad. You could have internal bleeding or broken bones." Becca walked over and stood next to Mark to show her concern.

Shawna was agitated with Becca's presence. "Look, Dr.

Thomas, I know you are the expert on everything but would you please just mind your own business and get me something cold for my face!" Shawna was like a mad dog marking her territory until she saw the way Mark looked at her with shock. She softened her tone. "I'm sorry Becca. I'm just in a whole lot of pain and I'm embarrassed. I should've seen the signs! I can't believe I let Brad hurt me like this." Shawna started crying profusely.

Mark sat down next to Shawna and held her like he had held Becca the night before. Becca thought she was going to be sick. She could not believe how quickly things had changed. "I'll get you that ice and some Motrin. You just try to relax, Shawna." Becca went into the bedroom to get the medicine. While she was there she looked at herself in the mirror and tried to calm her breathing. She did not want to let Shawna think she was getting to her. She had to stay in control. When Becca came back out of the room, she grabbed an ice pack out of the freezer and a glass of water. She made her way over to the sofa where Shawna was crying in Mark's chest.

Mark looked up and saw Becca looking at him in a confused state. He didn't know what to say. "Thanks Becca. This will do just fine to take the swelling down." Mark helped Shawna to sit up so she could take the two pills with her water. He then placed the ice pack on her eye and told her to stretch out on the sofa. "Just lay right here and rest Shawna. I have to talk to Becca for a minute but I'll be right back to check on you. Mark led Becca back to the bedroom and closed the door. "What do you think we should do?" He was pacing back and forth.

"What can we do? She doesn't want to call the police or the doctor. I mean she's a grown woman we can't make her do anything!" Becca was getting agitated. She knew something just didn't feel right about this whole situation.

"Well you don't have to get upset. I'm just trying to figure this thing out. I knew something wasn't right with that guy! I should've said something last night." Mark plopped down in the chair and held his head in his hands.

Becca couldn't believe it. Shawna had found a way to sabotage their vacation. Becca believed that Shawna was putting on an act just to get Mark's attention. "Look Mark, do you think that this could be an act? I mean it's a big coincidence that Shawna went through all this abuse and never showed any signs of fear or disgust with her boyfriend."

"Becca, I'm shocked that you would say something like that. What if it were you sitting there beaten up by your boyfriend? Wouldn't you want someone to believe you and help you through the crisis?" Mark looked at Becca in disbelief. "I'm going back out to check on my friend. Would you please see about Camille and Bryan?" Mark walked out of the room before Becca could respond.

On the ride back to Cleveland, Mark and Becca didn't speak much. The kids watched their DVD with their headphones on so that they wouldn't disturb Shawna curled up on the bench in the back. Mark pulled over at a rest stop so that he could fill the tank up and everyone could stretch their legs.

Becca was cordial when she spoke to Mark. "I'm going to take the kids in to use the restroom. Would you like to ask your wounded bird in the back if she has to go also?" Becca didn't care about the sarcasm. She was sick of Shawna's games. To lie about abuse was a new low.

"Don't do that, Becca. I would be treating you the same way if the situation was turned around. Let's not argue. We have another hour to go and I don't want to spend it on eggshells with you." Mark walked to the sliding door on his side and opened it. "Shawna, do you need to use the restroom?"

She was kind of groggy from the medicine. "Oh, yeah, thanks Mark. Do you think you could help me out of the van? My right side is still hurting." Shawna slowly sat up straight and reached out her hand to Mark. She glanced at Becca who was on the other side of him seething. When Mark gently took Shawna's arm and supported her body weight, she let herself fall into his arms as he lifted her carefully out of the van and placed her on the ground. "Thank you again Mark for helping me. I really appreciate your kindness especially now." Shawna touched his arm lovingly.

Becca was sick of the whole show. "Shawna, I'll take you from here. She stepped in between her and Mark and helped Shawna walk to the building. Bryan held the door, Camille went next, and then Becca eased through the door with Shawna. As soon as Shawna got inside the door Becca felt her stand up straighter and walk on her own with more stability. Becca was shocked. "Wow, Shawna you really seem to be moving a lot easier. I'm in shock! Especially since it looked like you were ready to pass out after Mark helped you from the van."

"Oh, I guess miracles are possible." Shawna half smiled at Becca and went into the restroom. Shawna was determined to drive a wedge between Becca and Mark and it seemed to be working.

On the way back to their vehicle, Becca noticed that Shawna was suddenly becoming more helpless again. As she helped her Becca spoke softly to her so that the kids couldn't hear. "Shawna, I know that you're playing games with us just to get Mark's attention but you betta' watch yo' self because Mark is not hardly stupid. He'll see through your games eventually."

"Oh, Becca, I'm sorry that you feel that way. I can't help the fact that my boyfriend lost his mind and started beating me up. I'd never try to manipulate Mark like that. And besides, he is too smart to fall for something like that because he didn't fall for my games when I was on top of him two weeks ago at my apartment." Shawna paused to let the venom sink in and spread throughout Becca's system. "Oops, that might not be such a good example because he did give into me that night. But Mark is always there to protect me when I need him. Isn't that just wonderful?"

Becca was speechless. She wanted to grab Shawna by her ponytail and yank her to the ground. In her mind, she just knew Shawna was lying but her heart was heavy. How was she supposed to ask Mark for the truth without sounding insecure and accusatory? Becca could have screamed bloody murder but she contained herself and chose not to respond to Shawna's lunacy because they had arrived back at the car.

Mark jumped out of the vehicle to help Shawna get back in the rear bench and then helped the Bryan and Camille. Becca had a funny look on her face that Mark had not seen before. When he closed the sliding door, Becca was already seated in the passenger seat looking straight ahead. He walked back around to his side of the vehicle, got in, and buckled his seatbelt and started the van. "Are you ok, Becca? You seem like you're in another world."

Becca only said a few words, "I'm ok, just in a hurry to get home and back to normalcy." Becca refused to look at Mark for fear her heart would betray her and her eyes would tell all her secrets. She leaned back in her seat and closed her eyes and thought about the stolen moments she and Mark had spent together over the weekend. What was she supposed to do now? He had not told her about being with Shawna on a date and definitely not about going to her apartment. Becca was tired of playing the fool. Maybe she didn't need to count Rob out. Since it seemed that there were just too many obstacles for her and Mark to get over.

Chapter 13

"Mom, MOM! Are you ready to go yet? Dad will be here any minute." Bryan was excited about seeing his dad again. It had been about two months since Rob's last visit and Bryan was anxious to see him in person.

Becca was upstairs putting the finishing touches on her makeup. "OK, Brian, I'll be down in about five minutes." Becca had decided to just kinda go with the flow of things especially after Shawna made a fool out of her on the way back from the resort a month ago. Becca's heart was broken to know that Shawna had been that intimate with Mark. So, when Rob called to say he wanted to come back and visit for a weekend it didn't sound like such a bad idea. He said that he wanted to take them bowling since that was Bryan's favorite activity. Becca figured that at least she knew what to expect from Rob.

Rob stood on the other side of Becca's door with a half dozen roses wrapped in red paper for the mother of his only son and a brand new metallic gold bowling ball for his little buddy. He was shocked when Becca agreed to let him stay with her and Bryan this time. But Rob was confident that this would be a turning point in their new relationship.

Bryan ran to the door when he heard the bell ring. "I got it mom!" He yelled back as he flung open the door to reveal his dad standing there smiling and bearing gifts. "Hey dad, how's it goin'? I'm so glad to see you!" Bryan wrapped his arms around his dad and gave him a big hug. Bryan stepped back so Rob could come inside.

"What's up big man? I'm doin' betta' now that I'm here with you." Rob looked around while taking off his black Carhartt jacket. "Where's yo' mom?" From there conversation a couple of weeks ago, it seemed as if Becca might be succumbing to Rob's charm. That, or either she was having a moment of weakness. Whatever the case may have been, Rob wasn't going to let this opportunity pass him by.

"Ma, Maaa!" Bryan ran to the steps and yelled up for his mom. "Come on down, mom. Dad is here!" Bryan went back to the living room and sat down next to his dad who had made himself comfortable on the plush red suede sofa. "So, dad, how long can you stay this time?"

Before Rob could get out an answer, Becca gracefully descended down the last few steps in a pair of black wide leg jeans and a hot pink cashmere v-neck sweater that was trimmed in silver rhinestones. Her black leather thick heeled ankle boots completed her outfit. Becca wore Polo Sport Cologne for women. The light fragrance engulfed the room. She spoke in a carefree tone. "How are you Mr. Harris? I hope I didn't keep you two boys waiting for too long." She smiled coyly at Rob and winked at her handsome son.

"Wow, Becca, you look good!" Rob stood up, walked over and slipped his right arm around her waist and pulled her close to him. Rob noticed that Becca didn't pull away like she usually did. So, he decided to take a chance and kissed her gently on the side of her face close to the corner of her perfectly berry glossed lips. "I don't think I've ever seen you glow like this, Becca. I hope my presence has something to do with it." Rob stepped back from her and with his left hand gave her the roses.

Becca was shocked. "Rob, you didn't have to do this. But you know I love them!" Becca could not get rid of the silly smile that had found a home on her face. It was wonderful to have a man chase after her for a change. "I'll go put these in a vase and I'll be ready. Bryan, go upstairs and turn off your television and grab your new tennis shoes." Becca walked into the kitchen, pulled a vase off her top shelf over the sink, and began to fill it with water.

Rob decided to test the waters. "Hey babe, why don't you let me help you with that? I don't want you to mess up that sexy outfit you wore just for me." Rob laughed as he stepped on the side of her and gently took the vase. He completed what she had started but he noticed that Becca did not move from his side. "Where do you want me to put it?" Rob turned toward Becca, stared into her beautiful brown eyes and smiled seductively.

Becca was blushing and didn't know how to respond.

Ordinarily she would have quoted a scripture or told him that he needed Jesus. At this moment, there was a battle going on inside of her that her spirit was losing. She knew just like with your natural body, if you don't work your muscles they will get stiff and weak. And Becca had been so concerned with the Mark and Shawna situation that she had not been taking care of her spiritual muscles. "Just set it in the center of the kitchen table." Becca thought it would be better to not even acknowledge the hidden suggestion in Rob's question. "I don't know what's taking that boy so long. Maybe I'll go upstairs and hurry him up." Becca was a little nervous.

Rob walked over to Becca and pulled her close to him. "Becca, I don't wanna play games. You know I'm fillin' you and I can tell you want me too. So let's just make it happen." He was so close to her he could feel her stuttered breathing.

"Wh-what are you talking about? Rob, there is too much unpleasant history between us. I don't think I can go back on unstable ground with you. Now, please, I think you need to let me go before Bryan comes downstairs."

"I don't think you really want me to let you go. That's why you trying to get loose 'cause you don't trust yo' self." Rob squeezed her so close that their lips lightly touched when he spoke to her. "As for Bryan, we're his mom and dad; it's natural for us to show affection to each other."

Becca could not believe that she was allowing Rob to hold her body as if she already belonged to him. She could feel her flesh melting in his strong grasp. Every time his lips touched hers while he was speaking, gentle bursts of electricity would explode throughout her body. "But Rob listen, this isn't a goo--" Becca was interrupted by Rob's tongue dancing in her mouth. It was unbelievable. He had never kissed her with this much passion and intensity. All she could do was let her body get lost in his embrace and return the passion that he was so freely giving to her.

"Mom, I'm ready to go!" Bryan announced as he bounced down the steps to the kitchen where his mom and dad stood side by side looking like they had something to hide. "Hey guys what's goin' on?" Bryan was now standing in front of his parents pulling on his jacket.

Rob and Becca answered together, "N-Nothing." They looked at each other and smiled nervously. Rob stepped over to his son and spoke confidently. "Man you're nosy. Ain't nothin' wrong with me and ya' mom. As a matter of fact, things are goin' pretty good." Rob winked at his son. "Now, let's go so I can kick yo' butt in bowling!" Rob gave his son some dap and they started walking toward the front door.

"Come on mom, we're gonna ride in dad's truck!" Bryan grabbed his dad's keys and his new bowling ball and jumped into the backseat of the cab.

Rob waited for Becca to grab her black leather jacket and helped her put it on. Becca locked the door to the house as Rob stayed close to her side. As Rob helped Becca step up into the front seat, she couldn't take her eyes off of him. She was so afraid that she was falling in love with him all over again. She even questioned whether or not she had ever really let go.

Mark couldn't understand why Becca was being so distant with him. Ever since they had returned from their vacation things had not been the same. At first he thought that Shawna might have said something to Becca, but it seemed as though she was finally moving on with her life. Shawna had not been around much. Mark decided to call Mrs. Donaldson, Becca's mom, to see if she could help him find out what to do about Becca. "Hello ma, how are you?" He made his voice sound light and carefree.

"Hey son, I'm doin' better now that I'm talkin' to you. Are you doin' alright?" Fran was not fooled by Mark's tone but she wanted him to open up on his own.

Mark paused briefly then spoke carefully. "Ma I'm fine. I just haven't talked to you since we got back from our vacation and I just wanted to know if Becca showed you the pictures of Bryan and Camille having fun at the resort?"

"You know she did. I tell you what those kids are growing

so fast! Pretty soon they'll be all grown up." Fran laughed and then calmly spoke. "I also saw a picture of my beautiful daughter with this tall, dark and handsome man. Do you know who this gentleman is? They looked so happy together." Fran chuckled as she spoke.

Mark laughed a little then sighed heavily. "Ma, it seems like that vacation was years ago instead of a month ago. Every time I try to call Becca she's always busy or too tired to talk. Do you know what's going on with her?"

Fran knew more than she let on. As much as she loved Mark like he was her biological son, she could not betray her baby girl's trust. "Well Mark have you been praying about the situation. Maybe there was something that happened on the trip that caused Becca to think she needed to give you some space. Only you can answer that one. But have you ever thought that maybe it's time for you guys to stop playing this silly cat and mouse game and have a long conversation about your future together?" Fran was hoping that with each word Mark was able to read between the lines.

"I don't know. Becca is my best friend and we share so much together I couldn't bear losing that kind of closeness with her. Oh, shoot, I don't know what to do! I have been praying and maybe I do need to come down there and surprise her and Bryan next weekend. Then we can sit down and just lay everything on the table. What do you think about that, ma?" Mark was tired of this guessing game.

"I think that sounds good. You can even bring the kids over to my house so you all can speak freely to each other. Besides, I haven't seen Camille in a while." Fran smiled to herself at the thought of her grandchildren.

"Thanks, ma that sounds good. Please don't tell Becca. I don't want her to come up with some crazy excuse for not being available." Mark heard his doorbell ring. "Ma, someone's at the door. I'll call you back with the details tomorrow. Love ya and thanks."

"You're welcome son and I love you too." Fran hung up the phone and proceeded to her bedroom to pray. She knew that Rob was there for the weekend and that did not make for a good combination. Fran didn't want Becca to make the same mistakes all over again.

When Mark opened his front door, Shawna was standing there wet from the rain. In the back of Mark's mind, he knew this wasn't the best idea but how could he turn his back on her after she had been through such a terrible ordeal with Brad. "Come on in Shawna before you catch pneumonia." He took her hand and guided her into the house. She seemed frail as she leaned on him.

"I'm sorry Mark I didn't know where else to go. I can't believe this is happening to me." Shawna cried into Mark's chest. She could feel him wrap his arms around her waist and she felt like nothing else could hurt her.

Mark was confused. He did his best to comfort her. He led her to the sofa where they sat down together. "What's going on?" Mark helped her out of her wet jacket and hung it over the dining room chair. He then pulled a dry hand towel out of the closet, sat back down next to Shawna and began to dry her face. She was shivering from more than just the cold rain. He was hoping that Brad didn't have anything to do with her condition. "You have to calm down, Shawna, and talk to me so I can help you."

Shawna gently took the towel from Mark's hand and wiped her eyes. She looked up at him with tear stained eyes. She knew that he was genuinely concerned for her. Shawna decided that she would dig a little deeper. "H-He won't leave me alone, Mark! He calls me all the time leaving nasty messages and threatening to hurt me again. I'm a nervous wreck!" Shawna wrapped her arms around her waist and bent her head over in shame.

Mark found himself getting upset with the whole situation. No matter what misunderstanding had transpired between him and Shawna, he couldn't tolerate the thought of a man putting his hands on this delicate woman or any other woman for that matter. "Shawna, why didn't you tell me all of this was still going on? Is that why you've been avoiding me?" Mark was trying to keep his cool.

"I didn't want to cause any more problems between you and Becca. It seemed like she was really upset with me on the ride back from the resort. The way she acted was as if I planned for Brad to go crazy and beat up on me! So I figured it would be best for me to just stay out of your way." Shawna sighed heavily. "I just want you to know that I'm sorry for trying to take advantage of you that night, a few months ago." A single tear ran down her face as she spoke. "You have treated me so well in spite of my bad attitude. Mark, you're really a good man."

Mark could not pull himself away from her gaze. She seemed so innocent and misunderstood. In some way he felt responsible for the terrible relationship Shawna had gotten herself into with Brad. "Look, Shawna, don't worry about all of that. I'm always here if you need me." He leaned in close to her and kissed her on the forehead. But something happened it was like he was magnetically stuck to her. Her perfume smelled of white cotton blossoms and it was intoxicating. Mark felt Shawna slip her arms around him and slowly lift her face upward toward his. It was like he was outside of his body and not in control until he heard his cell phone ring, which startled him. Mark looked at the screen and saw the familiar name. He cleared his throat. "Shawna, I have to answer this just relax and I'll be right back." Mark stepped into the kitchen and pushed talk. "Hey lady, where have you been hiding?"

Becca was standing in her bathroom upstairs looking at herself in the mirror as she spoke cautiously to Mark. "I've been right here buddy. I've just been extremely busy. How is Camille?"

"Oh you know Camille. I'm just trying to keep her mouth under control and herself out of detention. She's over Lena's house tonight." There was a slight pause in their conversation before Mark chimed back in. "And where is my son? Is he doin' alright?"

Becca lowered her voice a little. "Oh, he's great. We went bowling tonight. He really had a good time especially when he bowled a 93 the last game. We were so proud of him." Becca was so caught up in the pride of her son that she didn't realize what she had said.

"That sounds great but who is the 'we' that were so proud?" Mark was concerned with the possible answer that he might hear.

Becca knew she couldn't lie to him. She never could. "O-Oh, I thought I told you that Rob was coming down to spend more time with Bryan. Isn't that good? It seems like he's really trying this time." Becca cleared her throat nervously awaiting Mark's response.

Mark spoke carefully as not to show the disgust and disappointment in his voice. "Becca where is Rob now? Did he go back to Cincinnati or is he staying at a hotel?"

"There you go, Mark! We can't even have a sensible conversation anymore without you interrogating me like I've done something wrong!" Becca's voice turned to venom. She was sick of the guilt trip. "Look, Mark, I am not going to make excuses for the father of my son wanting to spend time with him. And if I choose to let him stay at my home so that they can be closer that's my business. I don't need you passing judgment on me! We've all made mistakes."

Mark was shocked by her attitude and guilt. Judging from the way she was talking Rob was probably in the next room waiting for her. His heart broke to hear Becca speak to him in this way. But what could he do? His situation wasn't much better. Besides, Becca was not his woman. She was free to do whatever she thought right for her family. Mark just always thought that her family included him. "Becca, I'm not going to judge you or go into an irate tantrum over Rob being there. You are an adult and you know what he's done before. All I want is for you and Bryan to be happy and safe. Well, it's getting late. If he has time tomorrow, would you have Bryan call me?"

Becca was blown away by Mark's quick change in mood. She almost didn't know what to say. "Yeah no problem, Mark. Sorry about going off. I'm just under a lot of stress right now."

"Well Becca, don't forget to pray. God has all of the answers you need. Have a good night." Mark hung up before she could say anything else. He kept his composure as he put his phone back in his pocket. He put some herbal tea on to boil for Shawna so she wouldn't catch a cold. As he was standing over the sink, he began to talk to God. "Lord, please help me to do what's right by Becca. She has been hurt so much and I just want to take care of them but not as a rebound. Show me what to do." Just as Mark turned to grab the tea bags, he saw Shawna leaning against the doorway to the kitchen watching him. "Oh, hey Shawna, I thought you were resting. I'm making us some hot tea."

"Mark you don't have to hide your hurt feelings from me." Shawna seemed to glide over to him. She pressed her body against his and touched his face gently with the palm of her hand. "Let me be the strong one for you Mark. You're always taking care of someone else. I can take care of you tonight." Shawna's movements were purposeful and without guilt as she started pulling his shirt from his pants and unbuttoning it to expose his toned, dark chest. When she saw that he was not pulling away, she knew that he was all hers.

"Come and lay down next to me, baby." Rob was already laying in Becca's bed with just a t-shirt and shorts on. He wasn't going to take a chance on her locking him out of her room tonight.

Becca was surprised when she saw him laying there. "Maybe this is what I need." She thought to herself. Becca smiled in the dark room nervously but was obedient to Rob's command. "Where is Bryan?"

"He fell asleep watching a movie so I took him to his room and got him ready for bed." Rob raised up and scooted close to her. "I do know how to be a good parent too, Becca." He could tell that something was on her mind even in the dark. It was obvious that she was vulnerable and he was definitely going to use it to his advantage. "Girl, why don't you just lay back in my arms and let me rub you down real good like I used to do when you were upset." His hands didn't wait for her to accept his offer. He slowly pulled her back so that she was lying directly in front of him.

Becca couldn't believe that she was allowing herself to get

sucked into Rob's chaotic world again. But it felt so good to lie in this man's familiar embrace that she started questioning her instincts. "Maybe he has changed. Rob has never spent this kind of time with us before. Isn't it good to give people a second chance?" Then she got agitated with herself for allowing thoughts of Mark to creep in. "If his love for me was deeper than friendship, then he would have tried to build a relationship by now. I'm sick of waiting on a dream that may never happen. Anyway, who am I to stand in the way of destiny? Maybe I'm supposed to be with Rob so that Bryan can have his biological parents together?" All of these questions ran through her mind like lightning. Becca didn't even know what reality was at that moment. All she wanted to do was live in the moment for once, and not worry about tomorrow. So, as she felt Rob's lips on the back of her neck and his strong right hand slowly gliding up her thigh and caressing her secret places, she just let herself slip into an illusion of happiness and satisfaction.

The rain seemed almost blinding as it pummeled the front windshield of her black Chevrolet Impala. Mary J. Blige's smooth crooning filled the car with thoughts of betrayal. Toya was not going to play the victim's role this time. As she sat in her rental car across the street from where Rob's truck had been parked in the driveway for the last three hours. The house had been completely dark for the last hour and a half. Toya's body was tired due to being in her eighth month of pregnancy but she had to see for herself what all these sudden trips to Toledo were all about. She didn't know what she was going to do. All she did know was that it was time to draw the line in the sand and let Becca Thomas know that she was not going to take her man. "That's alright." Toya spoke in an even tone as if she were talking to someone else in the car. "Since you didn't heed my warning, Mr. Harris, I'm gonna have to show you just how serious my love for you is. And Becca, you ain't seen drama like I'm about to bring to yo' life." Toya would not allow herself to cry. She just stared at the house all night long.

Chapter 14

R-R-Ring! *R-R-Ring*! "Hello." A hushed voice answered.

"Oh, I think I have the wrong number."

"Becca, you have the right number. I'm just whispering because I didn't want to disturb Mark. We were up so late last night and I just wanted him to rest. Did you want me to give him a message?" Shawna sounded like the happy wife.

As Shawna asked the last question, Becca could have screamed. To think that all while Mark was trying to play inquisitor with her life, he had been laying up with Shawna Lewis. "No Shawna, I don't need you to leave a message about anything! I'll just call him when he's not so busy! Goodbye!" Becca ended the call. She was furious. "Anybody but her!" Becca spoke out loud without realizing that Rob was standing behind her in the entrance to the kitchen.

"Who were you talking to?" Rob asked as he let out a stretch and walked over to Becca at the sink. "You sounded upset." He wrapped his arms around her and bent over to kiss her.

Becca lightly kissed him back and then slipped out of his embrace to walk to the stove. "Oh just some bill collector and she was about to make me burn the bacon." Becca was trying to keep her face straight. All she wanted to do was be alone so she could figure out what twilight zone she had stepped into. "How do you feel this morning?"

"Ahh baby, you know I feel great! I took a relaxing shower. The only thing that would have made it better would've been you in there with me." Rob chuckled and rubbed himself against her behind. He knew that after last night Becca was back on the hook.

"Rob, please don't do that. Bryan could come down any minute. I don't want him to be confused about our relationship." Becca turned the fire off and faced Rob. "There's still a lot of stuff we need to work out before everything goes public. Do you understand?" She was trying to appeal to his sensible side.

"No, I don't understand. I told you last night that you're the only woman in my life and I want our family back together. You act like you don't trust me, Becca! What else do I have to do to show you?" Rob was getting agitated. He was working too hard for her affection. He softened his tone and grabbed her up in his arms. "Didn't I please you last night? You should've let me go all the way and I bet you wouldn't be talkin' like this." Rob kissed her forcefully.

Becca snatched herself away from him. "OK, Rob, that's ENOUGH! You're doin' way too much for a Sunday morning." Becca was breathing heavy as she tightened her robe. "Breakfast is ready so you can eat. I have to get ready for church. Would you please make sure Bryan gets something to eat while I'm in the shower? I will send him down." Becca was trying again to stay calm.

"You're going to church? I thought we were all going to spend the day together." Rob grabbed a plate and put some eggs, bacon and hash browns on it. He sat down at the table and grabbed a buttermilk biscuit out of the basket that sat at the center of the table.

"We are going to spend time together at church. Then we can go to the movies or to the mall or something." Becca spoke in a matter of fact tone.

"No, *WE* are not going to church! I already went with you the other time. And besides, you go every Sunday! Can't you miss one service to be with your family?" Rob kept eating like the situation was settled.

"Robert Harris, I know you are not trippin' already! I don't believe you. All that talking about how you have changed for the better and this is how you act." Becca was adamant. Well, my son and I go to church on Sunday mornings and if you're not going you're going to have to find something else to do outside of this house while we are gone."

"Oh, don't even try it Becca! How you gon' act like you all holy when you were just lettin' me do stuff to yo' body last night that would make the preacher blush?! This is Rob you're talkin' to! You know I'm leaving tonight. So why can't we all just spend the day together without all the outside influences?" Rob smiled at her cunningly.

Becca didn't hear Bryan come down the steps. "Yeah mom, can we play hookie from church today? I wanna spend more time with dad." Bryan ran over and gave his dad a big hug while waiting for his mom's reply.

Becca didn't know what to do. All she knew was that she needed to be in the House of God today. She couldn't think straight. So, she decided to compromise. "Ok little man, you can stay home with your dad but I really have to go. I'll come home directly after service is over and we can all go out to dinner. How does that sound?"

"GREAT mom! Now we can play my video games dad and watch basketball." Bryan ran to his mom and gave her a huge hug. "You're the best!"

"Rob, please make sure he gets dressed before noon. I'll lay out his clothes for today." Becca went upstairs and proceeded to get ready. She could hear her baby boy's laughter fill the house. He was so happy. But she wasn't. Becca felt cheated and used all over again. She stripped down her bed and remade it with fresh linen. As she opened her blinds that faced the front street, she noticed a black car that she had never seen parked there before, but she continued on with what she was doing and figured a neighbor must have had company last night.

When Becca arrived at church, praise & worship was already going forth. She sat in the back section today because she felt so guilty. Her mom was down front singing with the Praise & Worship Team. It was almost as if she were beaming with this bright light from within. Becca wanted that light again. All she kept thinking to herself was how did she get here? Even though she tried to let go and just concentrate on the healing words of the songs.

"Excuse me, is anyone sitting here?" A very pregnant petite woman was standing next to Becca's bench.

"Oh, no one's sitting here. I'll slide down. Is this your first time visiting our church?" Becca smiled warmly and spoke softly.

"Yes. I'm from out of town, Cincinnati to be exact." Toya was trying to play the role of an innocent woman. "My name is Toya Browning."

"Nice to meet you, Toya. I'm Becca Thomas." Becca felt a little uncomfortable but figured it wasn't anything. As she tried to get back into the service, it seemed that this young woman kept staring at her. But she figured it was because she felt out of place.

After Pastor Samson gave the benediction, Toya stood carefully. "Thanks so much for letting me sit next to you. I really enjoyed the service." Toya was acting very shy and rubbing her stomach.

As they made their way to the front doors of the church that led out to the parking lot, Becca spoke carefully. "Um, Toya I hope you don't mind me asking but how many months are you?" She held the door so that Toya could walk through first.

"Oh, I don't mind. I'm about eight months. I'm having a little girl and I'm naming her Robbi, after her father." Toya could not hold back the smile that crept over her face.

"Wow, you don't have much time left. Where is the baby's father?" Becca allowed Toya to lead the way as they continued to talk. Becca couldn't quite understand why she felt connected to this stranger. She almost felt like a big sister.

"Well, here's my car. I know what you're thinking Becca. That he's probably no good and doesn't want anything to do with us. But that's not true. He is a wonderful man and he loves us very much. As a matter of fact, he left his first baby's momma to be with me. We're gonna be married after Robbi is born." Toya was trying not to get agitated.

"I'm sorry Toya. I didn't mean to pry. You just remind me of myself when I was pregnant with my son. I really believed in his father too but life has a funny way of throwing up detours unexpectedly." Becca chuckled to herself. Just then, she heard her mother calling to her from across the parking lot. She waved back to her. "Oh Toya would you like to meet my mother?"

"Well, I really need to check into my hotel. I'll be in town another week and I'll be back to the services here. Everyone is so cool. Thanks again, Becca. I'll be seeing you soon." Toya got into her car and pulled off before Fran walked up. Toya was definitely going to gain control of this little game that Rob had dragged her into.

"Who was that honey?" Fran hugged her daughter and watched the black Impala drive off.

"Oh, she's a visitor or maybe even a potential new member." Becca hugged her mom back. "You sure rocked praise and worship today. I enjoyed the new song." Becca smiled at her mom.

"How are you doing, baby girl and where's my grandson?" Fran looked in Becca's truck to see if he was sitting in the backseat.

Becca gave her mom a funny look and then tried to explain. "Listen mom, I need for you not to get upset. He's with his dad."

"Oh I didn't know Mark came down last night. But that's not like Mark to miss church." Fran was confused.

Becca cleared her throat. "Mom, Bryan is with Rob. He wanted to spend some more time with his dad before he left." Becca made her way to the driver's side of her car. She could see the shock on her mother's face.

"Becca Marie Thomas, I know you're not crazy! Why are you still dealing with Robert Harris? I thought you let go of that nightmare a long time ago. Come on Becca you're better than him." Fran was pleading with her daughter.

Becca's mind was spinning out of control. She was tired of thinking about every detail of her life. While everyone around her seemed to be living life to the fullest. "Look mom, there are some decisions I have to make on my own. It's called being an adult! Now

I really have to go. I'll talk to you later. Love you, ma." She hopped into her car and waved to her mom as she pulled off.

Fran couldn't believe that her daughter was falling for the same old nonsense again. She walked back into the church and fell on the altar in prayer. Fran prayed for the Lord to burn this bridge and to open Becca's eyes to the fact that all she needed to know was wrapped up in JESUS! All Fran could yell out was, "Free my baby, Lord!!"

Mark and Lena sat at her dining room table eating dessert while Camille was in the backroom watching a movie. Lena had asked Mark over for dinner because he hadn't been there in awhile. It seemed like he had been consumed with all of Shawna's drama. It was nice to have her big brother visiting.

"How are you feeling Mark?" Lena touched his hand gently. "You've been looking tired lately."

Mark smiled reassuringly at Lena. Usually, Mark was the one that was looking out for Lena but this afternoon Lena was being the concerned adult. "I'm doing fine, sis. I'm just doing what I have to do to take care of my family." Mark paused briefly to take a sip of his iced tea. "Well what's been going on with you?"

"Oh nothing much. I did get rid of T.J. I'm sure you're glad of that." Lena smirked at her brother. "Don't look so serious, Mark. I'm ok. He wasn't worth my time." Lena stood up and collected their dirty dishes.

Mark followed Lena into the kitchen. "So, what brought about this revelation? Don't get me wrong I'm glad you got rid of that garbage, but I'm just curious as to what miracle caused your blinded eyes to see clearly." Mark chuckled.

"Oh, now you're trying to be Mr. funny guy but that's ok. I got tired of him using me for a doormat so I stopped making myself available to him. I'm not gonna lie; it was hard at first but now I'm enjoyin' being single again." Lena laughed to herself while she ran water to start washing dishes.

Mark could hardly believe that Lena had finally started thinking better about herself. He was glad to see that she was finally growing up. "Well sis I'm really proud of you." Mark hugged his sister and gave her a playful nudge. It felt good to be with his sister it brought back memories of when the three of them were kids and they used to all have Sunday dinner together. It was times like these when he really missed his big brother and their mom and dad.

"How has Shawna been?" Lena wanted to ease into finding out why Shawna answered Mark's phone the other day.

"Oh, she's doing alright. Mark grabbed a hand towel and began drying the dishes that Lena put on the counter. "You know that crazy man she was dating is still trying to cause her problems? I had to take her to court to file a temporary protection order. I never would've thought that he was that kind of guy." Mark just shook his head as he put dishes into the cabinet.

Lena was getting sick of hearing Mark talk about Shawna like she was a victim. Nothing could be further from the truth. "Hey Mark what did you say that guy looked like?" Lena was curious.

"He was tall, white with blue eyes and brown hair. Why? I know you're not interested in that jerk!" Mark stopped drying a glass and gave her a stern look.

"Come on now, Mark; give me a little more credit than that." Lena paused briefly. She was concerned about going further but decided to push forward anyway. "The reason I'm asking is because my girlfriends and I were out a couple of nights ago at a club down on Kinsman and I know I saw Shawna in there with some white guy." Lena stopped washing dishes and turned around so she could see Mark's reaction.

"What are you talking about? You can hardly see anything when you're in a club. Why would you make this stuff up about Shawna?" Mark was starting to get agitated.

"Look Mark, I know that I saw her all hugged up on this Brad character. She didn't look like she was scared of him. As a matter of fact, the way they were grinding on each other was almost pornographic." Lena wanted Mark to see that Shawna was running a game on him.

"Why are you just telling me this now?" Mark was confused. He didn't know what to think. "I know Shawna can be extreme sometimes but this would be beyond crazy."

"Well ask her and when she gives you an answer, ask her why she's answering your phone?" Lena had a sarcastic stone.

Mark leaned against the wall across from Lena and rubbed his forehead. "Shawna has never answered my phone. Lena, I don't understand why you're so hard on her tonight?" Mark's phone vibrated in the pocket of his black pants. He pulled it out and looked at the screen. The number is familiar. He answered with a sigh of frustration. "Hello, Shawna. What's going on?" Mark did not make eye contact with his sister.

"Oh, nothin' much. I just called to see what you were up to. Are you at home?" Shawna sounded a little down.

"We're over Lena's house. She cooked dinner today. Where are you?"

Mark stepped into the living room and stood by the window.

"I'm just driving around trying to clear my head." She let out a heavy sigh and spoke slowly. "Brad called me today trying to apologize and he wants to meet me at my place to talk. All I want him to do is leave me alone."

Mark didn't know what to believe. He couldn't believe that Shawna could make up something like this. "Maybe you should come over here. I don't think you should be by yourself."

"Mark I don't want to impose upon your family dinner. I'll be ok." Shawna let her voice drop in hopes that Mark would hear the desperation. "I'll just give you a call later and if you're not busy I could just stay at your place tonight?"

All kind of bells started ringing and red flags flying in Mark's head. It seemed to him that Shawna had some other plans in mind. "Shawna, if you don't want to be alone the best thing for you to do is come over Lena's house now and hang out with all of us. We need to talk anyway." Mark paused briefly and continued with authority. "I will see you in about 15 minutes, right?"

Shawna couldn't believe Mark was acting like this. All she wanted to do was spend time with him alone. If she played her cards right, maybe she would get that opportunity again. However, the sound in Mark's voice let her know that he was not giving her a choice. "Ok, I'm not even that far away. See you soon." Shawna hung up the phone and couldn't seem to figure out why Mark was being a little cold toward her. She would just wait and find out. Her plan seemed to be working well and she tried to make sure that her and Brad were not seen together. So Mark couldn't know about that secret. Shawna decided that she wasn't going to worry about it and just continue to weave her web around him.

Becca arrived at home about a quarter to two. Rob and Bryan were in the backyard throwing a football around. She didn't disturb them. When she got upstairs to her room she changed into some blue jeans, a bright multi-colored sheer baby doll shirt with a red tank top under it. She also slipped on her red soft leather loafers. Becca pulled her hair back in a ponytail, sprayed some cologne and freshened her make-up. Before she left her room, she decided to call Mark again. She could still hear Bryan outside with Rob laughing and playing. Her heart beat faster with every ring.

"Hello, Becca, how are you?" Mark was surprised to hear from her but glad at the same time.

Becca knew she had to keep her cool in order to find the information she needed. "Hey, Mark, I'm doin' fine. How was church today?" She thought she'd try to play it normal.

"Oh you know we had a good time! Pastor asked about you and Bryan because it's been awhile since you guys have visited. I told him I'd let you know that he inquired about you. How was your service?" Mark tried not to show too much emotion but he was excited about hearing Becca's voice.

"Please tell your pastor that I said hello and we'll be back soon. Our service was good too. There was a young lady who visited with us today. She's from Cincinnati and may be moving here. She's also eight months pregnant. I gave her my cell number to call me." Becca was loosening up more and it really was starting to feel like old times until she remembered the incidents of that morning.

"So when do you think you and Bryan will be able to come for a visit. Maybe you can come Easter weekend? We all miss you guys." Mark paused because Lena and Camille were yelling hi from the background. "Did you hear the peanut gallery shouting?" Mark laughed.

It felt so good to hear all of them. Becca realized that she missed them too. "I'll have to check my schedule but are you sure you have room for us?" Becca had to know what was going on between him and Shawna.

"What are you talkin' about? Has there ever been a problem with me having enough room for you and my son? Why are you tryin' to trip, Becca?" Mark was confused about that question. He didn't want to get into an argument with Becca.

Becca's tone changed from light to serious. "Well, since Shawna is answering your phone early in the morning I figured that you guys were a couple now. Didn't she tell you I called this morning?"

Mark was furious that he had not seen through Shawna's games. He knew that Becca could not have made up the same story as Lena. His head was reeling from the questions that started popping up in his mind. "No, she didn't tell me you called. As a matter of fact, I had no idea she was answering my phone. I will take care of it. As for you and Bryan, I want you to know that there is no one that could ever take up the space in my heart or my home reserved for the two of you. Got it?" Mark's voice was strong and deliberate.

Becca was shocked by his response. "O-Ok, Mark. Well, we'll see you Easter weekend I guess. Call me later because I'm getting ready to take Bryan out for dinner. Kiss Camille for me and I love you, dude." Becca laughed and hung up the phone. She knew what she had to do. All of these games that were going on were draining. It was time to make some hard decisions.

Chapter 15

Rob sat across from Becca and Bryan at Red Lobster at a table in the back of the restaurant by a window. He thought that everything was going well. His son was enjoying being with him and Becca seemed to be falling in love with him all over again. "Hey Bry, how would you like your dad to stay with you a little while longer?" He gave his son a big smile.

Bryan was so excited that he yelled out enthusiastically. "Yes! Can you really stay longer with us?" Bryan stopped eating his fried shrimp to pay close attention to his dad.

"Of course I can. I'd do anything for you and your mom." At that point, Rob looked directly at Becca who was sitting there speechless. "Oh, I'm sorry, babe, is that ok with you?" Rob touched Becca's hand that was gripping the end of the table.

Becca could have screamed. She couldn't believe that Rob had tried to make it look like she really had a choice in the matter. He was up to his same old tricks. "Rob, don't you have to get back to your job?" She took a sip of her sweet tea.

"Oh, I already called my supervisor while you were at church and told him I needed a few more days off to be with my son. So everything's good." Rob winked at her and took a bite of his cheddar biscuit.

"Please mom, can dad stay another day?" Bryan grabbed his mom's arm and looked at her with his big beautiful brown eyes.

"Ok, that's fine, Bry. Now eat your food before it gets cold." Becca had a storm building inside of her that was almost uncontrollable. She couldn't wait to get Rob by himself. He had gone too far this time. Tonight she would have to draw the line with Rob.

"Thanks Becca. I just miss being with you guys so much. Maybe I can look for a job here so we can be together all the time." Rob tried to read Becca's expression but couldn't seem to get a feel for what she was thinking. He would make sure that tonight when he got her alone he would make her feel good.

They finished their dinner with small talk and basically kept the conversation centered on Bryan's favorite topics, cartoons and his game stations.

When they arrived home, Becca took Bryan upstairs to get him ready for bed. Rob went out in the backyard and called Toya on his cell phone. Her phone rang twice before she picked up.

"Hello, Rob." Toya answered with a calm tone.

"Hey sexy, how are you? I sure do miss you." Rob made sure he spoke in a low, seductive voice. He had to keep up this masquerade with Toya until after she had the baby and then he would dump her, get custody of their daughter, and raise his children with Becca. He figured that by then Becca would be so in love with him that she would forgive him for the lies and manipulation and they would be a family.

"Oh, I'm alright but you're daughter has been very active. I can hardly rest at night because of her kicking." She paused briefly and then spoke with concern. "Are you on your way home?"

"Well, Toya that's why I'm calling. It looks like I'm going to have to stay a few more days. Bryan is really having some trouble in school and I want to check out his teachers. You understand right?" Rob had to make his story sound good.

"Yeah, I guess. And what about Ms. Becca? How does she fit into this wonderful picture?" Toya tried her best not to sound agitated but she had to hear what lie Rob was going to make up next.

"Aw shoot! Don't start Toya. You know I'm not here for Becca I'm here for my son. She's not even an issue. She was trying to rekindle some old flame but I let her know right away that I've got a sexy, young woman and there is no hope for us to get back together. So, trust me she got the picture." Rob was trying to make a lie sound like the truth.

"Ok Rob, I believe you. Just remember what I told you before. You will never leave me. When I got pregnant, that was it. We are bound to each other forever. I love you baby and I'll be waiting on you to come home." Toya made sure her words were deliberate and stern.

"Well Toya, I'll call you back tomorrow. I gotta go make sure Bryan finished his homework. Try to get in bed early tonight and think about me makin' love to you." Rob chuckled full of lust.

Toya grinned at Rob's foolishness. She couldn't believe that he really thought she was that stupid. "Yeah, ok Rob, but I would much rather have you here in person than dreaming about you. But I guess I'll have to take what I can get. I love you boo, don't ever forget that. There is nothing that I wouldn't do for you." Toya waited to hear Rob return her sentiments.

"I know baby girl, I'll talk to you later." Rob hung up before she could say anything else. Toya was getting more and more possessive. Rob couldn't wait until the baby was born. He put his phone back in his pocket and stepped in the house and went into the family room to wait on Becca.

Becca ran Bryan's bath water and laid out his pajamas on his bed. She went downstairs to speak with Rob while they had some time alone. When she got to the bottom of the steps, she grabbed a bottle of water out of the fridge. Rob was sitting on the sofa in the family room watching music videos on BET. "Rob, can we talk?"

"Of course, baby. Come on in and sit here next to me." Rob patted his hand on the cushion next to him and turned the volume down on the television. "What's up?"

"Why didn't you talk to me first about staying longer? I don't like being caught off guard." Becca took a sip of her water trying to remain calm.

Rob was trying to focus on what Becca was saying until one of his favorite videos showed up on the T.V. "I know baby. I just knew you wouldn't say no in front of Bryan." Rob chuckled slyly. "Anyways, what's the big deal? I know you wanna spend more time with me so why do you keep tryin' to trip? Now let's watch this video." He tried to pull Becca close to him.

Becca had had enough she jerked herself away from him

and stormed up to the television then pushed the power button. "Look Rob, I can't continue with this nonsense! I told you before that I'm not the same person. I thought that maybe we could work things out but I've moved pass you and I wanna get my life back on track." Becca was not going to back down. Not this time.

"Becca, what the heck has gotten into you? I thought we were trying to work on a relationship so that we could be a family again! Why are you actin' like this?" Rob was confused and agitated.

Becca couldn't believe that she was in this situation again. She could hear her mother telling her not to mess with Rob. She had told her to wait on the Lord. But Becca was tired of being by herself. Even Mark had tried to warn her that Rob had not changed but she just didn't want to see. "I know Bryan is glad that you're here but we don't have to be together for you to have a relationship with your son. So please tell Bryan that you spoke prematurely and you need to get back to Cincinnati." She calmed down and stood still. "I'm not trying to hurt you, Rob. I'm just tired of playing Russian Roulette with my life."

Rob couldn't believe that Becca was shutting him down. He thought he had her wrapped around his finger. Now what was he doing to do? He couldn't let Becca mess up his plans. He was enjoying the comforts of her life too much. Everything was already set up: a nice home, a nice truck, and Becca's stable finances. He and his new baby would have it made and then he could finally get rid of his possessive, ghetto girlfriend, Toya. Rob stood up and walked over to Becca confidently. "Look Becca, I hear what your sayin' but I know yo' body wants me to stay. You always over think everything. Why don't you just go with the flow?" He pulled her to him and kissed her on her neck but he noticed that she didn't buckle in his arms this time. He ignored it and leaned in closer to taste her lips but she pulled away from him quickly.

"I'm going to go check on Bryan. He should be about done with his bath by now. I'll have him come down and say good-night. There are blankets in the chess and you can pull out the bed in the sofa. We will continue this conversation tomorrow." Becca started walking toward the back steps through the kitchen.

"Becca, I know you can't be serious! We were just together last night and now you want me to sleep on the sofa. You've got to be jokin'!" Rob was getting upset. She was not going to deny him his pleasure tonight. He knew that all he had to do was get her in a compromising position like before and she would change her tune. He decided to change his tone. "Ok Becca, whatever you say. I'll just come up and tuck Bry in so you don't have to send him down."

Becca just nodded and thought it was best not to say anything else. She proceeded up the stairs. To her surprise Bryan was already in bed.

"Hey mom, are you alright? Why were you and dad yelling?" Bryan had come down and heard some of their conversation. He was concerned about his mom.

"Oh baby, everything is good. Your dad and I weren't yelling. You know how I get when I'm trying to make a point. Don't be worried." Becca felt so bad that she had put her son in a position where he was worried about her. "Hey, guess what? I talked to Mark today and we're going to go to Cleveland for Easter weekend. He is excited to see us. What do you think big guy?"

"That sounds great mom. Did you tell him that my dad was here?"

"No Bryan. Mark didn't need to know that. You know that he gets concerned about the way your dad treats us." Becca was trying to get the conversation off of Rob but it wasn't working.

Bryan wasn't too sure how he felt about his dad staying anymore. "Mom, I want you to know that I'm ok if you want dad to leave. I just don't want you to be sad again. Dad doesn't make you smile like Mark does. Don't feel like you have to settle, mom. You're too good for that." Bryan sat up and hugged his mom tightly. He loved her so much.

Becca felt a tear stream down her face. "I love you too, big boy. You're so smart."

"Well does anybody love Big Poppa?" Rob chuckled as

he entered his son's room. He watched Becca stand up and start picking up clothes off the floor and putting them in Bryan's hamper. Rob noticed that she refused to make eye contact with him. "Hey man, you goin' to bed this early? Shoot, it's only 10:00." Rob made his way over to the side of his son's bed and knelt down.

"Dad, I have to go to school in the morning and mom usually has me in bed by 9:00. So I'm doin' pretty good tonight. We can do something afterschool tomorrow, Dad. Just me and you." Bryan smiled at his dad and said goodnight. He turned on his side and felt his dad pull the covers up over his shoulders.

"Good night son. I'll see you in the morning." Rob stood up and walked toward the door and waited for Becca to kiss Bryan on the cheek before he turned the light out. Rob allowed Becca to step through the door to the hallway first. He followed her to her bedroom door.

"Well, good night Rob. I guess will talk more tomorrow. Would you please try to think of a way to tell Bryan you can't stay as long as you thought?" Becca looked up at him and saw the intense stare he was shooting at her. She could tell by his body language that he wanted her. But Becca was tired of giving herself to men who were not worthy and had no right to her. "Ok then Rob see you in the morning." She walked inside her door and tried to close it but realized that something was obstructing its path.

"Look Becca, why don't we just talk tonight? We're both adults. I can just stay with you tonight so that we can get everything out on the table. How does that sound?" Rob pushed his body through the door and stood so close to Becca he could hear her breathing change. He just knew she was about to give in.

Becca's mind for a fleeting moment went back to last night when Rob had made her body explode. As bad as her spirit wanted to say no she could feel her flesh winning out. "There is no temptation that God will not make a way of escape." She heard the words deep down on the inside of her. As she heard it whispered each time stronger, she felt a presence surround and calm her. At that moment the phone rang. The loud sound of it seemed to tear down any hold that was drawing her to Rob. She reached for the phone lying in the chair next to the door and saw it was her mother. "Oh, Rob I really have to get this. Here's another pillow for you and have a restful night." Becca clicked the talk button before Rob could respond. She watched him back out of the doorway as she began a solid conversation with her mother. Becca closed the door and locked it immediately.

"Lord, I thank you!" Becca hadn't realized she had said the words out loud.

"What did you say, daughter?" Fran said in a confused state.

"Oh sorry mom, I just had to give God some praise." Becca was excited.

Fran began to rejoice with her daughter. She didn't know what had just happened but she did know that God was in control and that was all she needed to know. "Hallelujah! Becca let's pray." Fran prayed on the phone with her daughter until the Spirit of God fell in Fran's house and in Becca's bedroom.

"Thank you Jesus! Forgive me Lord! I'm so sorry." Becca felt her spirit lighten with every phrase. That night Becca knew she had received forgiveness from God for her sins and her salvation had been restored. She was not going to let anything or anyone take her peace again! When Becca got off the phone with her mother about an hour later, she fell right to sleep. It was the best rest she had had in a very long time.

Chapter 16

Becca was surprised when her cell phone rang with an unfamiliar number popped up on the screen. "Hello, this is Becca, may I help you?"

A familiar voice responded, "Hi, Becca, How are you? This is Toya."

Toya figured it was time to get to know Becca a little bit better.

"Oh, hello Toya. How are you doing? Are you feeling better?" Becca couldn't believe that Toya was actually calling her. "Is there something that you want to talk about?" Becca was concerned for Toya being in a new city and that far along in her pregnancy.

"Well, I was just calling to see if you'd like to go to lunch today? I found a couple of houses but I don't know the neighborhoods. Maybe you can help me go through the list and find which ones to look at?"

"Sure I can help. How about we meet at the diner on the corner of Glendale and South Detroit? They have great food. I can be there about 12:30 p.m. Do you know how to get there?" Becca spoke with sincerity.

"Yeah, I can map quest it or just ask for directions at the front desk. I'll see you there. Thanks again, Becca." Toya hung up the phone smiling to herself. Her plan was set in motion. She would finally get the information she needed to destroy this obstacle between her and Rob.

Mark answered the door when he heard the bell ring. It was time to set the record straight with Shawna. "Well Hello, Ms. Lewis. How are you this evening?" Mark smiled at Shawna as she stepped inside the door and he helped her take off her jacket. "Come on in and have a seat."

"Oh I'm good, Mark. I'm just trying to stay calm and not

become a nervous wreck." Shawna followed Mark into the dining room where Lena was clearing off the last of the serving dishes and putting out dessert. She had made a Key Lime Pie and an old fashioned Pound Cake. They both smelled delicious. "Hi, Lena, it sure looks like you cooked quite a spread today." She chuckled.

"Thanks Shawna, you know I'd do anything for my family." Lena smiled politely and winked at Shawna. "What brings you on this side of town so late in the evening?" Lena cut a piece of cake for Mark and set the plate in front of him.

"Oh just driving around trying to clear my head. So, I thought I call my good old friend Mark and see what he was up to." She paused briefly and looked at Mark as if they were the only two in the room then she lightly touched his hand that was resting on the table. "I'm sure glad I came over. Just seeing him makes everything seem better." Shawna laughed coyly and turned her attention back towards Lena. "I mean God forbid I would've missed all this great food. May I have a slice of that pie, Lena?" Shawna was playing the innocent role very well.

"Sure you can. Here let me slice that for you." As Lena slid the pie closer to Shawna, she picked up the sharp knife beside it and pretended to almost drop it, point down on Shawna's hand. "OOPS! Shawna, I'm so sorry. I don't know what got into me. I guess it seemed like I had a tighter grip on the knife than I thought. I suppose that's the danger in what things seem like… there usually apparitions of the true meaning."

Shawna looked at Lena with coldness in her eyes. She knew at that moment that Lena was hiding something and trying to make trouble between her and Mark. "Watch yourself, Lena you could really hurt someone with that knife. Maybe I ought to cut my own slice." Shawna picked the knife off the table and cut her own piece. Then she slid the pie back to the center of the table.

Mark looked at his sister and spoke carefully. "Lena can you help me get some ice from the basement?" He stood up and followed his sister out of the dining room after he looked back and spoke gently to Shawna. "I'll be right back with some ice cold Sprite, Shawna."

"What are you doing, sis? Are you crazy?" Mark was whispering to Lena in the basement.

"Naw, I'm not crazy! But that Heffer is psychotic! She's sitting up there like she is so wounded and hurt. Mark, that girl is full of it and I hope you see through that charade she's playing." Lena was leaning up against the freezer chest with her hands on her hips.

"I know full well what's going on but you have got to play it cool." Mark took his sister by the hand and smiled at her. "Your big brother is through being played. I got this one!" Mark hugged his sister and filled a bowl with ice, grabbed a 2 liter of Sprite, and proceeded back up stairs with Lena following behind him. "Here we are. Now Shawna, do you want a lot of ice or a little?" Marked grinned at her.

"Oh I guess I'll just have half a cup especially since it's crushed ice." Shawna smiled back at Mark.

Lena decided to go upstairs and check on Camille. She could hardly stand the sight of Shawna. "Uh, Mark, I'm gonna take a couple of cups of soda up to Camille and see what she's doing. Call me if you need me." Lena poured their drinks and before she walked out of the dining room she looked back at Shawna and spoke. "Shawna, if you're gone before I come down, have a safe trip." Lena proceeded upstairs.

Shawna stood up beside Mark at the table and slipped her arms around his waist as if in desperation. "Oh Mark I'm so glad we're alone. I didn't know how much longer I could hold it together." She laid her head on his chest and began to cry.

Mark was sickened by Shawna's touch but played it off well. "Come on Shawna let's go sit in the living room and talk." He led her to the sofa and they sat down together. Mark passed her some tissue. "Now what is it exactly that has you so upset?"

"I told you that Brad won't leave me alone. He keeps calling me and showing up on my job wanting to get back together with me. I keep telling him no but he just doesn't understand that I do not want him in my life. He's a manipulator and a liar and I can't trust him." She started to cry harder.

"Well Shawna, I know what you mean. It doesn't feel good to have someone you thought you could trust tell you lies and manipulate you. I've had some experience with that. The best thing to do is just cut them off completely." Mark was setting her up emotionally for a big fall.

Shawna was smiling on the inside. She thought her plan had worked perfectly. She just knew that after tonight she would have Mark Simmons. "Exactly, that's why I'm done with Brad. I just feel so stupid that I didn't realize what kind of man he was from the beginning." Shawna slides close to Mark and gently touches his face. "I guess that's what happens when you're trying to get over your heart being broken."

Mark decides that enough is enough. "Well, Shawna, if you're talking about what happened between us that night, I want you to know that I haven't thought about it since it happened. But what I have thought about is why I didn't see you for the vain, deceitful woman that you are." Mark stands and walks to the other side of the room.

Shawna is stunned by Mark's response. "Wh-What do you mean?" Shawna stands confused and disoriented as if all the wind had been knocked out of her. "Mark, baby, what has gotten into you? I've been nothing but honest with you." Shawna walks toward Mark and reaches for his hand but he pulls away.

"I want you to understand something very clearly, Ms. Lewis. There is not, nor will there ever be, anything between us. We are associates that work together nothing more. You got that?" Mark chuckles to himself with a surety. "You are really pathetic, Shawna, and I really feel sorry for you. Now, would you please leave my home? I have to see about my family."

Shawna was consumed with desperation as she began to plead with Mark. "Mark, everything I did so that you and I could be together. You just wouldn't respond to me any other way. I love you so much, baby. Can't you forgive me and we just move on with our lives?" Shawna ran to Mark's side and wrapped her arms around him and pressed her body tightly against his hoping to change Mark's mind about her.

Mark couldn't even stand the sight of her. He put his hand firmly on her upper arms and pushed her back from him. He spoke clearly and with purpose. "Look, Shawna, I will never trust you again. You did everything you could to tear up me and Becca's friendship. But it didn't work. I should have listened to her a long time ago."

Shawna jerks loose from his grasp in anger. "You JERK! I was ready to give you everything and you want to throw me to the side for Becca's big sorry butt! You must be crazy! Yeah, I did lie about Brad abusin' me and a lot of other things to get your attention. I listened to yo' sad stories about Becca and Bryan and it made me sick! Becca is weak. She could never satisfy a man like you and you want t throw me to the side. You've got to be kiddin' me!" Shawna laughed sadistically.

"Thank you, Shawna, for making this easier than I thought. Just forget you know me. You need serious help and I pray that you get it." Mark walks to the door and opens it. "Goodnight, Shawna."

Shawna gave Mark a cold stare and walked through the door then turned around quickly to spew out more insults. But just as she turned to face Mark again, he pushed the door closed in her face. He turned off the porch light and proceeded upstairs to spend the rest of the night with Lena and Camille. "Lord, I thank you for showing me what's real and what's not. Please show the same thing to Becca." Even though Mark conversed with his family, his thoughts couldn't help but rest on Becca. He couldn't wait to talk to her tomorrow. Mark decided it was time to tell Becca the whole truth. No more games.

Chapter 17

Becca sat in the diner waiting on Toya to arrive. While sitting there alone she began to think about how today was the day that Rob would be gone. She was tired of this nonsense with him. Becca would finally be free from the bondage that she again had become entangled.

Just then, Toya walked into the diner wearing a purple cardigan sweater over a black jumper that accentuated her eight month belly. She waved to Becca who sat facing the entrance to the restaurant. "Hey Becca, thanks for meeting me and sorry I'm a little late. Traffic was terrible trying to get over here from the south end of town. Have you ordered yet?"

"No, I haven't. I was waiting on you, my sister. How is the baby doing today?" Becca sat there in black pants and a silk, apple green blouse with a three-quarter length black jacket that emphasized all of her best assets. "I know you've got to be hungry so let's order."

As Toya sat across from her competition, she just couldn't believe that Rob was trying to leave her for this woman. Toya began to ask Becca personal questions to find something to build her arsenal. "So, Becca how long have you lived in your home?"

Becca was a bit stunned by the question but she answered. "I guess about four years. I live on the west side of town. Where is your list?" Becca wanted to get the emphasis off of her and on their reason for meeting.

"Oh, I'm sorry," Toya reached in her purse and pulled out a pack of folded papers. She handed them to Becca. "Here they are. There are about 5 listings on each page and about four pages. I hope that's not too much. I really want to find the perfect home for me and my family." Toya watched Becca closely as she unfolded the papers and began looking over the list. Toya wanted to try and rattle her cage a little more. "So, Becca are you married? Do you have any kids?" Toya shot the questions at Becca quickly.

Becca was shocked at Toya's questions about her personal

life and about the list of homes she had given her to look over. She felt somewhat uneasy about this whole meeting but she shook it off as being overly cautious. "No, Toya, I am not married but I do have one son." But before Becca could inquire about the housing list, their waiter walked up to the table.

Their waiter was a tall light-skinned African-American with dark features. He was very toned and wore a shirt that accentuated his physique. "Well good afternoon ladies, my name is Jonathan, and I will be taking care of you this afternoon. Would you like to start with something to drink?"

Becca responded first. "Hello Jonathan, I'll have a cup of hot apple cider and a garden salad with chopped turkey breast, shredded cheddar cheese and French dressing." Becca handed the menu back to the waiter and smiled.

"I like a woman who knows what she wants." Jonathan winked at Becca and then turned his attention to Toya. "Now, what about you lovely lady?"

Toya responded coldly to the waiter and did not smile. "I'll just have a cup of chicken noodle soup and some water with lemon. Thank you."

Jonathan tried to tempt her into ordering something more but Toya refused. "Ok, my Nubian Queens, I'll be right back with your orders. Turning his attention back toward Becca, he asked, "Will this be on one check or two?"

Toya didn't like being ignored, "It will be two." She was almost rude in her response.

Both Becca and the waiter looked at her with concern. "No, just make it one, Jonathan." Becca was surprised at the way Toya was acting. She just figured it was her hormones acting up from being pregnant. "Thank you, Jonathan." The waiter walked away shocked by Toya's attitude. When he was gone, Becca asked, "Are you feeling well?"

"Yes, I'm fine and I don't need you to pay for my food. I can manage just fine." Toya was getting upset. The more time she spent with this woman the more she couldn't stand her.

Becca couldn't believe this total switch in personality. She was beginning to think that maybe this wasn't such a good idea. At least they were in a public place, if Toya decided to flip out completely. "I didn't mean to offend you Toya. But I know what it's like to raise a child on your own and move to another city. So please allow me to be a blessing to you." Becca was sincere in her response.

"Yeah, ok but I told you at the church that my fiancé' is moving here with me. I'm not a single parent and I will never be. My man loves me and ain't nobody gonna take him away from me!" Toya let her hatred seep through in her protest.

An awkward silence rested on their table. Just as the sound of Becca's own breathing became too much, her cell phone rang. It startled her initially but then, she politely regained her composure and excused herself from the table. As she walked toward the area by the pay phone, she pushed the talk button on her phone and spoke in a confused manner. "Uh, hello. Is everything ok?"

"Hey beautiful, can you get off work early today? I really need to talk to you, alone." Rob tried to sound seductive and enticing.

Becca was tired of Rob's games. She just wanted him to go away. "No, Rob, I cannot come home early. I have a lot of work today. As a matter of fact, I am in a lunch meeting right now. I will speak to you later before you leave this afternoon." Becca was getting agitated. "Is there anything else?"

Rob was confused. He thought everything was good and that Becca was falling in love with him again. But now, something else was going on and he didn't know what had changed. "Ok, Becca I'll just talk to you when you get home." Rob hung up the phone with irritated. He thought to himself, "You will not mess this up for me, Becca Thomas. You won't throw me to the side!"

"Is everything ok, Becca?" Toya noticed that Becca looked upset. "Was it your boyfriend?"

"I'm fine, Toya, just trying to correct some mistakes that I've made." Becca sat down and pulled money out of her pocket to pay for the bill. "Look Toya, we're gonna have to cut this lunch short. I hope I've helped you in some way. I also apologize if I offended you in some way."

Toya refused to let Becca's seemingly kind gesture get her focus off her plan to get the man of dreams back. "Oh that's ok, Becca, thank you for your help. You don't need to apologize. I understand that you were just trying to look out for a sister. I hope everything works out with yo' man."

Becca just nodded. She didn't feel comfortable enough to tell Toya about her personal issues. "Well, if your still in town come Sunday, I hope to see you at church." Becca stood up and put on her leather coat.

"Thank you for lunch, Becca. I think I'm gonna sit here a little while longer and finish my tea. I'll call you if I decide to stay in town." Toya sat in her chair and began to sip her hot tea and look at the homes she found.

On Becca's way home from work that evening, she spoke with Mark. "Hey babe, how's it going?" It seemed like all her cares just melted away when she spoke to him.

"It's going. How about you? Is Bryan doing alright?" Mark was so glad to hear Becca's voice. Now, how was he suppose to tell her how much in love with her he really was especially now that he had taken care of the Shawna situation.

"I'm doing well and so is Bryan. He is at bowling practice this afternoon. How is Camille doing?" Becca was trying to keep his voice light so as not to alarm Mark. Their relationship seemed to be getting back to normal. However, there was another part of her that wanted to tell Mark everything. Her ordeal with Rob, the weird lunch she had just had with Toya, and of course how much she just wanted to be with him right now, at this moment.

"Camille is great. So, have you heard from Rob lately?" Mark had to find out if he still was trying to become a permanent fixture in Becca's life.

Becca spoke carefully. "Actually, yes. He called me at work this afternoon wanting me to come home early. I told him that I was in the middle of a meeting and I would talk to him later." She breathed a sigh. "I'm just ready for him to leave."

There was a brief pause before Mark spoke slowly. "Wait a minute, Becca, are you saying that Rob is still in town? I thought he left a few days ago. Why is he still at the house?" Mark could feel his blood heating up.

"Please Mark, don't start. I am done with the whole situation. I'm tired of arguing about the same thing. He thought things could be mended but they can't. He's leaving for Cincinnati tonight and I couldn't be happier." Becca tried to change the subject so that her stomach would stop feeling queasy. "What do you want me to make for Easter dinner?"

Mark could hear Becca's resoluteness in her voice. "Becca, I'm not trying to pry. I told you before that I just don't want Rob to hurt you guys again. But if he's really leaving today then I'm happy. Don't trust him, Becca. Stand your guard. I love you and I just want the best for you." There was an awkward silence that rested between them. Mark decided to break it. "Your famous pasta salad would be great. Just tell me what you need and I'll get it so you'll have everything you need."

Becca breathed easily again. It seemed their conversation had switched back to normal. "Now Mark Simmons, you know I'd have to kill you if I told you my cooking secrets." She chuckled and then continued. "I'll just go shopping when I get there. That'll be one less thing on your mind that you'll have to deal with."

Mark and Becca laughed and talked about the kids for another twenty minutes before they hung up. They both felt like their relationship was getting back to normal and in some ways growing into something they had only dared to dream about.

It was about 4:00 in the evening when Becca went down to the gym to let Bryan know that it was time to go. Bryan was playing basketball with a couple of his friends. Becca stopped at the entrance to watch her son. She was so proud of the young man he was becoming. She knew it was all because of GOD. "Bryan, we have to go. Your dad is waiting to say goodbye before he gets on the road." Becca tried not to smile too hard at the thought of Rob leaving. She was glad for the closure and release the LORD had given her.

"Ah Mom, can't I just stay for another hour. Donny's mom can drop me off. They live on our side of town too. Please mom, please let me stay. I'll still get home in time to say bye to dad." Bryan was hugging his mom so tightly and hoping that she would say yes.

"I don't know Bryan. How do you know Donny's mom doesn't have something else to do?" Becca was torn. She didn't want to be alone with Rob any more than she had to but she also knew how much her son needed this time with his friend.

Donny walked up to Becca and spoke respectfully. "Ms. Thomas, I already called my mom and she said it would be ok. She should be here in the next forty-five minutes. Coach Samson is still here in his office doing paperwork and he said it was ok for us to play ball until my mom gets here."

Becca decided that she would let her son spread his wings a little. "Ok, ok, but you two better be on your best behavior. Do you understand? Don't go anywhere with anyone else and stay together. I love you Bryan. Call me if you something happens. I'm going straight home." Becca grabbed her son and gave him a big hug and kissed him on the forehead. She also hugged Donny.

Bryan and Donny ran back to the middle of the court and began playing basketball again. Becca smiled to herself, turned to walk back down the hall to her office. Then she heard footsteps running behind her.

"Thanks mom, you're the best. Please don't worry about me. Love you much." Bryan hugged his mom again and then ran back to the gym.

On Becca's way home, she couldn't seem to fight an uneasy feeling that had crept into the pit of her stomach. All she could do was pray. "Lord, I don't know what this feeling is but

please protect my son. Encamp your angels around him and Donny."
She chalked it up to just being over protective. As she walked into
her home, everything was still and quiet. She called out for Rob but
she didn't get an answer. She thought back and realized that she
hadn't seen Rob's truck in the driveway when she pulled in to the
garage. Becca sat her briefcase down by the front closet and kicked
off her shoes. She hung up her leather jacket in the closet. She almost
got excited until she heard a hushed voice coming from the upstairs.
She proceeded up the stairs very quietly. When she got to the top,
she could see a light on in the guest bedroom and the door cracked.
She knew it was Rob's voice but why was he talking low and why
did he sound nervous? As she approached the door Rob's words
became clearer and more intense. Becca stopped just outside the
door and listened intently.

"NO! I'm tired of your weakness! It's over between us so
just accept it and move on." There was a pause. "Oh, baby, I will see
my baby! And if you keep on I'll take her from you!" Rob was
getting angry.

Becca couldn't believe what she was hearing. She knew
in her heart that Rob hadn't changed. He had been playing her all
along. Apart of Becca wanted to bust in on Rob and put him out of
her house. But then there was the other part that had to hear the rest
of the conversation.

"You're crazy, girl! Why would you come here and start
stalking me? Did you really think that would make me want you
more than Becca?" He laughed. "You don't have nothing! Yeah the
sex is good but that's it. Becca's gotta a good job, a nice home, nice
car. She's independent and the sex is out of this world! So just move
on Toya. I'll be there when the baby is born but I'm staying here
now." Rob's words were like daggers not only cutting Toya but
Becca too.

Becca's knees buckled and she fell against the wall. She
was shocked. She had allowed Rob to play her again. Not only that
but had put her in danger because of this crazy, desperate woman
who was definitely delusional. Becca wanted to scream from the pit
of her stomach. She knew Rob had heard her fall against the wall.
He opened the door with the phone still to his ear. Becca gave him a

cold stare and ran down the stairs to the living room and began pacing the floor. She couldn't say anything. Her mind was clouded and she felt like she was in a nightmare.

Rob saw that the charade was over and followed Becca down the stairs still yelling on the phone. "NO, Toya I don't want you! I'm done and you can't bribe me because Becca already knows. Oh yes she does. She's standing right here."

Toya demanded to speak to Becca so Rob handed the phone to her. Becca looked at him with hatred and contempt. At first she wouldn't take the phone, until he said it was the only way to get Toya to let go of this sick game. Becca took the phone and put it to her ear but did not speak.

Toya could hear Becca's breathing. "It's ok Becca, I understand why you don't want to talk to me but if you think about it I should be the one that's angry. You stole the man that I love, the father of my unborn child. We were making plans to be married until you and that bastard child of yours popped back into the picture."

Becca was outraged at the attack on her son. "Listen here, Toya. You have your facts all messed up. My son and I did nothing to lure your precious Rob from you. He came looking for us. So watch what you say! As a matter of fact, I'm done talking to you!" Becca clicked the end button on the phone and through it at Rob. She was furious. "How dare you allow that psychotic woman into our lives? You are worse than before Robert Harris and I want you out my house immediately. Enough is enough!" Becca started pacing the floor again. This time the house phone rang. Rob went to answer it but Becca yelled at him. "DON'T TOUCH IT! This is not your home! I want you gone before my son gets home." Becca picked up the cordless phone and spoke carefully. "Hello."

Toya's words were like poisonous venom. "I have your son so I'd suggest you not hang up, Becca. I tried not to have to go here with you but you seem to think that you are untouchable. Now who's in control?"

Becca chuckled in disbelief. "You are crazier than I

MY HEART'S BETRAYAL

thought. You don't have my son. You don't even know where…"
Becca stopped because she remembered that she had told Toya a
great deal about her life before she knew who she really was. Her
hands began to shake.

Toya knew things were starting to click in Becca's head.
"Ah ha, so I see you're starting to get the picture. You know you
really have to teach your beloved son not to be so gullible and nice.
As soon as he saw this pregnant woman struggling to get bags in her
car, he ran right over to help. He left his friend standing in front of
the school, across the street. So when I covered his face with a towel
soaked with Chloroform, it was easy to push him in the back seat of
my car and drive off with his friend staring and yelling after us.
What a shame. Oh well, now what are you gonna do, Ms. I have it
all together?" Toya ended the call. She looked back at Bryan passed
out in the back seat of her car and smiled to herself. If this was all
that was keeping Rob from being with her then she would remove
the obstacle. But first she wanted to torture Becca a little while
longer. She saw her phone light up she knew it was either Rob or
Becca but she was not going to ease their minds just yet she wanted
to have a little more fun.

Becca fell to her knees in the living room by the sofa. Rob
ran over to her but she swung her fists at him with everything she
had. He backed away from her and went to call the police. Becca
sat there crying and holding a framed picture of her little boy when
he was six years old. "Please Lord, help my baby. Protect him,
JESUS!" She screamed for her child while rocking back and forth
on her knees.

When Rob ended the conversation with the police, he
called Mark. As much as he hated it, he knew Mark was the one that
needed to be there with Becca. The conversation was short because
as soon as he gave Mark the information, Mark told him he was on
his way. There was no shouting match, no testosterone contest. It
was all about getting Bryan back safely. Rob knew at that moment
that Mark had stepped in and truly become Bryan's father. His heart
sank because he knew he was the cause of all this trouble. Rob
grabbed his keys and rushed out the house to go look for Toya and to
get his son back. It was time to stop playing games.

Chapter 18

Mark sped down the turnpike doing ninety miles an hour. He prayed that the Lord would make his car invisible to the police. Mark's soul motivation was finding Bryan and making sure he was ok. This was too much. "JESUS!" Mark let out a yell that permeated from every part of his body. He couldn't believe that Rob's psychotic world had now caused Bryan's life to be put in danger. It had to stop. "Rob Harris you're done reeking' havoc on my family!" Mark prayed silently all the way to Toledo. He knew he had to be focused so that he could support Becca.

When the bell rang, Becca jumped up from the dining room table with Fran right behind her, and ran to the front door. Her heart was beating so fast with hope that it would be the police standing there with her son smiling at her. As she flung the door open, a cold breeze swept over her that caused her insides to chill. Fran clutched her daughter as Becca's knees buckled in disappointment. Mark stood at the door solid and strong until he saw Becca's weak state. He rushed forward and grabbed the other side of Becca. He and Fran helped her to the sofa.

"Becca, just relax. I'm here honey. Everything is going to be alright but you have to hold it together." Mark held Becca close to him and rocked her back and forth. Fran sat on the other side of Becca rubbing her back and praying earnestly.

"Father in the name of Jesus, touch my daughter and bring my grandson back safely. I know You're in control, GOD and I trust only YOU!" Tears ran down Fran's face as she continued to pray fervently in the spirit.

"I'm tryin' Mark. But he's my baby!" Becca started crying profusely. I just can't sit here and do nothing. We should be out there looking for that crazy woman! Why Lord Why?!"

At that moment, Becca's cell phone rang; she picked it up off of the table and looked at the caller ID. She pressed the talk button and spoke as if it caused her great pain. "Where is my son,

Toya?" Becca was trying to be calm.

Toya chuckled in the phone. "Wow, you're a real piece of work, Becca! I would be hysterical if someone had taken my child. Maybe Bryan is better off with me. At least I know how to protect what's mine." Toya became serious. "I'm willing to do whatever it takes."

Becca's head was reeling. There were so many thoughts flooding her head at that moment and she didn't want to say something that would set Toya completely off and cause her to harm Bryan. Becca could hear her mother praying beside her faintly and a peace fell over her that calmed her heart. She couldn't explain why she just felt everything was gonna be alright. "Toya, I know you must be tired. Why don't you just bring Bryan home and we can talk about everything. I won't press charges. I just want to make sure all the children are ok. All this stress can't be good for your baby." Becca was trying to appeal to her nurturing side.

"Yeah right, Becca! You must think I'm a fool. Just because I don't have a bunch of fancy degrees and live a nice house doesn't mean I'll fall for just anything. You will never see Bryan again. You stole the love of my life and broke up my family; so now I'm gonna do the same thing to you. I hope you enjoy those sleepless nights wondering where he is and what he's doing, watching the minutes go by as you wait for the phone call that never comes."

Becca shuddered at the thought of never seeing her son again but she was trying to hold onto her faith. "But Toya, I didn't steal Rob from you. He never told me about you or the baby. Can't you see that he deceived both of us? Anyway, things weren't working out and I had already told him that we couldn't be together. I'm not in love with Rob!" Becca sniffled trying to keep her tears from overflowing. "Please, please don't do this, Toya, please! If you tell us where you are, we'll come get Bryan and this whole nightmare will be over. Then you and Rob can be together. As a matter of fact, I think he's looking for you because he's worried about you and the baby. So, see Toya, he does love you."

Toya was getting ready to respond to Becca when the

other line beeped on her phone. She did not say anything to Becca. She just clicked over. All Becca heard was silence.

Rob raced down the expressway toward Cincinnati. He knew exactly where Toya was going. She had always wanted talked about them moving to Tennessee. But he knew she would have to stop in Cincinnati to get her daughter before she went there. He figured he would try to call her one more time since he was about 20 minutes away from their apartment. "Hey, babe, where you at?" Rob spoke in his normal seductive tone. He knew she always liked that.

"Don't try it Rob! I know what you're trying to do and I'm not falling for it. I'm not gonna make it easy for you and you're whore to be together!" Toya was furious.

"Toya, you know I'm not playing games with you. Becca was trying to get wit' me but I ended it because I wanna be wit' you sexy and our baby. As a matter of fact, what you did was cool because now I'll have all my kids together and the woman I love." Rob had to pour it on thick because he didn't want Toya to shut down and not talk to him. "Why don't you meet me at our place and we can pack our stuff and head to Tennessee. Nobody will think to look for us down there. But we have to hurry."

Toya paused for a minute. Maybe, Rob was telling the truth. It would be nice for all of them to be together. She looked over at Bryan tied up in the chair with tape over his mouth. He could barely hold his head up from the Chloroform she had given him to keep him quiet. She rubbed her stomach as she felt the baby kicking. Toya knew she needed help. "Ok Rob, I'm gonna trust you but you betta' not play wit' me or somethin' bad will happen. I'm already at the house packing my bags. How long will it take you to get here?"

Rob breathed a sigh of relief. "I'll be there in about 10 minutes. Can you get my bag together too? I'm gonna stop by the bank and get some money for us."

Rob figured he would call Becca and let her know where they were going and come up with a plan so that no one would get hurt. Then Becca would see how much he had changed especially since he risking everything to get Bryan back. Rob just refused to believe that Toya would do anything to hurt him or his son. This nightmare would soon be over.

"I knew you loved me. All you needed was a reminder of how strong our bond is and now we're going to be together forever as a family. We'll be waiting for you. Hurry, babe, I can't wait to see you." She hung up the phone with a satisfied smile as one tear rolled down her face. She worked quickly so that they would be ready. This was it! She had finally won.

"Becca, do you remember anything that this woman might have said that can give us a clue as to where she might have taken Bryan? I know you're exhausted but when the police come we need to have information waiting on them. We don't want to waste any time." Mark opened the utility drawer on the right hand side of the counter and pulled out a blue pen and a small tablet. They only had a couple of more hours to wait before the police could launch a full investigation. Mark had just returned from driving around looking for Bryan. He had been to every side of town searching for Bryan to no avail. Mark stood at the counter writing while Becca and her mom sat at the kitchen table drinking hot tea.

"Did she mention family members or a special place she liked to go to?"

"I've tried to remember! I can't think of anything!" Becca put her hands to her head as she rubbed them through her braids with frustration. "All I keep thinking is that I let this crazy woman get close to me and now she could be doing anything to my son. How stupid could I be?" Becca started crying again.

Fran touched her daughter's hand and gave her some tissue. "Becca, God is going to see us through this storm but we have to hold onto HIS truth. I love you, daughter and it's time for you to concentrate on the details of every conversation that you had with this woman. Mark and I are here to help you honey, not judge you. We have all made mistakes in judgment. There is none that are none that are perfect." Fran smiled at her daughter and motioned for Mark to come sit down at the table on the other side of Becca.

Becca began thinking hard. Then something hit her like a ton of bricks. She remembered how Toya talked about her small apartment in Cincinnati. She didn't put it together then that she was talking about her place with Rob. Becca jumped up suddenly and went into the family room, grabbed an envelope that Rob had sent Bryan about six months ago. She walked quickly back to the kitchen and spoke with confidence. "I got it! This is Rob's address in Cincinnati. I bet she went back home to her safe place. Look Mark this has got to be it!" She handed the envelope to Mark.

He thought about it for a moment. Then he spoke cautiously, "When was the last time you heard from Rob? I know he hasn't called since I've been here." Mark paused briefly. "Do you think that he has something to do with all of this? You did say he was acting strange when you got the call and then disappeared."

"NO Mark! I know Rob has played a part in this mess but only by his unfaithfulness and deceit. I just don't believe he would go as far as to stage a kidnapping of his own son. Even Rob has some boundaries." Becca's mind couldn't help but still wonder. Could it be possible? Why hadn't Rob called her? She wasn't going to wait around and find out. Becca grabbed her cell phone and dialed his number. It seemed like the phone rang forever.

"Uh hey, Becca. Have you heard from Toya lately?" Rob tried to make his voice sound normal because Toya was listening intently.

"No, Rob, I haven't. But maybe you have. I haven't spoken to you since you hurried out of the house yesterday evening. The police will want to talk to you when they get here. How far away are you?" Becca noticed something different in his tone of voice.

Rob was getting a little nervous. But he knew he had to keep his composure if he wanted Toya to continue believing the lies he was telling her. "I don't have anything different to tell the police than you would. I never saw these tendencies in Toya. I just believe that when I talk to her everything will be ok and she'll bring Bryan back. So I'll call you later. I don't want to stop looking. Bye." Rob hung up quickly as not to have to answer any more of her questions. He looked over at Toya sitting in the passenger seat of his truck staring at him.

"Do you think she believed you?" Toya spoke calmly looking for any sign of regret in his eyes.

"Yeah, boo. Becca is so hysterical right now she'll believe almost anything. However, they are getting ready to talk to the police and she wanted me to be there. But you heard what I told her so we're good. By the time they realize what's goin' on, we'll be in deep in Tennessee." Rob mustered up a chuckle and leaned over and kissed Toya passionately. Then he looked back at his son still weak and confused from the drugs. He smiled and winked at him as if to say everything was ok.

Toya melted in Rob's kiss. Everything in her was reassured at that moment. She smiled at him and rubbed the side of his face lovingly. "Let's go baby. I can't wait for us to get out of this place." As Rob started the truck, Toya turned to her daughter in the backseat next to Bryan. "Buckle your seatbelt Casey and help your brother Bryan." Toya turned back around, gently touched her pregnant belly and gave a sigh of relief. This was all she needed and ever wanted to be complete.

Chapter 19

Mark and Becca decided to drive down to Cincinnati after the conversation with Rob. Becca found Rob's address on an envelope he had sent to Bryan last month. "Mom, are you sure you're ok with staying here?" Becca was putting her cell phone car charger in her purse.

"Yes, sweetie, I'll be fine. Someone needs to be here in case the police come up with something or somehow Bryan is able to make his way back home." Fran smiled at her daughter and hugged her. "Everything has to work out because we have the promise of GOD. So you and Mark go bring my grandson home." Fran reached for Mark's hand and prayed for their journey.

Mark helped Becca put on her coat, grabbed his jacket, and kissed Fran on her cheek. "Don't worry, ma, I'll take care of her. We'll keep you updated when we find out more information." Mark and Becca walked out of the house. He opened the door of his car for Becca and she slid into the car. Mark closed the door and jogged around to the driver side of the car. When he sat down in the car and closed his door, he started the engine and reached for Becca's hand. "We will get Bryan back, Becca. Just hold on." He put the car in drive and backed out the driveway as Becca stared at a picture of her son smiling back at her.

As Rob drove down I-75 south toward Kentucky, Toya fell asleep. Casey and Bryan were sleeping in the backseat also. He wanted to turn the car around and race back toward Ohio but he wasn't sure what she might do. So, he just decided to stick with the plan he had devised. Rob made sure that while Toya was sleep, he drove slower in order to kill time; hopefully, giving the police time to catch up to them so that this ordeal could be ended. Rob thought about the note that he'd left in his mailbox outside his apartment giving detailed directions on where they were going and what hotel they would be stop at overnight in southern Kentucky. He rubbed his forehead and took a glance in his rearview mirror at his son curled up in the backseat so drugged that all he could do was sleep. All Rob could think about was how he had allowed his son to get caught up in his nonsense. Rob knew this would be too much for Becca to forgive. He just hoped that she would at least let him visit Bryan.

Mark finally convinced Becca to get some sleep so that she could build her strength. She had been sleep for about an hour when her cell phone rang. Mark quickly grabbed it out of her lap before she woke up. "Hello." There was a brief pause. Mark became a little agitated but he spoke again. "I said hello. Who is this?"

"Hello, may I speak with Becca. This is Toya." Her voice sounded like a regular person instead of a crazed girlfriend who had been betrayed by her man.

Mark couldn't believe this woman. "Becca can't come to the phone right now." He spoke calmly and in a low tone so as not to wake Becca. "How is Bryan doing?"

Toya was a little shocked by the question but quickly became agitated. "Who are you? Where is Becca? I need to speak to her right now!" Toya was sitting in the car by herself. Rob had taken the kids into the rest stop to use the bathroom.

"This is Mark, Bryan's real dad and I need to know where you have taken him. Don't worry about Becca; anything you need to say you can say it to me, Toya." Mark was sick of this woman playing games with everyone's emotions.

Toya started laughing loudly. "Oh, so you're Mr. Wonderful. Well I don't scare that easily. You don't fool me Mark. Why are you mad? If you weren't so weak and would've just stepped up to the plate and told Becca that you were in love with her, she wouldn't have gave Rob a second thought. Then none of us would be in this mess. So don't be mad at me playa' 'cause I play to win!" Toya chuckled to herself.

Mark was furious but he couldn't get loud because he didn't want to wake Becca. "You don't know anything about me and I'm more of a man than Mr. Harris because I'm the one that's been takin' care of Bryan these past 11 years while he was off playin' house wit' yo psychotic self. I was the one makin' sure Bryan had whatever he needed. Don't get it twisted Toya, if you hurt Bryan in any way I will make the rest of your life a livin' HELL!"

Toya spewed out venomous poison, "Oh is that right? You are so pathetic! At least I had the guts to fight for the one I love and look what I've gotten, my man and part of yo' family, plus I'm drivin' yo girl insane. I couldn't ask for more than that." Toya was smiling so big.

A part of Mark was embarrassed because some of what Toya said was right. "You know nothing about me and Becca's relationship and what do you mean, you got your man?" Mark shook his head and gripped the steering wheel tighter. "Is Rob with you and Bryan?"

Becca started to stir at the loudness of Mark's voice. She awoke completely when the car swirved hard to the side of the road and came to an abrupt stop. "What in the world—Is that her? Let me—Is Bryan ok?" Becca was almost hysterical.

Mark was furious. He knew Rob was no good but this was just unbelievable. "Listen Toya, you tell that sorry chump, that if one hair on Bryan's head is hurt, I'm gonna jack him up!"

Toya saw Rob coming back to the truck with the kids and hung up the phone quickly. Just as Becca grabbed the phone out of Mark's hand. "Hello! Hello, Toya!" Becca dropped the phone from her ear. "Mark, are you crazy? Why would you talk to her like that! She has my baby boy. I don't believe you!" Becca began swinging at Mark hysterically.

Mark finally grabbed her arms and shouted above her shrieks with power and confidence. "I love you Becca Thomas! I have loved you for a very long time. Bryan is my son too. So understand my heart is broken just like yours." Mark loosened his grip on her and stared straight ahead trying to hold back the tears. Maybe if I had've of told you how I felt you wouldn't have let Rob back in your life again. But I was afraid of what it would do to our friendship. But I'm sick of all these games and secrets! Whatever happens—now you know the truth!"

Silence fell over the car. Becca's face was wet from the tears. She couldn't believe that after all this time she finally knew how Mark really felt about her. However, she couldn't process all of that at this moment. All she kept running over in her head was the phrase she heard Mark say when he was on the phone with Toya, 'Is Rob with you?' Could it really be? Becca's head was reeling. But she had to make herself focus so she could at least respond to Mark's unexpected declaration. "Oh, Mark, I don't want to sound cold—but I can't even concentrate on that right now. My life doesn't even matter. I just want my son back safely. Thinking that I needed a man to complete me is what thrust me into this nightmare! All I want to know is where Bryan has been taken. I apologize if that hurts you but I don't have the strength to deal with anything else, ok?"

Mark looked at the tears overflowing in Becca's eyes and all he wanted to do was make the pain go away. He gently pulled her close to him and spoke softly, "Becca, I see your heart and that's good enough for me. I still love you." Mark kissed her on her forehead. Then he looked straight in her deep brown eyes and spoke with confidence. "Let's go get your son!" With that statement he put the car in drive and sped forward. They were about fifteen minutes outside of Cincinnati.

As Rob was driving, he was thinking about how he got himself into this mess. He remembered when he first met Toya. She was so hot and sexy. She was full of life and boldness. Her street sense is what attracted him to her even more. It didn't bother him that she already had a child because Casey's dad was locked up in prison for armed robbery and assaulting a police officer. He wouldn't be released for twenty-five years. So Rob didn't have to worry about that aspect! He was just having fun and he thought Toya was too. Then, he noticed that she started getting overly possessive. She always wanted to know where he was. If he didn't call at least five times a day, she would get hysterical and confrontational. But Rob enjoyed the way she apologized. After awhile even that became boring. That's why he decided to go back to Becca. Rob thought he had everything figured out but he never thought things would be this bad.

Everyone in the car was asleep. But Rob heard a voice full of exhaustion call to him from the backseat. "Dad, what's going on?" Bryan's voice was groggy and his speech slurred. "Where's mom?"

Bryan tried to use his hands to help him sit up but discovered they were tied together with duct tape. Bryan's strength was minimal because of the high dosage of Chloroform. "Help me, dad, please."

Rob looked at his son in the rearview mirror. His heart broke to see his son in this state. Rob spoke in a low voice. "Hey man. I have everything under control. You are safe. Just relax and I'll take care of you." Rob could see at a second glance that Bryan was dozing off again. Rob looked over at Toya, who seemed to be sleeping peacefully. At that moment he decided that he just couldn't do it. Rob's choice altered the lives of everyone in that vehicle. "I know what I have to do."

Toya woke up in enough time to see the front of Rob's truck make a u-turn on the highway. He turned so sharply that Toya bumped her head on the side of the window. "What are you doing? Why are we going back the other way?" Toya held her head and readjusted herself in the seat. "Don't mess wit' me, Rob I'm not goin' back!"

Rob refused to answer Toya. He knew that he had to stay in control so he tightened his grip on the steering wheel and eased the gas pedal to the floor.

Becca and Mark stood at Rob's front door hoping that they would find some type of clue to where Rob and Toya had taken Bryan. The door was locked but the curtains were still open. Becca looked in the front window to find the apartment left in disarray. Clothes were strewn across the couch, dirty dishes left on the sofa table, and a garbage can knocked over in the dining area. Becca slowly stood up and tears began to slide down her face at the sight and the thought of her precious child having to be subjected to this dysfunctional lifestyle. "Where is my child, Bryan? I don't think I can take much more!" Becca's knees buckled but before she fell to the ground, she felt the strength of Mark's arm encompass her drained body. Becca just leaned into him and cried.

"Becca, it's gonna be alright. The Lord sees everything and HE is concerned about our lives. We have to continue to trust

GOD. We can go to the police station here in Cincinnati and file a report too." Mark gently wiped the tears from Becca's face and they started back to the car.

Becca stopped abruptly. "Wait a minute, Mark, before we leave let's look in the mailbox for some type of lead." Becca walked back to the box and looked inside. There was a small envelope leaning against the cold metal. Becca pulled the envelope out of the mailbox. She opened it, stared at it and then handed it to Mark.

When Mark read it, he immediately grabbed Becca's hand and guided her to the car quickly. The sped out of the driveway quickly and down the road to their destiny.

Toya realized that she had lost Rob. He had betrayed her for Becca. She became very quiet and just stared straight out of the window. She was contemplating her next move.

"Toya, baby, I know you don't understand what I'm doin' but it's for the best. This just ain't right. Look at my son. You've kidnapped him and drugged him and now he can barely stay conscious. What kinda stuff do you think is goin' through his mind? I can't have my son thinkin' that his dad had anything to do wit' this mess! Why couldn't you just trust that I was comin' back to you, Toya? This is some crazy crap! I figure if we turn back now I can probably get Becca to forget all of this and not press charges against you. Then we can just go back to our own lives.

Toya looked at Rob with a cold stare that could have cut him like a razor sharp blade. She just couldn't believe that Rob had betrayed her again for Becca. Everything was spinning out of control and she was tired of playing the fool. At that moment, Toya decided it would be better to sacrifice everything than to watch the love of her life find happiness with her enemy. She realized that she had come too far to turn back. She spoke low and deliberate. "I love you, Rob, I love you."

Rob was so proud of how he had taken control of the situation that he was totally oblivious to Toya's low chanting and the dark metal object she had pulled covertly out of her bag. As he glanced in the rearview mirror at Toya's daughter and his son, Rob felt something hard pushing into his side. "What is that?! What are you doing Toya?" Rob glanced down to see Toya holding a .45 tightly in her hand with her finger on the trigger ready to shoot.

"You know exactly what I'm doing, baby. I'm Fighting for my man!" Tears began to roll down Toya's face as she felt her finger grow heavy on the trigger. Nothing mattered anymore. She realized that her and Rob would never share a life together without Becca's interference. "I'm done playing games Rob."

Rob was sweating as he gripped the wheel tighter trying to think about what to do. He never thought Toya would go this far. Rob tried to mask the fear that had overshadowed him by speaking low and calm. "Toya, listen, this ain't the way. Let me pull o—."

Rob's voice was lost in the loud noise that rang throughout the vehicle. Then there was another loud ringing sound. Silence filled the air for a brief moment before tires were heard screeching to a halt and the sound of thunder against cement permeated the highway.

Mark and Becca sped down the highway toward the meeting place Rob had directed them to in the note. Becca found that she was feeling a ray of sunshine in this whole nightmare. She remembered the last time she held her handsome son in her arms. Oh what she would give to have him with her right now. "Mark do you remember the winter I had the flu. It was just before Christmas. Bryan was being so helpful. Whatever I needed he took care of his mommy." Becca smiled at the memory of her son washing dishes and warming soup in the microwave.

"No, Becca, we are not going to start that!" Mark was visibly upset but confident. "Bryan is alright., He may be a little scared but once he sees his beautiful mother he'll be good. Bryan is a strong boy and he's smart so don't start talking about I remember when... Ok?" Mark focused his attention back on the road again. They had crossed the state line into Kentucky about an hour ago.

Becca stared a Mark's profile as every part of his body oozed determination, faith, and love. She could see that he was just as torn up on the inside as she was. "Mark, I'm just tired of crying every ten minutes. I thought that if I could just think on the special moments it would renew my strength. I'm not giving up on my son. I know the Lord is taking care of him! All I have left is my faith. But I love you for having the same faith and being with me." Becca touched his knee and spoke with care. "But you need to know that it will be the sight of us together, mom and dad, which will settle Bryan." Becca turned her attention back to the road.

Mark could not respond because he had to jam on the brakes. His right arm flew across Becca's body to stop her from thrusting forward into the dashboard. Mark gripped the steering wheel tighter with his left hand and yelled out, "JESUS!" in a loud voice. The car stopped just inches away from the back end of a semitruck that was at a complete stop with the cab door flung open.

"Whew! Thank you Lord!" Becca removed her hands from over her face to see cars stopped all around them and people walking toward the left lane where a black F-350 truck rested on its top. The truck was banged up with smoke coming from it. The front end was smashed and there was glass and debris everywhere. Becca kept staring at the truck. Something about it was very familiar. All of a sudden she gasped for air.

"Becca, Becca, are you OK?! Breathe baby, breathe!" Mark didn't know what was going on with Becca. He unlocked her seatbelt so she could breathe and tell him what was goin' on. All of a sudden Becca jumped out of the car and ran toward the truck. "Wait, Becca, wait!" Mark called frantically as he chased behind her. "Where are you goin?"

Becca couldn't speak. All she could focus on was getting to the overturned, mangled truck. She couldn't speak. She didn't want to think about the obvious foreboding thought that kept creeping into her mind. This made her run faster. When she made it within 6 feet of the wreckage she saw an arm hanging out the window drenched in blood. Becca became hysterical and started screaming, "Bryan! Bryan! Lord please don't let him be dead!" Please GOD, PLEASE!"

Mark came up and grabbed Becca from behind. "Becca,

what is it? We shouldn't be this close to the accident. Tell me what's..." At that moment, Mark took a closer look at the wreckage and realized it was Rob's truck. He immediately broke through the crowd of emergency responders and police. When he got through, he saw a pregnant woman's lifeless body being pulled out of the passenger side and lifted onto a stretcher. Mark didn't know Becca was right behind him until he heard her scream out again.

"Toya! Oh my God! Oh my God! Where is my baby?!" She was crying and praying and calling Bryan's name. A police officer grabbed her and told her she had to step back from the scene.

"Ma'am, ma'am you have to calm down. Now who are you looking for?" The police officer was watching her carefully.

"M-my son, Bryan Thomas. He was in this truck. His father's girlfriend kidnapped him and we have been trying to find them. I know he's out here. He could be hurt!" Becca grabbed the police officer's arm pleading with him. "You have to find him! PLEASE!" Becca broke down crying again. She let out one last scream. "BRYAN! IT'S MOM! BRYAN, BRYAN!"

As if right on cue, a weak male voice answered from about ½ a mile up the road called back. "Mom, Momma!"

Becca could see another body being lifted up into another ambulance. She took off running again with Mark right behind her. As she got closer, she could see the young body clearly and she knew right away that it was Bryan. "Wait! Wait!   That's my son!" Becca arrived at the back door of the ambulance out of breath with great anticipation. "Bryan? It's me, it's your momma. Are you OK?" There was silence for a moment.

There was silence for a moment. Then the young man opened his eyes as if they were heavy cement blocks. But he opened them long enough to see his mother and Godfather standing side by side looking at him with so much love and relief. All Bryan could muster his strength to say was, "Momma, you found me." Then his eyes shut and he lost consciousness.

As the paramedics were preparing to close the door, Becca jumped in the back with them. "What's wrong with my baby?"

"Ma'am, he has serious head trauma. We have to get him to the hospital quickly. He also broke his left arm when he was thrown from the truck. You have to let us do our job." The paramedics allowed her to ride with them while they worked diligently on Bryan.

Becca remembered that she had to trust GOD. Even though, things didn't look good for Bryan, Becca knew that God always honored pure faith. She laid her hand on her son's leg and began to pray passionately for Bryan's healing. "Please Jesus, I need you to take care of my baby!" She rode the rest of the way praying within herself earnestly to the Lord.

Chapter 20

When Mark arrived at the hospital, he ran through the ER entrance in a frenzy looking for Becca and Bryan. In his mind, he was crying out to GOD on behalf of his God son. All of a sudden, as he rounded the corner, he heard a familiar voice call out his name.

"Mark, Mark." Becca was running on pure adrenaline. Her eyes were red from crying and her hands were shaky. "Mark," She fell into his arms and wrapped her arms tightly around his waist as Mark reciprocated by engulfing Becca with his arms. She laid her head on his chest and let the tears flood her eyes. "they won't let me see him! They said we have to wait until the detective gets here. My baby is back there with total strangers running all kinds of tests on him. Bry needs me! What do I do?" Becca looked up at Mark in helpless search of an answer.

Mark didn't really know what to say. He just pulled Becca close to him and whispered a prayer that only the two of them and God could hear. Soon after, a doctor came up to them and asked if they were kin to Bryan Thomas. Mark explained their relationship while Becca pulled herself together to speak.

"Doctor, how is my son? Can we see him now?" Becca was trying not to become frantic again.

The doctor looked at both of them and decided that it would be alright to break procedures just this one time. He spoke slowly and plainly so that they would understand. "Before the two of you go back there, I need to explain Bryan's condition. He suffered some minor scratches and bruising. He also broke his left arm which we have set and in a cast. However, we are concerned about the head trauma he received when the vehicle flipped over. Bryan keeps slipping in and out of consciousness. Each time he goes into an unconscious state it's a longer time before he wakes up again. The X-rays show that there is some swelling in his brain. We need to get him to surgery so that we can stop this."

Mark and Becca stood there in shock. It was as if the doctor was talking about someone else. Becca spoke first, "So, isn't that really serious when you have to go into someone's head? What if something goes wrong? Can't you treat it with a pill or a shot?" Becca could feel the heat of her tears flowing down her face again. Her breath started to stutter the more agitated she became.

The doctor helped Becca to a chair nearby. Mark sat next to her and the doctor across from them. "We have to make sure there is not any damage to his brain, Mrs. Thomas. I need you to give us consent to do the surgery so we can help your son. We have to hurry because time is crucial. Will you sign the release?" The doctor was very sincere and earnest.

Mark put his arm around Becca and whispered to her. "Becca, we have to do this for Bryan. You have to sign the form. The Lord will take care of him and guide the doctor's hand. Just believe, sweetie."

Becca's head was reeling. She kept trying to hear GOD but there was nothing but silence until the doctor spoke.

"Remember Becca that all things work together for the good to them that are called according to His purpose. You have to hold onto your faith in GOD. Please know that while you're praying out here I am praying in there. God knows."

"Becca felt a gentle peace come over her and she knew it was going to be alright. She reached for the clipboard and signed the form. The doctor stood up touched her gently and gave her a reassuring smile then rushed off to the operating room.

Mark looked at Becca and took her hands in his and spoke with so much love. "Becca, God has always taken care of you and Bryan. Don't doubt Him now. We are all back together and we are going to do things right this time. No more games. I love you both and no one's going to ever slip in and hurt you guys again." He kissed Becca on her forehead and held her tightly. "We better call mom and let her know what has happened."

Becca felt so safe in Mark's arms but she knew she needed some time to get into the arms of Jesus. "You go ahead and call her. I'm going to the chapel. I'll be back soon." Becca walked away but turned back to see that Mark was watching her. "I'm so glad you're here. Thank you." She turned back towards the direction of the chapel and disappeared down the hall.

Mark called Fran and explained everything. She told him to give her directions and they would be on their way. Mark had no idea that Lena and Camille were at the house too. He had no more strength to fight. So he conceded and gave her the directions.

When Fran entered the chapel to find her daughter sitting on a bench praying and wiping tears from her eyes, her heart melted for her daughter. She could see the pain and agony that was engulfing Becca. Fran was glad this whole situation was over but now there was another phase to get over and Fran believed that God would give them grace to go through it. As she made her way down the aisle, she was praying in her spirit.

Becca turned to see her mother standing there looking at her with so much love. "Hey mom." Becca jumped up and into her mother's arms. "I'm so glad you're here." Becca just cried in her mother's arms.

Fran didn't say a word. She just held her daughter and let her pour out. "You know this is not your fault." Fran's heart hurt to see her daughter in this state but she knew she had to hold onto her faith in God in order for them to make it through. "It's not over, Becca. Don't give up on God. He's gonna help us get through this terrible situation. Fran lifted her daughter's face and wiped her tears away.

Becca looked up at her mom and smiled. "I know mom, 'cause God won't give up on me." Becca hugged her mom tightly. As they were standing to walk out of the chapel, Mark came rushing in and grabbed Becca.

"What is it, Mark? Is Bryan ok?" Becca's breath became stuttered.

"Becca, the doctor just came by and said that Bryan is out of surgery and in recovery doing well so far. We can see him in a couple of hours." Mark pulled Becca close to him and embraced her with all the love he had. He looked at Faith and grabbed her hand as she waved the other one to the Lord. There family was mending and coming back together in a deeper way.

Chapter 21

"Yeah, mom, Bryan is in the backyard playing with Camille. He's fine stop worrying. Where is your faith?" Becca smiled to herself thinking about how far her son's recovery had come. It had been seven months since the accident. It was like Bryan had never been in such a tragic situation. The Lord had really done a marvelous work in Bryan. Becca was glad to be back at home with her family intact.

"Well you can't blame a grandmother for worrying about her only grandson. I'll never stop being concerned about the little man." Faith felt warmth come over her body knowing that her daughter and grandson were safe. "So is Mark there with you? Have you guys been talkin' about anything special?" Faith felt like Becca and Mark had waited long enough and it was time for them to move forward with their lives together. But she wanted to let them find their own way.

"No, mom, Mark is not here. He is in Cleveland. Camille wanted to stay with us. So I said ok. I'm going to take her back to Cleveland tomorrow after church." Becca was so happy that Camille and Bryan were enjoying each other. It was almost surreal. "Did you want to ride to church with us in the morning?"

"Sure. That sounds good. It's about time you started taking care of yo' mommy dearest." Fran laughed with her daughter. I'll be ready about 9:30 so that we can make it for Sunday School. OK?"

"Yeah mom that sounds good. I'm taking these two bowling with my friend Tonya Cooper, from work, and her two grandchildren. We should be back home by 8p.m. Then I can get them bathed and in bed by 9 so they can get plenty of rest." Becca went to the back door one last time wave them in so she could go upstairs and get ready for their outing this afternoon.

Fran was glad to hear that Becca was getting on with her life. "Well, I guess I'll talk to you in the morning, my precious daughter. Kiss the kids for me. Have a great time. I'm going to prepare dinner for tomorrow."

"Ok mom, I'll call you in the morning. I hope you're makin' a couple of Buttermilk Pies for dessert. I'm just saying it sure would be nice since that's my favorite. No pressure. Love you mom."

"Yeah right, as long as I make those buttermilk pies. Becca, you are so spoiled. I'll talk to you later. Bye." Fran hung up smiling to herself because she knew she was on her way to the market to make her daughter's favorite pies.

Becca was hanging up the phone as Bryan and Camille came rushing in the back sliding door. "Hey guys slow down. We all need to go upstairs and get ready for an afternoon of bowling and pizza. We have to meet Mrs. Cooper and her grandkids at 4:00 and it's already 2:30. Camille you can use my bathroom to take a shower and change your clothes. Bryan you go on up to your bathroom and get dressed. Both of your outfits are already pressed and ready to put on. Does everyone understand what they're supposed to be doing?" Becca looked at both of them with love and joy in her heart.

"YES!" Bryan and Camille answered together.

Bryan had more to say. "I'm ready to eat mom. Bring on the pizza!"

Camille co-signed. "Me too Auntie Becca."

"Ok guys well let's head upstairs." They all ran upstairs laughing and calling each other rotten eggs. When Becca got both of them in their prospective showers, she went into her closet to find something to wear. As she laid her hands on a blue jean outfit, she began to thank the Lord for all of HIS blessings on her family's life. Becca became so full that tears of joy began to roll down her face. "Lord, from now on I trust only You. Order my steps and only give me what you know is best for me."

It was about six o'clock when Becca and Tonya ordered went to the window to pick up their pizza and drinks. The children were having such a good time bowling and playing in the arcade. Becca wore her braids pulled back in a ponytail with her blue jean outfit and chocolate silk tank top under the jacket. Tonya also wore blue jeans with a melon colored blouse that highlighted her skin tones beautifully.

"I can't get over how wonderful Bryan's recovery has come along. You would never know that he had been in such a terrible accident. God is so good, girl!" Tonya high-fived Becca after they had set the food down on the table.

"I know Tonya. Sometimes, I just find myself staring at Bryan and my eyes well up with tears. I just become overwhelmed with so much joy. God gave us another chance and this time I'm doing things His way." Becca was resolute in her statement and Tonya could see the determination in her face.

"I'm so happy for you." Tonya felt a little hand pulling at her blouse. She looked down and it was her granddaughter, Nevaeh with her paper plate in her hand. "I guess that means you're ready to eat." Tonya and Becca laughed because the rest of the group had lined up behind her. Tonya passed out the pizza and Becca poured the drinks. The kids sat at the table in front of them so they could continue bowling.

About twenty minutes had passed and Becca was sitting across the table from Tonya when the question that was hanging in the air was finally addressed by Tonya.

"So, Becca, how's Mark doing? I haven't seen him at the school much or heard you talk about him much. Is everything ok between the two of you?" Tonya's face showed great concern.

Becca breathed a sigh before she answered. "I know Tonya. He still takes care of Bryan but I needed some time to just concentrate on my relationship with the Lord. You know what I mean, girl." Becca looked at Tonya with sincerity.

"Yeah, I know what you mean. I just hope you don't miss your opportunity with Mark. After you shared with me how Mark told you his true feelings about you, I thought that you guys would stop wasting time and go ahead and get together. But your spiritual life always trumps your fleshly desires. I just want to make sure you're ok." Tonya touched Becca's hand gently.

Becca let her mind slip back into a daydream about Mark

and her at the cabin on Valentine's Day weekend. She smiled to herself. " I'm better than ok. I am learning to put what I think I want on the back burner and go after what God wants. Yes, I love Mark, but I refuse to make any decision without my God's approval. I realize now I could have avoided a lot of pain and anguish if I would've just sought the Lord for what I needed to know instead of my flesh." Becca paused for a moment as a tear began to run down her left cheek at the thought of how God had restored her and healed her son. "I am so grateful to God, Tonya, because He never left me even when I walked away from Him, He continued to call my name until I came running back. How awesome is our God?!" Becca waved her hand in the air and gave Tonya a hi-five.

"Ooo-wee girl don't get me started up in this bowling alley!" Tonya was smiling back at Becca with so much happiness for her. She had been praying for Becca ever since Rob showed up at the school. So to hear Becca talk about her relationship with God with such confidence and enthusiasm made her soul leap for joy. "Becca, I am so happy for you. Don't worry about the thing with Mark because what God has for you is for you and that's all you need to know."

They spent the rest of the evening enjoying each other's company, watching the kids have a good time, and talking about the goodness of their Savior.

Chapter 22

Mark woke up early Sunday morning thinking about Becca and the children more intensely than he ever had before. He had a feeling of urgency to see them right away. So he decided to get himself together and drive to Toledo. He called his pastor and let him know that he would not be in church today because there was an urgent matter he had to attend to. Then he called his sister Lena to see if she wanted to ride with him.

"Of course I'll go with you, Mark. But I thought you told Becca you wouldn't be there until this afternoon?" Lena was groggy and confused but supportive of her brother.

"I did but what it's like the Lord woke me up this morning and told me what I needed to do immediately without hesitation. Then He gave me a peace like I never felt before in my life." Mark took a moment to reflect on the feeling that he just described to his sister. "So, I'll be over to pick you up about 8:30. That gives you about an hour and a half to get it together."

"O.K. I guess I can make that work. That means I'll have to cut short some of my beauty rituals this morning." Lena chuckled. I'll see you at 8:30."

Mark spoke in a serious tone. "Lena, I really appreciate you going with me and I want you to know that I love you much. I'll talk to you in a few." Mark hung up the phone and went to work preparing for their road trip. He wanted to be there for the start of service.

Becca sat in the adult Sunday School class in a pale blue two piece suit with beautiful sequins along the lapel of the jacket and around the hem of the skirt. Her shoes and purse matched her suit perfectly. Becca wore her braids up in a French Roll with ringlets gently cascading down the left side of her face. She looked beautiful. Her focus was on the children's review of their class. Bryan and Camille were doing a wonderful job of answering the review questions. The lesson for this week was "Seeking the Kingdom of

God". Everyone enjoyed the lesson.

When Sunday School was dismissed, Becca hurried the children to the bathroom so that they would not be walking during service. While her and Camille were in the ladies' restroom, Camille asked Becca a peculiar question.

"Auntie Becca, do you believe that God really answers our prayers?" Camille was very sincere.

"Yes, honey, I do. God is faithful. That's why we have to seek the Kingdom of God because then we will pray His Will not our own." Becca smiled at Camille and smoothed her hair back into her long ponytail. "Why did you ask that question?"

"Just curious because I've been praying for something for awhile now and it still hasn't happened yet." Camille dried her hands on a paper towel and looked up at Becca. "You really look pretty Auntie Becca. I wish my Uncle Mark could see you right now."

"Well thank you sweetie. I want you to remember that sometimes God doesn't answer us right away because He's fixing some things in us so that we will be able to accept the blessing that He has for us. But in the mean time you keep talking to God and believe that He will answer you. God loves you, Camille and He knows what's best for all of us. Are you ok?" Becca kissed her on the forehead.

"Yeah, Auntie, I'm good and I love you. I hope Uncle Mark let's me come back next weekend to stay with you." Camille gave Becca a big hug.

Becca felt good as they walked out of the restroom holding hands. Bryan was standing in the hallway waiting on them. He grabbed his mom's other hand and they walked in the Sanctuary together just as the Praise and Worship team began the first song, "What A Might God We Serve".

Mark and Lena made it to the church just as the choir was singing their second song, *"Grateful"*. Lena spotted Becca and the children sitting on the third row in the center section of the church and nudged Mark. She whispered, "There they are."

Mark felt his stomach start turning flips almost like he was back in high school, nervous to say hi to the girl he liked. He gently grabbed Lena's arm and spoke softly to her. " I need to go to the restroom. You go ahead and sit down I'll be right back."

The usher gave Lena a big hug and led her to Becca's row. Camille about jumped out of her seat when she saw her Auntie Lena sliding into the row and sit down between her and Bryan. "Hey Auntie, I didn't know you were coming to church today. Where is Uncle Mark?" Camille started looking behind her to try and spot her uncle but she didn't see him.

Becca could not stop grinning. She knew if Lena were here then Mark was somewhere in the building. She was just glad to have them there. She looked at her mom singing in the choir and saw her smiling unusually big back at her. Becca knew that he mom had seen him. Becca turned her attention back to the choir's melodic singing. She stood up and waved her hand because she was truly grateful to GOD for her family being all together and intact. Tears began to run down her face as she worshipped God with the others in the congregation.

The choir ended the song and exited the choir stand back to their seats as the pastor entered the pulpit and made his way to the podium. Fran gave Lena a big hug as she stood on the other side of Bryan. But Mark had still not returned from the bathroom. The pastor gestured for the congregation to be seated and began to make a few remarks of welcome and acknowledgement of people that were visiting their church today. Becca seemed to be the only one concerned that Mark was still had not made into the Sanctuary. She was trying not to be obvious. She leaned over to Lena and whispered, "Do you think I should send Bryan to check on Mark? He's been in there a little while."

Lena had to do everything she could to hold her composure. "He's ok Becca. I'm sure he'll be out in a minute." Lena turned her attention back to the pastor.

"Well saints it's so good to have our special visitors from Cleveland with us today. As a matter of fact, we don't really consider them visitors. They're family to us." The pastor was looking directly at Becca. "Before I get into the sermon, one of our brothers in Christ has asked for a space to have words. Now you all know that I don't usually do this so it must be special. Brother Mark you can come to the front.

Becca and her whole row turned around to see Mark coming down the aisle. Becca was so confused she didn't know what was going on. She tried to give Mark a questioning stare but he wouldn't respond. He just lightly touched her shoulder as he passed her.

Mark took the microphone that was on the floor and spoke calmly. He was a little nervous but he still had the same confident peace he woke up with this morning. "Praise the Lord saints! Hallelujah saints of God. I give honor to God who is the head of my life, to the pastor, who has so graciously given me this space to have words, to all the ministers, deacons, saints, and friends. I am so joyful today to be here with all of you. But I'm even more happy to see my family." Mark let his eyes scan over each one of them but then he rested them on Becca.

Becca couldn't even think straight. She didn't know what Mark was doing and it was making her very nervous. But she continued to try and look calm.

Most of you know that I am Bryan's Godfather and that I love him very much. As a matter of fact, he knows that I think of him as my own son. But what many of you don't know is that Becca and I have been friends for about 17 years now. We always joke with each other and say how we've been best friends longer than some couples have been married." Mark paused to clear his throat. He had his left hand in his pant pocket fidgeting with something. The congregation laughed in confirmation at his remark.

Becca smiled and nodded in affirmation of what he just said. She could hardly take her eyes off of him. She thought how handsome he looked standing there in his black pin striped three-piece suit with his crisp white collared shirt with gold and diamond cuff links, and a black satin tie. Mark wore these designer black leather wing-tipped shoes that completed his GQ look. No wonder the other sisters always salivated over him when he came to church. Becca continued to listen to her friend.

"I know you all are probably wondering why I up here today. I'm here because I know it was the Lord that woke me up this morning and told me to come and share with you. I want you all to know how much I respect and admire Becca Thomas. We've been through so much together: graduation, births, deaths, heartache, and joy. We've had arguments, shared secrets, and our life's ambitions and dreams with each other. We've even raised children together. Our friendship is strong because we never muddied the waters with romantic stuff. We just loved each other with agape love. But most of all, we kept God first. We were prayer partners. As you spend quality time with a person and get to know them- the good and the bad. You can't help but develop a deeper relationship with that person. I have had friends ask me for years when are you and Becca going to get married? Or why didn't you and Becca ever date each other? And my response would be the same, we're friends or we don't want to mess up our friendship." Mark paused again. This time he walked to Becca's row, smiled at her, and took her hand. He gently guided her to the front with him and then faced her. "Becca is a beautiful woman, mother, daughter, sister, and friend. She has overcome obstacles that would have devoured others because God is and has always had his hand on her life, even when she didn't know it. She truly is a virtuous woman."

Becca was so nervous being in front of the church with Mark saying all these wonderful things about her. She was so humbled because she didn't really feel that way about herself. But when she looked at him she calmed down.

"Becca, I wanted to say this in the House of God, with the congregation and our family as witnesses, I have obtained favor with the Lord because I found you." Today, I knew what I had to do when I woke up and I've been excited about it all day." The congregation held their breath as Mark kneeled in front of Becca and pulled out a small black velvet box.

Becca could feel the heat rushing through her body and her

hand shaking. She never expected anything like this. They hadn't even talked about moving forward in their relationship. She just began to pray in her spirit that this was truly in the Lord's will.

Mark spoke carefully and with such great emotion. Almost as if her response would be life or death for him. "Becca, I've loved you for a long time but it wasn't until we went through this last storm that I realized how much in love with you I had fallen. I could not have special ordered a more gifted, anointed, and beautiful woman of God to spend the rest of my life with. You are my sunrise and my sunset, my clear starry night, and my calming breeze, you're my confidant and my best friend. I know that as long as we continue to keep God first in our lives he will continue to strengthen our love for each other make us one. I don't want to spend another moment without you. So Becca Marie Thomas will you honor me by becoming my queen and letting me love, honor, and cherish your for the rest of my life?" Mark was looking at her with such intensity. He wanted her to feel all the love that he had been hiding for so long.

Becca was speechless. It was like she was in some type of dream that she never wanted to wake up from. It wasn't until she heard her son yell out that she snapped out of her trance.

"Mom say YES!" Bryan was so excited. The whole congregation burst into laughter.

Becca got down on her knees with Mark as tears just streamed down her face and spoke with confidence and love. "Mark James Simmons, as long as we stay in this position together before the throne of God, our marriage will be like the man that built his house on the rock. No matter how the wind blew and the storms raged it did not falter because it was built on a sure foundation. I promise you that I will love you with everything that is in me and raise our children in the fear of God. Thank you for finding me." Becca couldn't speak anymore the love she felt for Mark was too much to contain.

Mark opened the black box and pulled out a 3 karat princess cut diamond solitaire with 2 baguette diamonds on each side set in 14 karat gold. He placed it on her left ring finger and kissed her gently on her forehead and softly on her lips. He stood up and then helped her up. The congregation erupted in praise to God and thunderous hand clapping. Mark then beckoned for Fran, Lena, and the children to come to the altar with them. He turned to the pastor and asked for prayer that he may lead his family as God intended.

Becca stood next to Mark at the altar with their family all around listening to the pastor pray and anoint each one with blessed oil. She realized at that moment that once she had finally made the decision to trust God completely with every area of her life, all she needed to know was in Him, and what He had for her was unimaginable and far better than any plans she could have made for herself.

The End

ABOUT THE AUTHOR

Patrece L. Tolbert lives in Ohio where she is an ordained minister and faithful servant at her church. She has one son and is very proud of him and his accomplishments. He is truly the joy of her life. Patrece loves spending time with her best friend, prayer partner, and beautiful mother. Ms. Tolbert is a graduate of Central State University and Jesup W. Scott High School. She is a member of the National Sorority of Phi Delta Kappa, Inc. Beta Gamma Chapter. Patrece has also written, directed, and produced six gospel plays. Her goal is to share the gospel of Jesus Christ through literature and theater so that the lost, bound, backslidden can be saved, delivered, and restored.

Made in the USA
Lexington, KY
22 October 2014